WHATEV
BY KIM HUNTER

Table of contents

Whatever It Takes
Copyright © 2008 by Kim Hunter 2008

The right of Kim Hunter to be identified as author of this
work has been asserted in accordance with sections 77
and 78 of the Copyright, Designs and Patents Act 1988.

All rights Reserved

A CIP catalogue record for this title is
Available from the British Library.

This is a work of fiction.
Names, characters and incidents originate from the
writers imagination.
Any resemblance to actual persons, living or dead is
purely coincidental.

Other Works by Kim Hunter
EAST END HONOUR
TRAFFICKED
BELL LANE LONDON E1
EAST END LEGACY
EAST END A FAMILY OF STEEL

Web site
www.kimhunterauthor.com

PREFACE

Life was once a fairground where all the rides
were free.
Everything was magical for all the world to see.
But that was in my childhood and things were
different then.
Everything was wonderful and everyone was
friends.
Now the fairgrounds gone from town and
nothings left upon the ground.
Just dust and dirt and longed for dreams and
people
with their silent screams

Roxy Baxter

<u>PROLOGUE</u>

Tess Davey struggled from the station with her luggage and didn't have a clue where she was going. Lately the weather had turned cold and the nights had started to pull in. It was just past seven and already the light was waning. Walking along the platform, she headed in the direction of the exit and hoped that the taxi rank wouldn't be empty. In comparison to the capital, Spalding was a small place and unlike London, when all the taxis had a fare and had driven off into the distance, you had no option but to walk. Lady luck, if that's what you called it, was shining on Tess and a single remaining cab stood idle in the rank. So different from the black hackneys that she'd become used to, Spalding's idea of a taxi came in the form of a ford sierra or cavalier. Opening the door, Tess placed her luggage onto the back seat. When the driver asked 'Where to', she had to stop and think for a moment. With no job and nowhere to call home, there was only one place and one person left that Tess could call on for help. The journey was made in silence. After several attempts on the cabdriver's part to make conversation, which had fallen on deaf ears, he'd given up and concentrated on the task in hand. Tess stared out at the cold Streets that had in the past held excitement for her. Now they seemed small and uninviting. Pulling up outside the address, she paid the fare and hoped with all her heart that Sophie Milligan was home. Ringing the doorbell Tess stood on the step with her shoulders slumped. After what seemed like an age the door finally opened and the next thing she heard was hearing the high-pitched scream of excitement. Sophie hadn't thought she'd ever see her friend again and now it was like all her Christmas's had come at once.

Jumping forward, Sophie embraced Tess and in turn kissed her on both cheeks. For Tess, this show of emotion was too much to bear and she suddenly began to sob uncontrollably. The sight of her friend's pain shocked Sophie to the core. Tess had always been the strong one, had always been the one to look out for her. 'Hey! Hey come on now, things can't be as bad as all that.'

Tess sniffed loudly and through continual sobs and sniffs, she tried to talk

'Oh yes they can, you've got no idea.'

Unlike the past the roles had now been reversed and it was Sophie's turn to be strong. Grabbing the suitcases she invited her friend inside. She couldn't help but notice just how much weight Tess had lost. A few weeks earlier the young woman was more than a few pounds on the heavy side. It wasn't just her size, Tess had aged. Her face was drawn and there was something else, something that for a moment Sophie couldn't put her finger on. Suddenly it came to her; Tess's eyes looked dead, as if a light had gone out somewhere deep inside. The flat was warm and welcoming and after seating her friend on the settee, Sophie made two cups of strong hot coffee, one of which she liberally laced with brandy.

'Drink this.'

The fumes from the cup wafted up into Tess's nostrils and she momentarily turned her head away. Sophie studied the woman sitting before her but she didn't speak. Slowly Tess sipped at her drink and gradually the tears began to subside. The gas fire flickered and gave the room a warm glow; it was the first time Tess had felt warm in over forty-eight hours. When she stood up and removed her coat, it was like a green light to Sophie Milligan. Having given her friend just long enough to compose herself, Sophie was soon back to normal and bombarding Tess with one question after another. Tess Davey was tired and really not in the mood to talk, the trouble was she'd turned up on her friend's doorstep out of the blue and the least she owed her was an explanation.

'Oh Soph! How could I have gotten things so very wrong?'

Sophie Milligan sat down on the settee and gently placed an arm around her friends shoulder.

'Maybe I could answer that if I knew what the hell you were talking about.'

'Sorry I forgot it's been such a long time since we last spoke. You're never going to believe what I have to tell you, not in a million years.'

'Try me.'

'It's a long story.'

'I don't care if it takes all night. You need to unburden yourself and neither of us is going anywhere until you have.'

Tess drank the last of her coffee and placing her cup on the table, began to speak.

CHAPTER ONE
6 Months Earlier

Climbing the steps of the building that had been like a second home to her for more years than she cared to remember, Tess Davey felt full of apprehension. Today was make or break. Today she would find out if she was on course to conquer her demons or the possibility that she would have to begin at the start and find a new career. If the latter was the case, then she didn't have a clue what path to follow. Pushing hard on the heavy glass doors, she swiped her identification card in the slot and gained entry into the inner sanctum that was Spalding's head and only police station. As usual the place was full of hustle and bustle and the phones rang out constantly from every direction. Some may have found the atmosphere claustrophobic but it gave Tess a warm feeling. People passed by quickly in all directions. Some with their heads buried in paperwork as thick as war and peace, others deep in conversation with fellow officers and some on a break making their way to the canteen. Tess, slightly overweight and with mousy brown hair, had never attracted her share of the opposite sex. Somehow it hadn't bothered her and the strong friendship she'd built up with female colleagues had somewhat compensated her for the lack of a love life. By no means gay, she had concentrated solely on her career. It was something Tess had dreamed of since she was small and even if a man had shown interest, she probably would have rebuffed him. Sophie Milligan was one such colleague and walking towards her friend, stopped when she saw Tess Davey approach. Sophie Milligan lacked female friends as Tess lacked Male and the two had

1

had formed a solid bond since joining up.

'Hi! Tess, how are you?'

'Not too bad thanks Soph, on your break?'

'Yeh, why don't you come and have a coffee? Oh Tess I've just realised, it's today you hopefully get the nod isn't it?'

Tess smiled. Her friend was scatty to say the least but the two had been in more than one scrape together and she knew that Sophie truly was a mate who'd stick by you through thick and thin. Glancing at her watch Tess saw that she was at least half an hour too early and sharing a drink with a friendly face was far more appealing than sitting on a bench outside the boss's office.

'Actually Soph, I have got time for a coffee and I could do with some moral support.'

'Then cappuccino and support it is, mind you I think frothy coffee is hoping for a little too much. We'll just have to do with a cup of Mrs Talbot's instant.'

Tess laughed as Sophie linked her arm through her friend's and the two women headed to the noisy but familiar canteen. As usual it was Tess who stood in line for the drinks while Sophie took a seat. It had been that way the whole of their friendship but it wasn't something Tess minded. Sophie Milligan could never last from one payday to the next and had owed money to each and every officer in the station at some time or other in her career. Finally the two sat facing each other with a steaming cup of liquid that could marginally pass for one of Brazil's lesser-known brands, placed in front of them.

'So what time are you in with the big chief?'

'In about twenty minutes and I'm not looking forward to it one bit. What if it's not what I want to hear, where do I go then?'

Sophie Milligan placed her hand tenderly on her friend's

arm.

'Just take one step at a time love, it's no good getting up tight about something that may or may not happen. If things don't go the way you want, you'll just have to think of something else.'

Tess smiled at the enormous amount of faith her friend had in her.

'It's nice to know I have someone on my side.'

'Always, now drink up. I don't want to make you late, you know what a funny bastard he can be if you upset him.'

Wanting to kiss her friend before she left Tess thought better of it. It didn't pay to show any emotion in a police station. The slightest show of affection here could brand you a lesbian or even worse a serial lay. Tess would do anything not to bring any trouble to Sophie's door, not when she wouldn't be around to protect her.

'I'll call you later.'

'Ok kidda, good luck'

Tess Davey walked along the corridor and felt as uptight as she had on her first day in the force, nearly ten years earlier. Nervously clearing her throat, she tapped lightly on the highly polished door. The words 'Chief Inspector Shepherd' printed neatly on a brass plaque did nothing but heighten her nervousness. The seconds that it took for her to be ordered in seemed like hours and she could feel herself begin to perspire. Lifting her arm above her head, Tess sniffed in deeply at the seam of her crisp white shirt. Satisfied that there was no odour she was about to lower her arm as the door opened. Lifting her eyes but eyes but not her head, she was met by the gaze of a stern looking grey haired woman wearing spectacles. Mildred Short had been secretary to many Chiefs over the years and took her position seriously. Tess felt as if the woman was silently tutting her and she could feel her cheeks begin to flush.

'The Chief Inspector will see you now Miss Davey, please go inside and take a seat.'

Without a reply Tess did as she was asked and walking into the pristine office, saw that a chair had been strategically placed in front of the large desk. Chief Inspector Shepherd didn't look up from his papers and although she knew this was all textbook psychology, it made her feel uncomfortable. Placing her handbag on the floor she took a seat and remembering to keep her back straight, neatly crossed her legs. Several minutes later and Chief Inspector Shepherd finally placed the paper he'd been reading onto his desk. After sighing heavily, he took in a deep breath.

'So Detective Davey, you want to leave our happy little band and head for the bright lights?'

'That's right Sir.'

'Can I ask why?'

Tess, whose hands had been placed one on top of the other and positioned gently on her knee, could feel the clamminess of her palms. She didn't know why this man should make her feel so awful and could only put it down to the fact that he had a reputation for being mean and could make or break someone's career with a stroke of his pen. Swallowing hard she allowed herself a couple of seconds before answering.

'It's personal Sir.'

'Personal or the fact that you think it's a fast track to promotion?'

'Nothing could be further from the truth believe me. I've enjoyed every last second of the time I've spent here but I need to be in London and my only option was the Met. If I am not given that opportunity Sir, then I will have no

alternative but to leave the force. Forgive me if you think I have an over inflated ego but it would also mean the loss of a damn fine officer. I'm good at my job Sir, it's just that I can no longer carry out my duties here due to family reasons and those I would rather not go into.'
Expecting a stern lecture to say the least, Tess was astounded at his next sentence.
'Detective Davey I know it's been a tough time for you of late and I have studied your file very carefully. You are an exemplary officer and therefore I have reluctantly recommended your transfer. You begin at Agar Street Station a week from today, though why you chose that particular location beggars belief. I also realise you have personal things to sort out, so I've arranged for you to take time off until then to get yourself ready.'
Tess stood up and forgetting herself was about to walk round the desk and hug her boss. Before she was able to make that mistake, a knock at the door brought her back to reality.
'Thank you Sir, thank you so much.'
'Not at all and I hope that if the bright lights ever dim, then you will come straight back here.'
'I will Sir and thanks again.'
Passing the stern looking secretary in the doorway, Tess nodded to her as she pulled the door closed behind her. Out in the corridor, Tess Davey punched the air with euphoria as she walked along.

Back home, she surveyed the small cramped living room that also doubled as her bedroom and was happy at the realisation that there really wasn't much packing to do. Only a few items that had been dotted around the fully furnished rented flat, that in reality was only a studio, had long been placed neatly into cardboard boxes.

If her request had been denied then her belongings would still have been joining her in London but the journey would have been tainted with sadness. Now it felt as if a whole new world was opening up to her and she was giddy at the thought of it all. Soho wasn't exactly a dream destination but it was where she had to be and she was going to make the most of it. Packing an overnight bag, Tess headed for the station and the long journey that lay ahead of her to the city. This would only be a flying visit but she had to find somewhere to live and seven days wasn't long to do that and move her belongings. The carriage was stuffy and cramped, making the air seem thick. Every seat was full and no one attempted to make conversation, forcing the minutes to drag by until it seemed as if time was standing still. Three hours later and as her train pulled into Kings Cross station, Tess let out a huge sigh of relief. A short ride in a taxi saw her soon walking the Streets and alleyways of Soho. The location was ideal. Her new station was close by but far enough away not to cause her too many problems or at least that was what she was hoping for. It didn't take long for Tess to realize that it wouldn't be a case of popping into the nearest estate agents and finding somewhere to live. For one thing she hadn't been able to find one, she wondered if once you arrived in Soho, you never left. After walking around for over an hour she became thirsty and called into the first pub to hand. The Ace of Spades was unusually quiet and much to her relief, she had no problem being served. The barman could immediately see that Tess wasn't local and his trying to be friendly was mistakenly taken as a come on.

'Not from round here?'

Tess studied the man's face and saw that he was no different from the blokes in Spalding who fancied their chances with every girl on a Saturday night.

'So?'

'Wo! Hold on there a minute babe, only being friendly. No need for you to go getting all defensive.'

'I'm not defensive, nor am I looking to be picked up and neither am I anyone's babe. So if you don't mind I'd rather be left in peace. That's unless you can be of some real help but I doubt that very much.'

'Try me!'

'Ok! I'm shortly moving here and I need to find somewhere to live but it's proving more than a little difficult, any suggestions?'

The barman scratched his chin as he thought and then walked over to the mirrored counter. Picking up what she thought was a business card; he walked back to face her.

'Aint no flats to rent round here babe, not unless you're a brass and looking at you, I somehow can't imagine that. Landlords are too scared to entertain anyone straight see, in case they phone old bill. Anyway, this old girl runs a B & B and it's perfectly respectable I might add. I only send over bodies that I think she'd like and you fit the bill.'

Handing Tess the card, he held onto his end for a second longer than was necessary which made her feel uncomfortable and she ended up snatching the small piece of paper from him. It didn't faze the barman, only made him smile and leer at her in a way that had her skin crawling in seconds.

'Anytime you're back round this way call in, maybe we can get together one night?'

His sentence ended in a question but it wasn't one she intended to answer. Instead with the card clasped tightly in her hand, she made her way outside. Hailing a cab,

Tess blurted out the address and was about to climb inside when the cabbie locked all the doors.

'Not so fast darling! I suppose I could make a few quid here but I'm feeling fucking generous today, so your luck's in. Take the next left at the end of this road and you're there, hardly worth a cab fare, now is it?'

Tess Davey's cheeks reddened with embarrassment and after a curt thank you; headed in the direction she'd been told. Just as he'd said Manette Street soon came into sight and as night was fast approaching, Tess felt nothing but pure relief. The Street was a miss match of buildings and she was surprised when she reached the address on the card. The house and its neighbours on either side were all that remained of a once fine Georgian terrace. Number seventeen, unlike the adjoining properties, appeared to be in pristine condition and the brass letterbox and numbers shone so brightly that she could see her face in them. Lifting the heavy lions head knocker, Tess stood back and waited for the door to be opened. The woman who greeted her was not what she'd imagined in her wildest dreams. Agatha Goldstein, Agi to her friend's, was seventy if she was a day. Standing no more than four and a half feet tall, the peroxide blonde hair and scarlet lipstick made the woman resemble an aging prostitute more than a property owner. Tess managed to stifle her shock and gave the most genuine smile she was able to muster.

'Hello, I'm sorry to bother you but the barman at the Ace of Spades said you may have a room available?'

Agatha Goldstein returned the smile and immediately Tess could see a lifetime of lines etched upon the woman's face.

'Come in sweetie and we'll see what we can do.'

When the heavy door closed behind her, Tess looked

8

around the amazing hall and couldn't believe what she was seeing. The place was absolutely beautiful and she could visualise some ambassador living here but never the woman who stood before her.

'Nice isn't it? Most people have a shock when they first come in. I inherited it all from a, well let's say a lifelong friend. Anyway I don't understand why Duncan sent you, as I only take in male lodgers.'

Tess was embarrassed and turned to open the door.

'I'm sorry to have bothered you Ms?'

'It's Agatha, Agi to me friend's and don't be so quick to rush off. Just because I don't normally do something, don't mean I can't change my mind now does it? Duncan knows how particular I am and if he felt you was good enough then it'd be downright rude not to have a chat. Come on through and I'll make us both some tea.'

Tess did as she was asked and followed the woman into a fabulous farmhouse style kitchen.

'Take a seat love while I do the business.'

The kitchen was warm and inviting and as she began to relax, Tess realised her feet were starting to throb. With her legs hidden under the large pine table, she slowly slipped off her shoes. Agi laughed out loud; there wasn't much that escaped the attention of this Streetwise old bird.

'Bastards aren't they?'

'Sorry?'

'Heels love! God knows why we wear them but men like them so I suppose that's reason enough.'

Agatha Goldstein placed a large teapot and two mugs onto the table and took a seat opposite her guest.

'So what do you do for a living sweetie, don't tell me you're on the game because I don't take any brasses, no matter how nice they are.'

9

The woman's words shocked Tess but she also wanted to laugh. She'd been mistaken for many things in her life but a prostitute wasn't one of them. Frumpy clothes and being several pounds overweight should have been enough to convince the women but then again this was London and it took all sorts.

'No, no! Of course I'm not. I've just landed a job in one of the city firms as a secretary and I have to start next week. Finding somewhere to stay was a lot harder than I thought and Duncan was just helping out a damsel in distress, that's all.'

'Glad to hear it sweetie, slippery road to ruin is the game I can tell you.'

Tess didn't feel like delving any further but she somehow sensed the old woman could tell more than one interesting story.

'I've got a small room at the front that might suite you. Its sixty-five quid a week with two weeks up front. I don't allow any hanky panky and you must be discreet at all times. I have several regular gentlemen lodgers and I don't want them upset. So would you like it?'

'I would Agi, thank you very much.'

'No need to thank me sweetie I've got a feeling were going to get along just fine. Drink up and I'll show you to your room. I take it you need to stay tonight?'

'Yes, yes I do, though I won't be moving in properly until next weekend if that's all right?'

'Fine by me sweetie.'

The room was small but smartly furnished and as Tess gazed around her, Agi smiled to herself. It would be good to have a bit of female company for a change; she just hoped the young girl wasn't running away from trouble. Soho made more than its own share of trouble and Agatha Goldstein knew that the area didn't need any

10

more, no matter how small.

'Right Dearie I'll leave you to it. I expect you're knackered after all of your travelling. The bathroom is at the end of the hall and excuse my other lodgers if they leave the seat up or piss on the floor but you know what men are like and gawd bless them they'll never change. Breakfast is seven until eight thirty, definitely no later. Night!'

'Night Agi and thanks.'

As Tess heard her new landlady descend the staircase she could just make out the words "You're welcome." Removing her night dress from the overnight bag, Tess quickly undressed. Her bed, like the rest of the house's furnishings was top quality and the large downy mattress completely moulded around her body. Within a few minutes she was fast asleep and experiencing the best nights rest she'd had in many weeks. The following morning after a well-cooked hearty breakfast, Tess Davey made her bed and collected her overnight bag. Making her way to the front door she was met by Agi coming out of the sitting room.

'On your way back lovie?'

'Yes but it won't take me to long to sew up the few loose ends I'm leaving behind.'

About to turn the doorknob, Tess was startled when the old woman placed a hand on her shoulder and gave her a peck on the cheek.

'You take care of yourself, you hear?'

'I will and thanks for everything.'

As Tess walked from the house, Agi Goldstein smiled to herself and hoped that the young woman wouldn't change her mind about returning. Agi needn't have worried as Tess was desperate to return, desperate to get things moving and begin a whole new life.

CHAPTER TWO

Travelling back to Spalding that morning, Tess suddenly remembered that she hadn't phoned Sophie. It was the first time she'd ever let her friend down but it didn't lessen the guilt. Watching the rain as it ran down the windowpane, Tess placed her hand on the glass and could feel the cold from outside. Unlike yesterday, the carriage was relatively quiet and void of commuters, so she fished out her mobile and tapped in her friend's number.

Knowing it was about to switch to voice mail, Tess almost hung up when she at last heard Sophie's sleepy voice.

'You took your time, not interrupting anything am I?'

'I wish! No I'm off duty until tomorrow so I thought I'd have a lay in.'

'And now I've ruined it for you! Sorry.'

'Don't be silly Tess. Now how did you get on? I was expecting you to call me last night.'

'I know and I'm sorry but you know how it is. Things just seemed to snow ball and before I knew it I was in London. Listen Soph, instead of going over everything on the phone now, how about we go out to dinner tonight? My treat!'

Tess knew that if she hadn't added those last two words to her sentence, then the answer would have been a firm no! She could imagine that her friend was probably living off baked beans until payday and eating out was definitely off the agenda.

'I'd love to. Where shall we go, what about Othello's?'

'I'm treating you to a meal, not taking up a second mortgage. I was thinking more on the lines of the wine bar in the high Street, they say the pastas out of this

12

world.'

'Then the wine bar it is. I feel like I've been starved for weeks so I can't wait.'

After the two women agreed to meet at eight that night, they both hung up. Tess Davey continued her journey home and Sophie Milligan went back to bed. The train was smooth and before long Tess drifted off to sleep but it wasn't to be a peaceful slumber. Unable to wake herself from the nightmare she knew was about to happen, Tess sighed within her own dream and waited for the pain to start all over again. As with every night's sleep since the news had arrived, albeit with the exception of last night, she found herself sitting at her desk in the police station. Replacing the handset Tess was feeling as proud as punch. The team had just nailed a serial paedophile and it had been a case in which she herself had played a large part. Her colleagues were already lining them up in the local pub and she had just taken a call of congratulations from the chief himself. All in all it had been a very exciting day, the kind of day that most police officers only dream of. Visualising her rapid promotion, she was startled back to reality when the telephone on her desk again burst into life.

'Hello!'

'Tess? Oh thank the lord I've got hold of you.'

Realising who her mystery caller was Tess sighed in annoyance. Her mother the eternal drama queen was once more spoiling any fun she was having.

'What is it this time mum? Washer gone on the kitchen tap?'

Instead of her mother's usual chastisement, all that could be heard was a gentle sobbing emitting itself from the handset. Without further conversation, Tess hung up. Grabbing her coat and bag, she drove as fast as possible to her parent's house. The ten-minute journey passed in a blur and it wasn't until she pulled up outside the smart fifties semi, that she realised she couldn't even remember getting there. As if on autopilot the car had turned down the numerous streets and avenue's without her even realising. Running up to the front door, Tess let herself in with the key that her father had insisted she keep in case of emergencies. The house was eerily silent and as she walked towards the front room, something on the stairs caught her eye. The large manila envelope had the local hospital stamp on the front. It was identical to the many she saw regularly in her work. People's lives or what was left of them at least, neatly folded and placed inside the dirty coloured beige package. Slowly sitting down on the bottom step, Tess had an awful feeling of foreboding. Instinct told her to go to her mother but at the same time she felt compelled to look in the offending envelope. Placing her arm inside, she could feel something smooth and cold. Withdrawing her hand she could see that it held her father's gold watch. Pressing it to her chest she began to cry and it was several minutes before she looked up to see her mother standing in the doorway.

'Finally got here I see but too late as usual. I should know better than to expect anything else from you.' Margaret Davey was a tall upright woman, a pillar of the community or that's what she thought of herself, even if no one else agreed. Her acid tongue had been experienced by most that she came into contact with and Tess and her father had not been the exceptions. As far back as she could remember, Tess had loathed the woman and if it hadn't been for her father, she would have happily placed herself into care. Albert Davey had been the complete opposite to his wife and loved by everyone.

14

If anything needed to be done, then Albert was your man. Hard working all his life, he asked for nothing but gave everything he could. Cruelly his payment came in the form of a loveless marriage, ruled with an iron rod by his dictator of a wife. It wasn't until the day Tess arrived, that he felt he had a real reason to live. Albert totally adored his daughter; she was the first thing he thought of in the morning and the first person he wanted to see after a long day at work. When Tess finished her training, there had been no prouder father at the passing out parade than Albert Davey.

'Are you just going to sit holding that damn watch all day?'

Margaret's usual sharp tone brought Tess back to reality with a slap and she stared into her mother's cold eyes.

'What happened?'

'Heart attack, said it could have happened at any time. Trust your father to let it be in the middle of Sainsbury's. I was absolutely mortified, everyone was staring at us and to top it all off he had to go and wet himself.'

Tess couldn't believe what she was hearing. Standing up and still with her father's watch clutched tightly to her chest, she walked from the house as Margaret chased after her.

'Where are you going, I need you!'

'Mother you've never needed anyone in your entire life. Let me know when the funeral is.'

'Suppose I don't, suppose I just let you miss your own father's big day.'

'Big day!, you really are sick in the head woman and you will let me know because the shame of having your only child not turn up to her father's funeral, would embarrass you more than anything.'

With that Tess got into the car and drove back to her

small but welcoming flat. Over the next few days she threw herself into work and if it hadn't been for Sophie letting the cat out of the bag, no one at the station would have known about her father's death. Finally the curt phone call she'd been waiting for came. Her mother informed her of the date, time and place the funeral would be held at, and then slammed the phone down on her daughter. Sophie Milligan accompanied her friend to the service. They tip toed across the church's flagstone floor trying to be invisible and when they sat at the back of the church; Sophie thought it was more than a bit strange. The place was full of her mother's friends but Tess couldn't recognise any of her father's pals. It would be just like her mother not to have informed them. Margaret Davey had always thought of her husband as beneath her and the men he worked with and looked upon as friends, were common and below her social level. After the service the congregation walked over to the small adjoining graveyard. The priest said a few words and it was finally over. Tess turned to leave but was stopped by her mother's hand.

'Not so fast madam, I have a few things to say to you.'

'For Christ's sake mum! Dad's not even covered over and you can't resist having another go!'

Margaret gave Sophie a steely glare, which told her in no uncertain terms the woman wanted to be alone with her daughter.

'I'll be off now Tess, you two obviously have things to discuss. Call me later.'

With that Sophie made her own way home and hoped she'd done the right thing leaving her friend with that dragon of a woman.

'Right Tess I want you to come back to the house.'

'What to show a united front to all the blue rinses you've

invited back? I don't think so.'

'There are things I need to give you, things your dad wanted you to have. Don't you want his last wishes to be carried out?'

Margaret knew those words would do the trick; the girl would do anything for her father.

'Ok! ok! but I'm not staying long.'

'Don't worry it won't take long, it won't take long at all.' Linking her arm through her daughters and stopping all Tess's attempts to disengage herself from her mother, the two women, if only in appearance, portrayed a family united in grief. It had turned out just as Margaret had wanted.

Back at the house the wake was already in full swing when they returned. Margaret's bridge club had prepared a spread of boiled ham sandwiches and china cups full of orange stewed tea were being handed round. After graciously shaking hands with a select few of the mourners, mother and daughter at the request of Margaret made their way upstairs. With the door firmly closed Margaret turned to her daughter and at last let down her guard. Removing a small wooden box from beneath the bed she slowly and precisely opened its lid. The contents resembled any other box of family papers but the look in her mother's eyes made Tess feel afraid. Margaret Davey sifted through the top few layers until her hand rested on what she'd been searching for. Removing the large folded document, she handed it to her daughter but before letting go couldn't resist a vengeful sentence.

'Right you little bitch! Take this and let's see it wipe that snide look off your face. I've waited for twenty-five years to see this and believe me, it feels good.'

Tess snatched the paper away from her mother and gingerly began to unfold the stiff document. Slowly she

17

began to read its contents but for a moment couldn't take in its words. Margaret Davey began to laugh in an almost hysterical manner and only stopped when Tess's hand engaged with the woman's cheek.

'You vicious, spiteful old woman. You've waited patiently for all these years to tell me I'm adopted? Well let me tell you something, I'm glad, glad that I wasn't spawned from a dried up old bitch like you.'

Tess turned and walked from the house, leaving her mother standing open mouthed. Margaret wanted to feel triumphant, had waited years for it and now that the deed was done she felt nothing but emptiness. Staring into the ornate wall mirror Margaret brushed back her hair, re applied her lipstick and with a fixed smile on her face, went back to join her guests. Tess didn't call Sophie that night, she needed to be alone to take in the enormity of the news she'd just learned. After reading the adoption papers several times, she finally began to cry. Slowly at first, then pitiful gut wrenching sobs for all that she had lost. Each tear felt as though part of her was draining away and she began to think her life so far had been wasted. She didn't know who she was or where she belonged and it hurt more than she could ever have imagined. The love she had for her father was real enough and no matter what she was told, he was and always would be just that, her dad. He was the one who had comforted her when she was sick, who'd stopped the bullies when they had taunted her mercilessly at school and who, much to Margaret's disgust, had attended every single play she had ever appeared in. No, there was no way that Tess would ever deny the love she had for her father but out of this came a small sense of happiness, happiness that she never had to acknowledge that awful woman again. Pouring herself a large glass of wine, Tess

18

sat down on the snug little sofa bed, which almost filled the tiny space of her living room and again opened up the paper. Slowly she began to read and it took every ounce of concentration she had to take in the words.

Born - March tenth nineteen seventy-six. Suffolk.

Mother - Janet Sayers (Deceased).

Father - Unknown.

Siblings - Twin girl.

Adopted March twenty first nineteen seventy-nine - aged three.

Scanning the information, Tess's eyes kept drifting back to the penultimate line. Siblings, she not only had a sister, she was actually a twin. Then and there she knew that there was no alternative but to find that person, a need far greater than any other she had ever felt before. Nothing mattered as much as feeling whole and until she had the answers, that feeling would be an impossibility to ignore. Suddenly Tess woke with a start and was grateful that the nightmare had finished only half way through. Slightly disorientated she looked around the carriage and remembered where she was. The train began to slow and wearily she stood up and removed her bag from the overhead storage rack. The journey had tired her and right now the last thing she wanted was a night out with her best friend but go she must. After all Tess didn't know when she'd get to see her friend again, it certainly wasn't going to be in the near future. That thought alone gave her concern. Sophie was a good mate but not a particularly good policewoman. Tess had watched the woman's back on more than one occasion and now she was going to be out there alone. For some reason Sophie rubbed people up the wrong way and she wasn't really liked at the station. Tess had always found her scatty, funny and best of all a loyal friend but for reasons unknown to her, others saw Sophie in a different light. Trying to dismiss her fears she disembarked and made her way home. Sophie Milligan was a big girl now and it was time she stood on her own two feet, if that was at all possible.

CHAPTER THREE

Back at the flat Tess glanced at the mantle clock and
seeing that it was only just after midday, decided to take a
nap. With everything that had gone on in the last couple
of days she was exhausted and there was plenty of time
before her dinner date. Lying down on the small sofa still
fully clothed, she closed her eyes and sleep swiftly came.
Seconds later she was back in the nightmare and it was
the day after the funeral. Given a week of leave at the
insistence of her superior, Tess had made the journey to
Ipswich in Suffolk to seek out the local Department of
Social Services. It had crossed her mind to deal with the
matter by telephone but then she had thought better of it.
There were bound to be questions she would forget to ask
and then have to call back several times trying to get the
answers. No this was something best done on a face to
face level, though she had no idea what she was going to
learn and that thought alone made her nervy. Deciding to
call just to ask the name of who she needed to see, she
was surprised when Donald Plaslow informed her he
would be the person in question. Tess was even more
surprised when he informed her he'd had a cancellation
and could see her at ten the following morning.
Replacing the receiver, she decided to get an early night's
sleep in preparation for the drive but it wasn't to be and
memories of her father and the life Margaret had led them
both, invaded her mind every time she closed her eyes.
Finally the alarm burst into song and as she leant across
the bedside table to stop the ear piercing bleeps, Tess felt
totally drained. Showering and dressing casually in jeans
and a sweater she at last closed the door to her flat and
began her journey. It didn't take as long as she thought

and her early arrival gave her time to explore the town and try to get a feeling of what her roots might be. Ipswich was a pretty place and the fact that it was situated on the shoreline made her feel warm inside. Maybe her family were struck down by some terrible tragedy. Maybe until that day they had been loving and close knit and only circumstances beyond their control, had been the factor that had torn the family apart. Tess, normally a level headed person, chastised herself for trying to make things seem like a fairy tale. Knowing deep down that after reading 'father unknown there was going to be nothing nice in the information she was about to receive, she reluctantly pushed open the main doors of the Social Services building. The receptionist told her to take a seat while she tried to locate Donald Plaslow. Doing as she was asked, Tess looked around at the grim office and wondered how many other poor people had learned the truth about their roots in this god forsaken place.

'Miss Davey? Donald Plaslow, very pleased to meet you. Do come this way.'

The man was elderly and Tess imagined that he was past retirement age and had been allowed to stay on due to the nature of his job. His heavy lidded eyes looked like they carried the weight of the world and she knew that this was one job she wouldn't want in a million years. Her own line of work carried many down sides and a lot of the cases she worked on were heart wrenching but this, well this was somehow different. People came here full of hopes and dreams, full of anticipation that there really was someone out there who loved them and were as desperate to be reunited with their family as she was. Then there was poor old Donald who had to shatter more dreams than make them. Poor old Donald, who had to be the bearer of the news, that they were never wanted, that these people had been cast aside like an unwanted gift. Taking a seat in the cramped office that was brimming to capacity with confidential files, Tess wondered to herself how the man coped with so much pain and hurt every single hour of every working day. Sitting behind his ministry issue desk, Donald Plaslow put on a pair of horn rimmed spectacles and smiled in Tess's direction. Tess handed over the document she'd been given by her mother and waited for his opinion. Expecting to be blocked at the first hurdle, she was surprised when the man stood up and began rummaging through a rather dilapidated filing cabinet.

'Most of my earlier cases are in here; all the newer ones are dealt with by the younger people. The department allowed me stay on after my time, just to close as many remaining files as I could but I know I'll never see it through to the end.'

Inwardly Tess smirked, she felt like the cat that had got the cream. Her police training had taught her to evaluate every situation and she had been bang on target when it came down to Donald Plaslow. After handing her a large orange folder that was so crammed with papers it had to be held together with string, Donald sat back down in his chair with a thud.

'I really am too old for this but at least I have another satisfied customer.'

He smiled at Tess but she didn't know if satisfied was really a suitable phrase to use. She began to untie the string and was stopped by the man's words.

'My dear those papers are for you. Take them away and read them at your leisure.'

For a moment Tess was speechless.

'I didn't think I'd be allowed to, I thought they would be

23

government property?'

Again Donald smiled at her.

'A lot has changed in the last few years my dear and not all for the good I might add. Today any adopted child has a right to a copy of their file, no matter how harrowing the information inside. Those papers are your property and a copy will also be here for any siblings you may have. Of course it's a different story for the birth parents. They have little or no rights and the times I've had to deal with heartbroken mums, desperate to find the child they gave away years earlier. Listen to me! you don't need to hear all this. No, you take your papers away with you Miss Davey and I hope they bring you some peace of mind and happiness, no matter how small.'

After shaking the man's hand and saying thank you over and over again, Tess Davey left the building. Still in a state of shock at how easy it had all been, she slowly made her way back to the car. The sun was shining and Tess put on her sunglasses ready for the journey. The pile of paper work sitting on the passenger seat caught her eye and she had to fight the urge not to peek inside. Deciding not to open the file until she was in the safety of her own flat, Tess was well aware that she didn't need any distractions on her mind while driving. That was easier said than done and even though she didn't look inside; it didn't stop her mind from going into overdrive about what secrets were lurking beneath the orange package on the seat beside her. Finally after pulling up outside her flat Tess took in a deep breath. Staring at the file for a few moments more, she snatched it from the seat and ran inside. It had suddenly turned chilly and she wasn't sure if it was due to the time of year, or the fact that she was scared to death regarding what she was about to learn. Igniting the small gas fire in the tiny living room, it wasn't long before she started to feel snug and just a bit more relaxed than she could have hoped for. Walking through the archway she opened the fridge and poured herself a liberal glass of wine. Replacing the bottle she closed the fridge door but only made it half way to the sofa before thinking again. With a feeling that it was going to turn into a long night, she returned to the kitchenette and retrieved the bottle. Making her way back to the task in hand, Tess thought of unplugging the phone from its socket to stop any interruptions. Knowing that she could be needed by someone stopped her. The next two hours told Tess many things she was desperate to know and many she would have preferred to remain secret. She learnt that her birth name had been Susan Sayers and that the Davey's had changed it within a week of the adoption. In a way she was glad, she liked her name and at the moment, it was the only thing in her life that felt right but her twin sister, whose name was Sally hadn't been so lucky. Then again on reflection, Tess thought that maybe she was the unlucky one. Their mother Janet had misused every substance known to man and after a heavy drinking binge had been killed by the man she was living with. Alec Watson had tried to plead mitigating circumstances but was found guilty of manslaughter and sentenced to eight years in prison. The two small girls had been placed in care and while Susan was quickly adopted, Sally had gone to one foster home after another. The records stopped when the girls reached sixteen and Tess's only lead to her sister was the last known address of her foster parents. There and then Tess Davey had only one aim in life, to track down her other half, track down Sally Sayers in the hope of making herself feel whole again. The shrill ring of the Telephone startled her and she swiftly picked up the receiver.

Wiping her brow she glanced at the mantle clock and saw that it was six thirty.

'Hello?'

'Hi Tess it's Sophie, just ringing to check the time. I couldn't remember if we said eight or eight thirty?'

'Eight and it's a good job you called, I was engrossed and lost all track of time.'

'Mind in overdrive with everything that's going on?'

'Yeh something like that, anyway I'd better start getting ready.'

'Ok, bye!'

Tess was relieved that Sophie had telephoned but she felt guilty at not sharing her news of the last few days with her friend. The trouble was she was having enough difficulty dealing with it herself, without a second party asking every question under the sun. Sophie Milligan could talk for England and sometimes to Tess's annoyance, didn't know when to shut up. After showering and carefully applying her makeup, Tess chose a smart pair of navy trousers and a pale pink blouse. Standing in front of the mirror, she was about to pull on the trousers when she caught sight of her reflection. Her ample bosom and pear shaped hips made her sigh in exasperation. She wondered if her twin was identical but deep down she hoped not. God hadn't been kind to Tess when it came to looks and she didn't want anyone, especially her sister, to suffer the way she had over the years. Finally after dressing, she smoothed down the fabric of her blouse and took one last look. Inwardly Tess groaned and muttered under her breath.

'You can't make a silk purse out of a sow's ear.'

It was a phrase her mother had used many times over the years but even saying it to herself now, hurt more than she would admit. Her mousy brown hair, though clean, still hung limply around her shoulders and Tess wondered if the rest of her family looked the same. Thinking that she might be chilly, she grabbed the first coat that came to hand and left the flat to meet her friend. Sophie had been told that after a massive row with her overbearing mother Tess needed a change of scenery and had applied for a transfer. The reasoning had been readily accepted by her friend and now Tess was again feeling guilty. The walk to the wine bar had her mulling over the possibility of disclosing her real motives for the move. After having a battle of wills within her own mind she reached the wine bar and decided to come clean about everything that had gone on. It would make for an interesting evening if nothing else. Sophie was perched at the bar on an impossibly high stool, where she flirted with anyone who passed by. This had not been an entirely wasteful exercise as she had four empty glasses lined up in front of her. Tess laughed to herself; she really was going to miss the girl. Sophie glanced round and let out a somewhat inebriated shriek.

'Tesssssss!!!!!'

Slightly embarrassed, Tess joined her friend and after being shown to their table, ordered a jug of water for them both.

'Water! Tell me you're having a laugh?'

'No I'm not Soph! I have a lot to talk to you about and I need you to be sober. There will be plenty of time for drinking when I'm done.'

Her serious tone made Sophie Milligan sit back with a worried expression on her face but Tess didn't begin her tale until her friend had drunk two large glasses of water. Throughout the courses and there were many, as Sophie could not only talk for England but eat for her country as well, Tess revealed her story. When she finally finished or at least where the file had abruptly stopped, she looked to her friend for a reply. Sophie sat stunned for a moment.

'Well fuck my old boots.'

After all the tension, this outburst had even Tess in a fit of giggles.

'No Tess don't laugh, I'm being serious here! Whatever are you going to do now?'

'What am I going to do? Find my sister of course.'

'How?'

'Well! The Social file may have ended but I did a little investigating of my own.'

'You never did?'

Tess laughed again at the sheer shock on her friend's face but the shock didn't stop Sophie Milligan shovelling spoon after spoonful of ice cream into her mouth. Tess knew that Sophie was storing up reserves. It was another week until payday and desperate times called for desperate measures.

'I tracked down the last family to foster Sally and I telephoned them.'

'No!'

'For goodness sake Soph stop being so dramatic and listen to what I'm saying will you?'

'Sorry, sorry Tess and then what?'

'They are called the Parsons and they seemed very nice, although they hadn't heard from Sally in over twelve years.'

'So she left them when she was only sixteen?'

'Let me finish and I'll tell you. It seems a man came to see her, a Lenny Layton. The Parsons didn't like him and tried to stop him having anything to do with Sally. The next thing they knew, is that she'd run away. They didn't know where but as this Lenny Layton came from London they assumed that's where she went.'

'So that's why you're off to the smoke, I thought it was a strange choice.'

Tess took a large swig of the wine that Sophie had ordered and placed both palms flat on the table.

'I had Tony in I.T look up this Layton bloke on the computer. Seems he has a lot of form and has done more than one stint at her majesties pleasure. The only other information is that he frequents the Soho area. I'm not that interested in him but I do need to find my sister and the only lead I have so far is him. It may come to a dead end Soph but I have to try. If I don't then I'll spend the rest of my life just wondering.'

'So this is our farewell dinner then?'

'Looks that way, though I dare say I'll be back if the trail runs cold. Sophie all this could take quite a while and I'm asking you as a friend not to say a word about any of it back at the station.'

For a moment Sophie looked offended and Tess wished she hadn't spoken her last sentence. Then out of the blue Sophie Milligan came out with one of her classic one-liners.

'Cross my heart and hope to fucking die!'

Tess Davey laughed until the tears streamed down her face, while Sophie stared at her friend wondering what was so funny. The two women spent the remainder of the evening drinking and talking about old times but both knew that it would be a very long time, if ever, that they would share this kind of intimacy again.

CHAPTER FOUR

The next day was her last in Spalding and Tess woke with the mother of all hangovers. After drinking what seemed like a gallon of water, she downed three painkillers and hoped the thumping pain in her head would soon subside. Within the next twenty-four hours she was due to start her new job and turning up looking like one of the walking dead, didn't make for a good impression. An hour after waking she had rousted herself and was now dressed and ready for the taxi that was expected any minute. The last of her possessions or at least the few she'd chosen to take with her, were either packed inside one of the two suitcases or the small cardboard box that she could just about manage with the rest of her luggage. Taking one last look around the place that had never quite felt like home, she closed the front door and got into the cab. Sophie Milligan hated goodbyes so had said her farewells last night. She wasn't aware that her friend had given notice on the small flat and that she had no intentions of returning to the town that now held nothing for her. Tess had thought it best to leave her friend with the thought that maybe she would be back one day. She had promised faithfully to keep in touch by phone and had every intention of doing so, at least in the beginning. Placing her car keys inside an envelope and securing the tab, Tess pushed the package into a post box at the station. She knew that Sophie would love her car and if push came to shove, she could sell it if times got hard, which they frequently did. The train journey was a mixed bag of emotions. Her head swam with memories of all the happy times she'd shared with her father and of all the laughs she'd shared with

Sophie. It was also scary that she could now possibly meet her sister, who until recently she didn't even know existed and just the idea was mind blowing. By one that afternoon Tess had arrived in the heart of the British sex industry and had found her way to Agatha Goldstein's house. The taxi driver hadn't helped with her luggage and had tutted rudely when she took longer lifting out the heavy cases than he would have liked. Tess threw her ten-pound fare through the small sliding window that protected the driver from any assaults and she imagined there were many due to his utter bad manners. Knocking wearily on the door she waited to be let in. Seconds later and Agatha could be heard walking along the house's inner hall and unbolting the door. After the long journey, Tess was eternally grateful that the woman was home and not out shopping.

'Tess I'm so glad to see you, good trip down?'

'Long and tedious and I'm just glad I won't be making it again for a while.'

Reaching down she started to lift the first of her heavy cases and was stopped immediately by Agi.

'No no dear, leave those. Mr Seaman's home today, he'll be more than happy to help I'm sure. Geoffrey, Geoffreeeey! Come here and lend a hand will you.'

A small portly man in a silk smoking jacket was standing next to Agi in an instant. The sight of the odd little characters made Tess want to laugh but she was too well mannered to show her amusement. The two women walked into the house and along the hall into the kitchen. From behind her Tess could hear Geoffrey Seaman struggling with her bags but Agi totally ignored his labour.

'Take them upstairs Geoffrey there's a good boy. Leave them inside the small room at the front then I'll start your

31

dinner, all right?'

Huffing and puffing Geoffrey began his task and in almost a whisper Tess heard the man reply 'For you my queen! Anything.

'What a nice man Agi, has he been with you long?'

Agi Goldstein stopped making the tea and gave Tess a wink.

'More years than I care to remember and when we get to know each other better, I'm going to tell you a few stories that'll make your hair curl.'

Tess smiled and holding the fine china cup between both her palms, relished the hot beverage.

The following morning and not totally unexpected, Tess entered the dining room to find a feast set out in all its glory. There were all the usual ingredients that made up a traditional English breakfast but also kedgeree, grilled kidneys and kippers. This type of food seemed so uncommon these days and Tess knew that either Agi came from a prominent family, which was doubtful to say the least or she was going overboard to make her guest feel welcome. Either way it wasn't going to go to waste and shortly after she sat at the table, Tess was joined by Geoffrey Seaman and the cook herself Agi Goldstein.

'Agi what a marvellous spread!'

'Why thank you Dearie, can't have you going off to the city on an empty stomach now can we?'

Tess smiled and hoped this wasn't to be a daily occurrence or she would soon need to invest in an entirely new wardrobe. Thirty minutes later and feeling fuller than she would have liked, Tess said her goodbyes and headed off to work. A fine mist of rain had just begun to fall and Tess pulled the collar of her coat up tight around her neck. Walking to the top of Manette Street, she made her way along until she reached Charing

Cross road, when the heavens suddenly opened. It wasn't far to the station but after all that food she just couldn't face the walk. Getting drenched as well, would have truly got the day off to a bad start. Hailing a cab she jumped inside and gave the driver directions. The Agar Street building was very traditional in style and Tess knew it had been standing long before it was ever a police station. Pushing open the heavy brass covered door, she walked up to the counter and informed the desk sergeant that it was her first day and she had been told to ask for a Detective Reynolds. After insisting on seeing her identification, the sergeant, Tommy Radcliff, led her through a side door and up two flights of stairs. The place smelled of stale tobacco and Tess guessed its patrons didn't adhere to the government's new non-smoking policy. The idea of the staunch anti smoking Chief Inspector Shepherd ever being sent here on secondment brought a smile to her face. Not that that would happen in a million years but it was still a funny thought. Walking along the corridor, Sergeant Radcliff stopped at a rather stained and battered looking door.
'You'll find him in there and good luck.'
Tess nodded her thanks then tapped lightly on the door.
'Enter!'
Sheepishly walking in, she was surprised to see a small badly decorated room that contained two tired looking desks. Seated at the better of the two, was a man who she would later find out, looked much older than his years. His appearance was so scruffy and dishevelled that he could easily have been mistaken for a tramp. The odour of stale scotch hung in the air and by the state of the room, she guessed the office doubled as sleeping quarters most of the time.
'Tess Davey Sir, I'm your new number two.'

Joe Reynolds sat upright in his chair.

'Come right in then girlie and let's have a look at you.'
His manner deeply offended her but she thought better
than to complain on her first day. Joe studied her for the
next few seconds and as his eyes moved up and down her
body, Tess began to feel uncomfortable. Finally after
giving her the once over, D.I Reynolds smiled and
revealed a mouthful of miss matched teeth. His hair was
dark but prematurely streaked with silver and Tess could
see that he had once been a handsome man.

'Well I can see you aint from these parts.'

'How?'

'Too fresh faced that's how! Fuck me the bastards round
here are going to run rings round an innocent like you.'

'Sir I may be from an area that you would refer to as the
sticks but let me tell you something before we even get
started.'

'Fire away girlie but make sure it's brief.'

'Please don't call me that! My name is Tess or Detective
Davey if you prefer to be formal. I have been in the force
for over ten years and the last five have been in C.I.D. I
was one of the leading officers who brought down the
Carlton paedophile ring. I have witnessed more brutality
than most people could even dream of, so don't patronise
me or treat me like a rookie straight out of cadet school.
Is that brief enough for you?'

'Yeah! Now take a seat. Your desk is over there.'
Doing as she was told, Tess took up residence behind the
battered table whose top contained nothing more than an
A4 pad and old-fashioned dial out telephone. Her new
boss stared at her as she opened up her handbag and
removed a few items. First was the ornate silver framed
photograph of her father that she positioned to the left of
her pad. Next an array of brightly coloured pens and

pencils complete with their own holding tray. As she fished for her Dictaphone she heard a snigger from across the room. In such a short amount of time her new boss was really starting to annoy her.

'Is something the matter?'

'Nothing at all it's just been a long time since anyone bothered about neatness and the likes in this nick.'

'Well maybe it's about time they did. Doesn't the Chief bother about things like that?'

'Don't make me laugh. When he's not on the golf course, he's out to lunch with one villain or other. Old Bateson's just biding out his time until retirement.'

'So does any work get done in this place?'

'Not much, well not by me anyway. I show my face out on the Streets now and again but that's about as far as it goes. The rest of the time I just shut the door and stow away in here. No one seems to bother about this office, so if you need to do a spot a shopping then feel free.'

With that D.I Reynolds or Joe as Tess would soon come to know him, placed his feet up on the desk, put his hands behind his head and closed his eyes. Tess was furious to think she'd left a buzzing station to come to this. Shepherd must be laughing his socks off but then a thought sprung to mind that until now hadn't occurred to her. If no one bothered where you were or what you got up to, she could have all the free time she liked looking for her sister. To top it all, she would even be able to do it in an official capacity without anyone raising an eyebrow. Tess Davey sat back in her chair and took up the same position as her superior.

Her first day was turning out better than she could have imagined. The remainder of the day was spent collating papers and folding neighbourhood awareness leaflets. Unlike her own, Joe's desk resembled a minefield of pens

35

and white sheets.

'Sir is this all you do all day?'

Joe grinned and Tess couldn't make out if he was laughing at her or at what she'd just said.

'Doing nothing and making it look good is hard work and it's took me over three years just to perfect it.'

Tess didn't know how to reply to that, so she didn't. Instead she carried on with the menial task she'd been given. When four o'clock came, Joe Reynolds sat bolt upright as if an inbuilt alarm had just signalled. Yawning so wide that Tess could see every part of his inner mouth, he slapped his lips together.

'Well that's another one out of the way.'

'Another one?'

'Day at the grind stone Tess! I think it's about time to knock off and have a few jars. I like one or two, just to help wind the day down. You coming?'

About to say no she had second thoughts. Maybe it wouldn't hurt to get to know D.I. Reynolds a little better.

'Yes, yes I'd like that thanks.'

'Don't get too excited, you aint seen the place yet.'

Holding open the door, Joe beckoned her into the corridor. The unlikely pair silently made their way out of the station and onto the Street. Joe Reynolds took massive strides as they went along and Tess was finding it difficult to keep up with him.

'Hey there! Slow down a bit it's not a race you know.'

'Aint it?'

They didn't speak again until they were standing outside The Ship and Shovel on Cravens Passage.

'Listen Tess! Maybe this wasn't such a good idea, being your first day and all. I mean we don't want to tire you out now do we?'

'Tire me out? I've done nothing but sit on my backside

36

all day. Are you sure you're not just a little embarrassed or is it that your drinking buddies don't know what you do for a living?'

Joe Reynolds turned his face away from her and Tess knew she'd hit the nail on the head. Placing her hand firmly on the brass fingerplate she began to push.

'Come on Sir, I won't let on about your little secret and the first drinks on me OK!'

Smiling, they both entered the not so clean public house. The floor looked like it hadn't seen a mop in weeks and the four people sitting at the bar, appeared to have taken up residence. Two coloured youths were playing pool and stopped to eye up Tess as she walked to the bar. As her jewellery was always kept to a minimum, she was of no interest to them so they resumed their game within seconds. The landlord already had a scotch waiting for Joe and looked a little bewildered when he saw his most regular customer wasn't alone. Drummy Stevens, one of the four at the bar, had a grin as wide as the ocean and Joe slapped the old man on the back as they reached the bar.

'Well, well, well! Old Joey Reynolds has gone and got himself a lady friend. What do you reckon to this lad's? Wonders will never fucking cease.'

His three amigo's sitting alongside him all burst out laughing at Drummy's words and both Joe and Tess could feel themselves begin to blush. Neither of them tried to deny it, there wasn't any point and besides Joe liked the feeling that he was still able to pull a pretty young girl, at least as far as his friends were concerned. Tess on the other hand didn't want to cause any further embarrassment and she could see by the look on Joe's face, that part of him was enjoying the attention. The crowd laughed and joked and when the conversation

37

turned to work, Tess informed everyone that she was in computers in the city. Drummy Stevens made a sound that came out not quite as he'd hoped.

'Wooooo! A city worker in the Ship and Shovel whatever next?'

Everyone laughed and it wasn't long before Tess was being asked if she could lay her hands on a cheap piece of kit. When she explained that she only worked on computers and didn't sell them, interest dwindled fast. They assumed she was a high flyer and when she admitted to doing a menial job like Joe, she became just another drinker. After two hours and rather more alcohol than she would have liked, Tess pulled Joe Reynolds to one side.

'I have to be going now Sir.'

Grabbing her arm, he pulled her into a corner.

'Don't call me that in here for Christ sakes! In fact don't call me it full stop. From now on its Joe, Jesus I'm only forty five and you make me sound like I'm ready for my pension.'

Tess nodded.

'Sorry Joe.'

For everyone else's benefit, she raised her voice an octave.

'See you at work tomorrow Joe.'

Outside in the fresh air her head suddenly started to spin and she hailed a taxi, desperately wanting to get back to Agi's. Inside the Ship and Shovel, all conversation had turned to Joe's new lady friend and he basked in the admiration. His drinking cronies, after spending a couple of hours in her company, were all of the opinion that she was a thoroughly nice piece. Joe had to agree but the comment started him wondering. What was a nice girl like Tess Davey, doing in a shit hole like this?

38

CHAPTER FIVE

As Tess opened the front door to Agi's house, grateful that the day was finally over, Roxy Baxter was just about to begin hers. Sighing, she finished applying the last touches to her makeup. It was so routine nowadays that she could almost put her lipstick on with her eyes closed. The weather had been turning cold over the last couple of days and she was dreading standing on the Street tonight. With both hands she grabbed at her tights through the flimsy material that barely passed for a skirt and gave them one final hike towards her waist. Picking up her oversized handbag, she checked for condoms, tissues and wet wipes. Happy that her supply would be enough, she switched off the light and walked from the flat. Being on the ground floor was noisy at times but the neighbours, living similar lives to her, kept themselves to themselves. Berners Mews was a good ten-minute walk from the centre of Soho but Roxy didn't mind. She liked to distance herself, as much as was humanly possible, from her work but the cold night air would do little to help get her in the mood for work. During the daylight hours she could pretend that she was just like anyone else and not the cheap brass that she had become. It had all been so different when she was in the care home. Then she'd studied hard and was a top achiever. Roxy was so sure she wouldn't turn out like the others, that she'd been determined to prove them all wrong and make something of herself. It now all seemed like so long ago. The dreams and expectations that had been her only goal were now just ashes along with the rest of life's rubbish. Only one person had ruined things, had shattered her dreams and his name was Lenny Layton. Like the devil incarnate, he'd turned up on the scene, promising her anything she wanted. Walking along she wondered how it had all turned out so bad and how in hells name she going to get off this roller coaster that ultimately would see her in an early grave. All the girls on the Street were going to stop as soon as they had enough money, trouble was there was never enough or that's what they told themselves and Roxy was no different. She thought to herself that deep down maybe she was different, if only in the fact that she knew there was no getting out, whereas all the others would try to convince themselves that eventually things would change for the better. Now crossing Oxford Street and entering Soho Square, Roxy saw the first of the dealers starting to emerge for the night's trade. It was a pitiful sight and made her feel like crying. Young lads mulled around waiting to score and if they hadn't quite enough reddies, were willing to sell their bony little arses for enough to get high. Denzel Howard was a friend of a friend and he called out as Roxy hurried by, desperately trying not to be seen.

'Hey Rox baby how you doing girl?'

Waving but not stopping, she continued on her way.

'Got some blinding gear babe want a sample?'

For a moment she was tempted to stop and do a deal but thought better of it. If Lenny found out she was off her nut before she'd turned a trick, well it didn't bear thinking about. No, by the time she'd earned her keep he'd be waiting with enough gear to blow her mind for all eternity. All she had to do was get through the next few hours, and then she could get away from this sordid life at least for a while.

'I'm pukka Denz but thanks anyway.'

He didn't bother to continue the conversation. If there was no chance of a sale, then he wasn't going to waste time on a brass, no matter how good looking she was and Roxy was definitely that. Standing five feet eight in her stocking feet, she had long black hair and a figure to die for. Perfect bone structure, coming from only god knew where, Roxy was a natural beauty and this would give her the added advantage of lengthening her career on the street. If you were only blessed with minimal beauty, you somehow aged much quicker and most of the prostitutes in the area had aged far beyond their years. Reaching Greek Street, Roxy could smell the lure of Soho in the air. It was the sweet sickly smell of cheap perfume, alcohol and the great unwashed. Night people or the lower classes at least, didn't seem that keen on soap and water, something she found not only disgusting but also strange. Even if you were lucky enough to work out of a flat and have a maid, things were still grim. All the rooms and she'd been in many had as much stock of air fresheners as most chemists. A lot of men didn't know the meaning of personal hygiene and she'd actually heard of one girl who'd hurled up her dinner while still on the job. It had been a joke on the Streets of Soho for months. The punter had got so turned on by her vomit, that he'd paid her double. High class pros couldn't be told apart from the wealthy but a crack head brass or rent boy could be smelled a mile down the road. Every nonce and pervert would be out on the Street within the next hour and it made her skin crawl. Roxy hated what she had become but she would have done a deal with the devil himself, if it meant looking good and working out of one of Park Lanes finest. Instead she'd been given a duff hand and it had come in the form of Lenny Layton but she knew deep down, that however much she moaned about him, she would love the man forever. Continuing along until Old Compton Street came into sight, she entered the small doorway at number ten. The hallway stank of urine and other bodily fluids but it went unnoticed. Right at this moment Roxy was just glad that she didn't have to be alone. Carmel Jones had been a brass long before Roxy had arrived in the smoke. She was well know for taking care of waifs and strays and had taken in Roxy on more than one occasion when Lenny had had a skin full and turned on the girl. The high platform boots that were Roxy Baxter's trademark didn't stop her climbing the stairs two at a time. Bounding into the flat just as Carmel came out of the bathroom, she gave the older woman a fright.

'Fuck me girl, you nearly gave me a fucking heart attack. Thought it was Old Bill finally catching up with me.'

Dropping her bag on the floor, Roxy flopped down on the heavily soiled sofa and placed her arms behind her head.

'Sorry Carm. I just couldn't wait to get here tonight that's all.'

The woman still dressed in a cheap housecoat, laughed. 'Right, like this is the fucking Ritz and all. You jacked up already girl? Only you know what'll fucking happen if he catches you!'

'No I aint and anyways I can take care of Lenny, without me he's nothing.'

Carmel Jones pushed aside the beaded curtain that tried to disguise the hovel of a kitchen.

'Sure he aint darling but all the same don't let him hear you say that.'

The two women laughed, although both knew that what had been said was the truth plain and simple. Handing Roxy a glass that appeared not to have seen water in its entire life, Carmel sat on a hard chair by the window.

'Get that down your neck, warm the cockles of even the hardest brass will that.'

The vodka was neat and Roxy winced as it hit the back of her throat. It was the same scene night after night but it didn't make her medicine any easier to swallow. With both their glasses dry, Carmel fetched the bottle from the kitchen.

'Do the honours babe, while I finish putting me face on.'

Roxy sniggered to herself and couldn't resist having a snipe at her only friend.

'This bottle won't last that long Carm, should I pop to the offie and get another?'

Carmel continued to apply mascara and didn't flinch at the girl's remark.

'You're a cheeky cow Rox but I love you. Chuck me fags over will you they're on that sofa somewhere.'

Doing as she was asked, Roxy turned and began to fish about under the cushions until she found what she was looking for. Pulling out a crumpled packet of Bensons, she grimaced when she saw a used condom had adhered itself to the packet.

'Carm you dirty bitch, look at this!'

The older woman, mascara brush still in hand, glanced over towards the sofa. When she saw the limp sheath of latex dangling down from the packet that Roxy held high in the air, she burst out laughing. Instantly she began to cough, deep racking hacks that brought tears to her eyes. Trying to speak while laughing and coughing, made her double over and Roxy thought she was about to peg it right there and then.

'Carm! You all right?'

Carmel Jones, unable to speak just waved her hand.

When the coughing had finally subsided, she got up from the table and walked over to where Roxy sat. Taking the offending item, which the girl still held in the air, she peeled off the condom and threw it into the bin. Lighting a cigarette, she drew in deeply and after a small cough, winked at her friend.

'Ahhh that's better. Sorry about that Rox, only I was little bit the worse for wear last night. Mind, if you'd seen the ugly bastard, you'd have needed more than a glass of the hard stuff. Paid me extra as well! I think he was just grateful to finally get shagged the ugly cunt!'

'Carm aint you got no boundaries?'

'Listen sweetheart! It aint going to last much longer and I need to get in as much cash as I can now. If that means fucking a wino, then I would if he'd got the reddies. I mean let's face it, half the bastards we sleep with stink. At least this one was clean Rox; at least I could be grateful for that.'

Roxy Baxter wanted to jump up and embrace the woman. To her Carmel was the kindest sweetest person she had ever met and also the person with the shittiest life.

'When I get off the game and set up in some nice little place, I'm going to have you come live with me Carm. Then we won't have to have any smelly, ugly, drunk bastards in our lives ever again.'

Carmel placed a hand on the young girls shoulder and looked deep into Roxy's beautiful eyes. She really was a stunner and Caramel wondered how long it would take for her beauty to fade. Over the years she'd seen many girls come and go and some of them could easily have been models but sooner or later the life got to them. If they didn't end up dead, then they turned into old hags just as she herself had become.

'Sweetheart let's not even go down that road again. You're always dreaming of the day your knights going to charge down Old Compton and save you. It aint going to

44

happen babe, you know it and I know it.'

Roxy stood up and took a step back, distancing herself from Carmel's touch as she did so.

'Thanks for that mate! Of course I know it but it doesn't stop me wishing does it? If I can't have me dreams then I might as well top myself here and now. Aint you ever had a dream Carm, don't you ever snuggle down at night when your shifts over and imagine what it's like. Imagine a nice house and a warm bed and things?'

Carmel Jones sat back down and poured herself another stiff drink, offering the bottle to her friend when she'd finished pouring.

'Course I have. When I started out, there was no bigger daydreamer than yours truly but you have to stop it see. If you don't, you'll end up going fucking crazy girl. There's nothing to bring you down like waking up in this shit hole day in day out. If you hold onto all of them fantasies for too long, all you end up with is a big fat depression and in our line of work,

that aint any good for no one. Why don't you turn the telly on Rox and I'll finish doing myself up?'

Roxy got up and walked over to the small portable television that was perched on the top shelf of a wall unit. Standing tall in her platforms, she had no use for the stick that Carmel kept close by to change the channels. East Enders had just come on and she stood in the middle of the room mesmerised. All the characters looked so well and happy in their own miserable way. Everyone seemed friendly not like the narky sods she'd come across on her numerous visits to that particular area of the smoke. As the title credits began to role, Carmel Jones appeared in the doorway in all her finery.

'All ship shape and Bristol and ready to sell me arse!'

Roxy smiled at her friend as she eyed the woman up and

down.

'Don't scrub up to bad for an olden do I?'

Roxy didn't have the heart to disagree and just nodded. Though not a natural beauty by any standards, tonight's get up did nothing to improve matters. Carmel tried her hardest but the thick make up and gold lam'e dress only showed exactly what she was. Roxy knew that with her makeup toned down and clothes more suited to her age then Carmel, could in a dim light, pass as respectable but the woman was stubborn and would be offended if Roxy made any suggestions.

'Then let's go to work Miss Jones.'

'After you Miss Baxter.'

The two women descended the narrow staircase and entered the now bustling Street. Men of all ages mulled around the area, that at this time of day

became their own. There wasn't a drop of interest shown in the females who passed them by. If on the other hand Carmel and Roxy had been well-toned males, it would have been a different story. As much as Roxy hated her life, she loved the buzz that was Soho in the early evening. Most Streets became deserted after six o'clock but Old Compton was the exception and she couldn't think of a better place to live. Tackling the traffic on Charing Cross road was dicey and it was at times like these that Roxy wished she only wore flats. Once they had made it safely to the other side, they walked along in silence but with arms linked until Leicester Square came into sight.

'Fuck me Carm! My feet are bleeding killing me already. Look what say we head back to the Admiral? At least it's a bit more nearer home territory.'

Carmel sighed deeply but with the endless traffic, her annoyed attitude went unheard by her friend.

'Rox you can do what you like but I need reddies and this area has far more business at night than Soho. So what's it to be, a nice little earner or going home to Lenny with a measly few quid and a guaranteed shiner to boot?' Roxy didn't reply and the pair continued to walk until they reached the corner of Garrick Street and New row. The Corner House had long been a favourite with Carmel and it was somewhere a brass could be comfortable and not get hassled. It was common practice to bung the landlord a few quid and he was happy to let a girl ply her trade, though no brass ever paid up front. As normal the place was still relatively quiet but that would change in the next half hour.

After ordering a couple of vodka and cokes, the two sat down at one of the small tables that hadn't had a wipe down in ages. The surface was sticky and they both had to pull their glasses up hard before they carried on slowly sipping their drinks. Neither wanted to buy more alcohol than was necessary and if lady luck shined on them tonight, they wouldn't have to wait long for a refill. Before their glasses were empty the door opened and two grey haired men walked in. Their suits, a dead giveaway, told the girls all they needed to know. Not exactly city types, they were still well turned out and Carmel winked at Roxy to do the business. As if on autopilot she stood up and walked over to the bar. Positioning herself next to one of the men, she accidentally bumped into him.

'Sorry babe I was just trying to get another drink.'

The man grinned and revealed what Roxy could immediately see were ill-fitting dentures. She felt like gagging but instead put on her best smile. At first glance he assumed she was just a young girl out for the night but after spying Carmel in all her finery, knew exactly what the score was. Turning to his mate, he then raised his

47

eyebrows suggestively. Roxy wore a low cut top and her small pert breasts jiggled as she pushed past. Her nubile figure had his mind doing somersaults. It had been his fantasy for years to fuck a minor and although this one was well over the age of consent, her body said different. Mick Jennings felt as though all his birthdays had come at once and he wasn't about to let the opportunity pass. Feeling the first stirrings of an erection, he moved in for the kill. Eyeing her body from top to bottom, he couldn't think straight. Her high black leather boots almost met her micro mini but not quite. A few inches of flesh were exposed and his mind went into overdrive imagining what the feel of her would be

like. This girl was to die for and years of experience, or so he thought, told him she was gagging for it. He took a moment out and turning to his mate, whispered.

'Up for a bit of fanny Bert?'

His friend eyed both women and decided to go along with the offer, only if he got to choose.

'Must say Mick I aint had a good shag in a while but I want her! You'll have to take the wrinkly or you're on your own mate.'

Mick Jennings looked in Carmel's direction and rolled his eyes. Under normal circumstances he would have backed out sharpish but he was desperate. Roxy had got him so worked up, that he'd have serviced a granny if that was all that was on offer.

'You're a right cunt! Bert Hawkins but I guess I aint got no option. How much is it love?'

Winking at Carmel, Roxy thought for a moment.

'For me it's fifty but my friend does reduced rates for pensioners, so she's thirty.'

'You're a cheeky cow Roxy. Come on then, let's get down to business.'

48

The men purchased drinks that were downed in one, and then swiftly escorted the women outside. Being a regular, Carmel knew exactly where to take the punters. The back yard of the Corner House was quiet and dimly lit. Carmel's trick, had her dress lifted and had slipped himself into her in seconds. He wanted relief, nothing more and wasn't about to try and pleasure something that resembled the bride of Frankenstein and that was in a good light. Carmel Jones had long since stopped the practice of safe sex. The only punters interested in her nowadays set the rules and she was in no position to argue. Bert Hawkins had other ideas. Not only had it been an age since he'd had sex, it had been years since he's shagged anything under fifty. Slowly he slipped his hand up Roxy's skirt and touched her cool soft skin. He instantly felt his penis harden at the realisation she had no knickers on but as Bert tried to kiss Roxy on the lips, she turned her head sideways. That was a definite no no even with a young man but with this perv she knew she would vomit. When his fingers started to roughly explore her, Roxy's felt a tear trickle down her cheek. After a couple of minutes she couldn't stand it any longer.

'Are you going to get on with it pal, only I aint out here in the fucking cold for the good of me health'

Bert took offence at being spoken to in that way and slammed Roxy hard against the wall.

'Hold on there a minute pal! You don't get in without a jacket on.'

Bert Hawkins had just about had his fill of this mouthy little whore and releasing his penis, forced his entry into her. Roxy was taken aback by his rough manner and she was so dry, that the pain was excruciating. Luckily for her he ejaculated after three or four thrusts and she quickly wiped herself clean. Carmel who'd finished

49

some time ago, waited by the gate for her friend.

'All right babe?'

'The bastard hurt me Carm and he didn't wear a rubber.'

'Take no notice babe; they're all fucking wankers. He looks a clean sort so I doubt you've got anything to worry about, though I wonder if he can say the same.'

'You cheeky bitch, I had the all clear from the clinic just the other month.'

The pair laughed out loud as they strolled along but Roxy was shaken. Oddly, in the few years since she'd been on the game, this was the first time a punter had cut up rough and she didn't like it. When the women were reinstalled in the pub waiting for their next trick of the night, Carmel pulled a man's wallet from her handbag and passed it to Roxy.

'What's this?'

'It fell out of your tricks pocket when he walked by.'

Roxy laughed out loud.

'Carm, I didn't think you did dipping anymore.'

'Like to keep me hand in now and again and besides, the bastard deserved it. The way I see it, they use us and on this occasion it was time for a little pay back. Open it and see how much there is.'

Roxy unsnapped the clasp and pulling the black leather apart, flipped through the notes.

'One twenty, a hundred and fucking twenty Carm! I wouldn't want to be in his shoes when he gets home to his old woman.'

'If he can afford to dip his wick Rox, then he can afford us a little bonus. Quick stash that away, fresh meats just walked in!'

'Shouldn't we leg it in case they come back?'

'Babe there's no way they're going to come back and kick up a stink. For a start they'll both be bricking it in

50

case their old women find out and they aint going to march back in here and admit to shagging a couple of brasses now are they?'

This was turning out to be a good night and Roxy Baxter was now glad that they hadn't turned round and gone back to the Admiral.

CHAPTER SIX

A short distance away and still on the fringes of Soho,
Lenny Layton sat in the Kings Head on Gerrard Street.
He hadn't seen Roxy since early that morning and he
hoped she was doing a good trade tonight. He'd spent
most of the day in the Trocadero centre trying to push a
pocket full of crack. Some days it was easy if the place
was full of youngsters but today had been slow. He was
into Maxi the Jamaican for a lot of gear and if he didn't
settle up soon, knew what the consequences would be.
Lenny didn't like the stuff himself preferring heroin to
any buzz that crack could offer. Although the day had
turned out poor, he still had enough cash to get a good hit
and if his girl came up trumps, then Maxi would be off
his back as well. Starting to feel a bit clammy, Lenny ran
his fingers through his thinning greasy hair and hoped
young Bobby Race wouldn't make him wait too long. He
hated dealing with kids but when needs must and as hard
as he'd tried in the past, he couldn't get Maxi to supply
any shit. Maxi always said that even dealers had
standards but Lenny knew it was just down to profit
margins. Maxi Trueman would have sold his granny if
the price was right. The Kings Head had two main doors.
One set at an angle in the corner and the other facing
straight onto the Street. It was a perfect place to meet,
with plenty of escape routes if the Old Bill ever showed
their faces. The doors opened and Bobby Race entered.
Heading straight for the corner booth, he knew exactly
where to find his customer. Not taking a seat he leered in
Lenny's direction.
'Starting to cluck yet you old cunt!'
Lenny smiled but the beads of sweat stood proud on his

forehead.

'Nah not me mate. Good gear is it?'

Bobby hated all his shots. To him, druggies were the scum of the earth but it paid a good wedge so he could put up with them, at least for the time it took to do the deal. Trading since he was fourteen, there wasn't much you could get over on Bobby Race. Already having served a five stretch and only now twenty-three, he hated everyone with a vengeance. Any conscience he might have had regarding what he dealt in was eased by his own words 'I don't push it onto people, they contact me. Supply and demand, it's as simple as that'. They were the two sentences he practiced over and over again. The ones he'd used with Old Bill and the ones he'd repeated to his dear old mum, on one of her monthly visits when he was still banged up. Removing a couple of wraps from inside his jacket, he swiftly passed them over to Lenny.

'Shits shit aint it? Now hand over me dosh.'

Lenny Layton was about to barter then thought better of it. Knowing the little ponce, he'd take it straight back and then do a runner. No Lenny was too near the edge now, he needed a fix and he needed it now. Passing a twenty over to the boy, Lenny snatched up the two small parcels and gripped them tightly. Standing up he looked all around but Bobby had already disappeared. Leaving the pub, Lenny crossed Shaftesbury Avenue and made his way through Soho. He was desperate to jack up but at the same time he needed to be at home. He had never been one to fill his veins in a doorway, and it was also a personal thing. When Lenny came down from a high, it had to be in his own bed. It was a cold night but Lenny was sweating. Removing his beaten up old jacket, he placed it on his shoulder. No one paid any attention

53

to him as he passed by; he was known by all and hated by most. He was too far down on the food chain to be of any interest to Old Bill and too much of a scumbag, to work for any known faces except dealers. Reaching the flat, Lenny's hand shook as he fumbled with the key. Finally he heard the lock click and slamming the door behind him, lent against the cold paintwork. His breathing was laboured and coming in short gasps now, such was his need to get high. Stumbling into the bedroom, he felt under the bed until his hand at last made contact with a small tin box. Clutching it tightly, he started to remove its contents but after five minutes he was no nearer to getting his fix. Cooking up on the middle of the bed and filling his syringe, he tried to administer his treasure but it was useless. Finally he lay stomach down on the floor and began the first of many press-ups. After so many years of abuse, raising his blood pressure was the only way of finding a vein. Stopping and feeling along his arm, Lenny eventually found a spot and managed to administer a hit. The high was unbelievable and his last thought, was that Bobby Race didn't know the quality of his own gear. Roxy Baxter finished her last trick at just past midnight. Wiping her mouth with the back of her hand she had difficulty standing. It had been a long night and the boots weren't helping. Carmel had disappeared hours ago and now she was left to walk home alone. With her last punter out of sight, Roxy let her weight be supported by the back yard wall. Removing her takings she flicked through the notes, hoping that she could take out a cab fare and Lenny wouldn't be any the wiser. Exhaling deeply she smiled, all in all it hadn't been a bad night and she was two hundred and fifty smackers better off. After making her way back onto Charing Cross road she hailed the first hackney that came into site.

'Berners Mews and don't bother taking the fucking long way round because I'm local!'

'Well in that case darling, show us your fucking money because I've been done over by brasses before.'

The driver's words had cut her to the quick. She should have been used to those sort of comments by now but deep down, she still couldn't accept herself as a prostitute. Reaching inside her bag, Roxy pulled out a twenty and flashed it in front of the man's face.

'Fucking good enough for you?'

The driver didn't answer; instead he pulled away from the curb so sharply that Roxy was thrown back into the seat. 'Fucking arsehole' she muttered under her breath. Any other time she would have given him a mouthful, the likes of which he'd never heard before but she was worn out and just wanted to get home. Due to the late hour, the journey took less than five minutes and when the cab pulled up outside the block of flats; Roxy didn't bother to thank the driver. Taking her change she also didn't offer a tip and disappeared into the flat before he had time to complain. All the lights were on and she called out to Lenny but there was no reply. Unzipping her boots, Roxy kicked them off and left them where they landed. Entering the bedroom she saw why he hadn't answered her. Lenny lay diagonally across the bed and was so far gone, he wouldn't have noticed if the house was on fire. Slowly undressing she sighed at the sight in front of her. He was hard enough to live with at the best of times but seeing him as high as a kite, made her loathe him with a vengeance. Rolling him onto his side she was just able to get onto the bed when she had a thought. Feeling inside his pockets she removed his remaining wrap of heroin. If Lenny was in a good mood he would score for her, obviously tonight had been bad. Roxy knew that by morning he would be clucking and if she used his gear, well it didn't bare thinking about. Deciding to replace it she reached over him to put the wrap back, when her eyes caught sight of the sheets.

'You dirty filthy bastard!'

The smell of urine had begun to fill the air and Roxy was livid. Instead of replacing his stash, she reached inside the bedside drawer for a piece of foil. Unlike her boyfriend, Roxy wasn't into jacking up. The thought of sticking a needle into herself made her shudder; no she had her own preference when it came to administering drugs. Chasing the dragon was enough to get her to sleep and a lot less painful than Lenny's own choice. Pouring the contents of the packet onto the foil, she held a lighter underneath. Instantly the powder turned to liquid and gripping a straw between her teeth, Roxy inhaled deeply. Two goes on the foil and her eyes were heavy, she didn't care about anyone or anything, and she was now ready to sleep. The next thing she knew was being shaken awake by Lenny. His breath hot on her face smelled disgusting and she tried to wriggle free but as skinny as he was, Lenny had a strength that she couldn't match.

'Where is it you thieving little bitch?'

'Get off me Len, you fucking stink.'

His fist landed clean on her jaw and she felt the pain immediately. Desperately she tried to turn her face away, knowing if he marked her badly, then work would be out of the question. Lenny always acted first and thought later. He didn't give a second thought to the real earner in their home, the only person who could supply his drugs when he was having a bad week and bad weeks were recently becoming more frequent. Grasping a handful of her hair he held it up, stretching her neck until she

56

thought it would snap.

'I needed a pick me up last night and you were so far gone that I couldn't ask.'

'So you fucking nicked it? You fucking nicked off the only person in this world who cares about you!'

Feeling his stomach start to churn, Lenny knew it wouldn't be long before the sweats came and he had nothing to dampen the cravings.

'Now what am I going to do? I'm fucking starting to cluck and not a scrap of gear anywhere.'

Hauling her to her feet, Lenny picked up Roxy's coat and pushed her towards the door.

'Get out there and fucking find me something and don't be long about it.'

Walking back into the room she hoped she would be able to pacify him but it wasn't going to work.

'Look Len it's early morning and there won't be no one about. Let me make you a hot drink and I'll pop out a bit later and get you fixed up Ok?'

Again she felt his hand, only this time it connected with her mouth and she winced as the flesh split. Licking the blood away with her tongue, she knew she was on a hiding to nothing if she continued to argue. Quickly pulling on the high boots, Roxy snatched her coat away from him and ran from the flat. Outside was cold and desolate and Roxy couldn't see another soul in the whole Street. Soho was lively at night but until mid morning, only businesses stirred. Entering the square she knew she was stupid to even hope that Denzel would still be around. He wasn't and now she was in turmoil. Leaving the flat in such a panic she hadn't stopped to pick up any cash, what he thought she was going to use to buy any gear with was beyond her. A thought crossed Roxy's mind. No money, no drugs and she realised Lenny knew

57

that as well. Lenny Layton may well be starting to cluck but he was still as sharp as a razor. Roxy knew fine well that if she went back home he wouldn't be there and neither would her hard earned money. Continuing to walk, she soon ended up on Old Compton Street. Making her way up the familiar staircase, Roxy knocked hard on the door and hoped Carmel didn't still have a punter in tow. Her friend had a knack of taking home her last trick of the night, something Roxy had never been able to understand. Maybe it was just the idea of being alone in the small hours that she didn't like. For all prostitutes it was a time of day when it really hit home just what they did for a living. Luckily, Carmel Jones was alone and the hammering on her door was a sound she couldn't be bothered with. It was too early in the morning, so turning over she buried her head under the pillow. Still the loud incessant sound continued.

'All right! All right I'm coming!'

Dragging herself from the bed, she fumbled around in the pile of clothes heaped high on the floor. Finally she found what she was looking for and pulled on a heavily soiled housecoat. Roxy leaned against the wall while she waited for her friend. Forgetting about her face, it wasn't until the door opened that she gave it a second thought.

'Fucking hell girl! Whatever have you done? On second thoughts don't bother it was that cunt Layton wasn't it?'

'Oh Carm whenever am I going to learn hey?'

The older woman led her inside and after seating her on the hard chair by the window, prepared a pot of tea for them both. With a small tin that contained a few plasters, pins and some cotton wool, Carmel Jones proceeded to patch up her young friend as best she could.

'Well he's really put the kybosh on you earning again in a hurry. What was it this time?'

Roxy told the story and didn't leave out anything. Carmel had been round the block more than once and she could tell a mile off if anyone was lying. Anyway Roxy couldn't see that she'd done anything wrong.

'Rox, why do you put up with it? I mean you're a good looking girl who could pull just about anyone. Instead you lumber yourself with a tosser like Layton. Even I can do without a man like him and at my age you can't be that choosey.'

Roxy held the cotton wool tightly to her lip and suddenly the tears started to fall.

'I know Carm and you're right but Lenny has always been there for me and I don't know if I could face life on my own.'

'Of course you can you daft cow! Why don't you go home and get your stuff and move in here with me. I could do with some help on the rent front. What you say?'

Roxy Baxter mulled over the offer for a few seconds. She realised that she had to get away from the one person who swore his undying love for her but in fact was sucking the life right out of her.

'Ok, I'll drink me tea and then go back. That low life won't be home for hours, not now he's got all me money.' Sipping her tea, she winced as the hot liquid touched her lips. Knowing that if the pain was this bad when all she did was drink, then her face must look a real mess. As Roxy set off to collect her things, Carmel slowly closed the door behind her. Having seen the same scenario a thousand times before, she knew that Roxy would make up with Lenny and the whole unhappy scene would begin again. If only she could have her time over but then deep down wasn't that what every brass wished for. Collecting the cups she walked into the kitchenette and swore that if

59

she couldn't get Roxy out of this life, then the least she could do was try and protect her. The only thing was, when it came down to Lenny Layton, the man was totally unpredictable. There wasn't anything that would shock Carmel when it came to that animal. She just wished her friend would wake up to him once and for all, before it was too late!

CHAPTER SEVEN

Tess woke with a start. She'd been resident in London for almost a week and boy had that time dragged. Wearily she rubbed at her eyes and glanced at the bedside clock. Six am and she was already wide-awake. Joe Reynolds was so lazy and being in his company every day, she'd spent most of her time sitting bored to tears at her desk. Deciding she may as well get up, she hoped that perhaps due to the early hour, she would have a chance of slipping out of the house without Agi hearing her. Her enthusiasm for the banquet breakfasts was wearing thin and she didn't know how much more food she could eat. Agatha really was a lovely old lady but she couldn't be making much from the money Tess paid her. In fact, Tess knew that the food alone would come to well over her rent. After showering and trying to be as quiet as she could, she made it to the hall. Collecting her coat from the hallstand, she silently slipped out into the fresh morning air. It really was a beautiful day and Tess decided that for the first time since her arrival she would walk to work. At the top end of Manette Street she turned right onto Charing Cross road. It dauntingly seemed to stretch ahead for miles and she now wished she'd gotten a cab. This main thoroughfare was just beginning to come alive and she casually window-shopped as she strolled along. At last she turned off the main road and the station was almost in site. Passing the Adelaide Street shopping centre, Tess realised that all the walking had made her hungry and right at this minute, she would have eaten anything Agi put in front of her. It was eight thirty and only one place was open, the Silver Spoon café. It catered mainly for tourists but opened

61

early, in the hope of luring in any passing workers that might fancy a full English. Tess pushed open the door and was greeted by a man with a smile that seemed to take over the whole of his face. Theo Domingo was a jolly looking man, who greeted all his customers with the same enthusiasm, as Tess was now about to experience. He liked the police to use his premises as it kept away undesirables and he didn't get any pressure from protection mobs. A healthy discount kept all the local and not so local nicks, as regular clients. Joe Reynolds had introduced Tess to the place on her second day, though she hadn't been in since.

'Miss Davey! 'Ow nice ta see ya again so soon! Please cumma dis way I 'ave a lovely table for yow.'

Tess wanted to giggle. The man's accent was a mixture of Spanish, Italian and god knows what else. She didn't know if he was a very bad actor or if it was just the fact that he'd lived in several different countries throughout his colourful life. Either way she decided not to delve, as Theo's stories could last for hours or so Joe had told her.

'Thank you Mr Domingo.'

'Please calla me Theo, all ma good friends do.'

'In that case Theo, I'd like a full English with toast on the side and a cup of tea please.'

'Comin' righta up.'

The food was excellent and after almost clearing her plate, Tess once more set off for work. She hoped today would be different; that today maybe she could actually do some work. Apart from copying a few files, her time so far had either been spent in the Ship and Shovel with her boss, or monotonously sitting at her desk folding leaflets. It seemed her wish was about to come true. Entering the normally laid back station, Tess was met by an unusually busy reception. Tommy Radcliff glanced up from a pile of papers and rolled his eyes, as much as to say "It's a total fucking nut house Tess". Smiling she made her way upstairs to find the corridor to her and Joes office full of people milling around. Looking closer, she could actually see them coming out of the room.

Entering, she was a little startled to find Joe already sitting at his desk. Though new to the station, Tess had soon learned that an early start for D.I Reynolds meant ten thirty at the earliest.

'Morning Sir!'

The look he gave her told Tess all she needed to know, he wasn't a happy man. The room appeared different somehow and as she glanced around, it dawned on her that everything had been replaced. The desks, chairs, even computers and she couldn't wait to find out what was going on. Fifteen minutes later and they were finally alone.

'So Sir, what's all this about?'

Joe Reynolds stood up from his new chair and walked towards the radiator. Standing with his back to Tess, he looked up at the newly placed picture of the Queen and began to speak.

'That miserable bastard Bateson's been suspended. Something to do with a local crim but I haven't got all the gory details yet.'

'Well that's good news isn't it?'

Joe's reply came in the form of a shriek and Tess sat back in her chair with surprise. Her boss may have been a bit on the lazy side, well in all honesty he was downright idle but he had always seemed so mild mannered.

'Is it fuck! They've now brought in some hot shot to shake up the station and we've got to be at a briefing in ten minutes'

His words were like music to her ears but she knew it

would be prudent not to show her happiness. In the beginning she'd thought the lack of work would give her free time to find her sister but as she hadn't made much progress in that department and things hadn't exactly gone to plan, having something to do would be a relief.

'Oh I see! Best make our way downstairs then.'

Opening the door she stood holding the handle as her boss slowly and with much reluctance, walked towards her. The incident room, situated on the ground floor, was large and packed to capacity. Many of the faces Tess hadn't seen before and she wondered if they had been brought in or were part of the fixtures and were as lazy as her boss. In all probability they had crawled out of the woodwork and had only come in to work to show themselves in a good light to the new boss. Tommy Radcliff came over to join them and the expression on his face was nearly as bad as Joe's.

'What a fucking turn up for the books mate!'

D.I Reynolds removed a cigarette from his pocket and after accepting a light from his old friend the Sergeant, inhaled deeply.

'Turn up for the books! I'll tell you something for nothing Tom things aint never going to be the same again. You mark my words.'

The mood was sombre and small groups of people were huddled together, obviously whispering about what was going on. Finally the door opened and a tall, rather elegant woman came in. Dressed in an expensive navy suit and with her hair piled high on her head, she resembled a retired model more than a chief of police. The room was eerily silent as she made her way to the front and leaned against another of the newly installed desks. Scanning the room her eyes fell upon Joe.

'Put that cigarette out now!'

Joe smirked at her request but walked over to find an ashtray all the same.

'Right let's get down to business. My name is chief inspector Annette Windsor. That's not a name any of you will get to use but all the same it's nice to put a name to a face. To all of you I will be addressed as Ma'am and I insist on the respect that goes along with that title. I am aware that gossip regarding Chief Inspector Bateson must be going through this station like wild fire and I am not about to fuel the flames any further. That's not to say the Internal Investigations Command isn't looking into things. While all that is going on, I shall be running things here. I have a reputation for being hard but fare and if any of the officers in this room have a problem with that, see me after.'

This sentence was directed towards Joe. She didn't take her eyes off him the whole time she spoke and it didn't go unnoticed by Tess.

'Before I explain what's going to happen, I would just like to tell you of a government ruling that came into force quite a while back. All Met premises are non-smoking but I expect the memo regarding that, didn't manage to arrive at this station for some reason.'

Her tone was sarcastic and once again her eyes rested on Joe.

'Now then let's get down to work.'

Standing up, she walked to a large flip chart that had been strategically placed for all to see. Turning the first page, she revealed an in-depth map of Soho and the surrounding areas.

'This ladies and gentlemen is our new target. I plan to clean up as much of it as I can and I will not leave a stone unturned in doing so. Has anyone got a problem with that?'

Several people shuffled their feet but most kept their eyes fixed firmly on the ground. It was nothing new to her and Annette Windsor had been brought up to speed before accepting the post. She was aware that many of the officers fraternized with the local criminals. She was also aware that not a lot of work got done, police or otherwise. Turning the next page on her chart, she revealed the names of all the people in the room. Each of the deadwood officers had been paired with someone that Annette thought could help bring them back into the fold, although this view wasn't voiced.

'I want as many dealers taken off the Streets as is humanly possible. I also want the number of Toms reduced. I don't care that many have been here for years and that some of you might actually be on friendly terms with them. Results will be monitored closely and god help any of you who don't come up to scratch.'

Pointing to the chart she smiled at her audience.

'You have all been paired up with new partners to freshen up your wits so please feel free to see who you're working with from now on. On that note I will leave you all to get on with the job in hand and we'll have another get together in a few days to see how things are Progressing.'

The room remained silent until Annette Windsor had closed the door, then all hell broke loose. People jostled with one another to get to the front, all desperate to see who they had been assigned with. Tess stood at the back with Joe and waited for things to calm down. When the officers had left, all muttering under their breath, she made her way over to the chart. Slowly she scanned the list and was happy to see her and Joe's names were side by side. He was lazy and sometimes a miserable old git but deep down he was growing on her. Walking back to where her boss stood, she was annoyed to see that he'd lit another cigarette.

'Sir, you really are hell bent on making our lives difficult aren't you?'

'You listen to me Tess! I'm not having some jumped up tart coming in here after all these years and telling me what to do.'

Making her way to leave, she looked back over her shoulder as she spoke.

'I don't think you've got much choice in the matter Sir, do you?'

That afternoon Tess got to grips with her computer. Her I.T skills were good but the Met had a totally different system than she'd been used to in Spalding. It was no good asking Joe for help, as he was still sulking over the briefing and Tess had a funny feeling it would be the blind leading the blind anyway. Several hours later and just as her shift was about to finish, she was summoned to the chief's office. The call didn't unnerve her, unlike her meeting with Chief Shepherd, she was actually looking forward to getting to know this woman. Tapping lightly on the door she waited until called.

'Enter.'

The office was pristine and not at all feminine. No family photos adorned the walls, not even the obligatory pot plant on the windowsill.

'Take a seat D.C. Davey. Now I've called you in because you're the newest recruit to the station. The short time you've been with us wouldn't have been long enough to taint you, as it has all the others. Tess, may I call you Tess?'

Detective Davey was in awe of the woman and gingerly nodded her head.

'I want you to be my eyes and ears.'

Tess hadn't been expecting this and her nerves began to surface. Her senior could see immediately that the young woman's head was in turmoil. Annette Windsor had been in the force for over twenty years. Starting at the bottom, she had painstakingly worked her way up and she wasn't finished yet. At forty-two years old, the post of commander was at the top of her achievement list. That said she had to prove herself amongst these Muppets and clean up the area if she ever wanted to be considered for the post. Realising that Tess had immediately put up a guard, she changed tactics.

'Tess, why did you join the force?'

'Pardon?'

'You heard me! Why did you join?'

Tess had to think quickly and knew that the correct answer was imperative.

'To protect and serve. To uphold the law and apprehend as many criminals as possible.'

'Bull shit!'

'Pardon Ma'am?'

'Tess you have just given me the bog standard reply and we both know that deep down, the reason for you joining up was something totally different.'

Tess was gob smacked. She knew that she either had to continue proclaiming her love of the law or be straight with her new boss.

'I'm adopted Ma'am. As an only child, I had to put up with the wrath of a very overbearing tyrannical and dictatorial mother.'

'So by becoming a police woman, you could be the one to dish out the orders?'

'Something like that but please don't think I'm a bully. I treat everyone the same and without blowing my own trumpet, I'm a good policewoman.'

68

'I already know that or you wouldn't be sitting here now.'
Annette Windsor smiled at the young woman, who so
reminded her of herself many years ago. Removing a
bottle of scotch from her top drawer she poured them
both a drink. Tess didn't like whisky but as the
atmosphere had lifted slightly she didn't want to
antagonize the chief. Slowly she sipped at the liquid and
her boss laughed as she downed her own drink in one.
'You've just proven yourself to me, by being honest. If
you'd have continued with the politically correct
explanation, then our meeting would have been over
immediately. Tess there are a lot of rotten apples in this
barrel and no one can be trusted. I've had good reports
about Joe Reynolds, even if he is a bit work shy and
Chief Inspector Shepherd holds you in very high regard.
You two being the only ones who I assume are not bent,
means you will become my A
team.'
'Ma'am, there's no way Joe would ever spill the beans on
any of his colleagues.'
'I'm not asking him to. All I want is to have a handful of
people I can call on if necessary and luckily for you two,
you've got the job. Now go back to Joe and explain all
that I've said. I dare say he's calmed down by now.'
Tess returned to her office more confused than ever but
the sight of Joe made her smile. New office furniture or
not, there he was with feet upon the desk fast asleep, or
so she thought. Suddenly but with his eyes still closed,
he began to question her.
'So! What did the bitch want you for?'
Tess repeated every word that had been said and she
could see that Joe was becoming more and more agitated.
'That bitch wants us to be grasses and I don't use that
term loosely.'

69

'It's not a case of that Joe. She has to do a clear up and there are a lot of bent coppers on this patch. She doesn't want us to drop them in it, on the contrary actually. We're to carry out our work as normal, or in your case abnormal.'

'Cheeky cow!'

'What Chief Windsor wants, are some eyes and ears out on the street. If we know of any dodgy dealings within the station, then she just wants us to tip her the wink. That's all.'

'Fuck me Tess, how long did you say you'd been in the force? You're as wet behind the ears as a day one rookie.'

His words offended her deeply and this time she wasn't about to hold back.

'Now you listen to me Joe Reynolds! I want to do my job to the best of my ability. I don't want to sit around here all day playing games or spending the remainder of my working hours down the pub. The chief has shown an interest in us and even if you have no desire to rise in the ranks, I do. Now it's been a long day and I'm going home.'

Without another word Tess grabbed her bag and marched from the room. Joe Reynolds resumed his position of earlier and closed his eyes. Grinning to himself, he thought that his new partner was a feisty little thing when she got her heckles up. Things around here were suddenly becoming interesting.

CHAPTER EIGHT

Maxi Leroy Trueman had arrived in England with his parents at the tender age of five. By the time he'd reached his teens, he was well and truly on the way to a life of crime. Proud to be called a 'Yardie' though he didn't hanker for the sunshine of Kingston. There his family had been poor and nothing more than low class citizens. Here in the UK the world was their oyster, or so Solomon Trueman was heard to say on many an occasion. Maxi's father Solomon, gained employment with London transport and had hoped that Maxi would follow in his footsteps. Maxi on the other hand had always wanted more. He didn't see the point in just surviving, even if that meant a shorter life, it would be worth it. Lady Truman was a typical Jamaican mother and in her eyes the boy could do no wrong. Every day she would pass the youngster a five-pound note before she headed off to her cleaning job at the local school. Maxi always accepted the cash gratefully but would sneer at his parents behind their backs. An only child they doted on him and he could have had the world at his feet but that wasn't for Maxi. By the age of eighteen he was dealing on a regular basis and bringing home more income than both his parents combined. The flash clothes and up to the minute trainers gave the game away and his father soon gave him an ultimatum.

'Clean up ya act bwoy or yah can git outta dis howes fa eva.'

Maxi Truman didn't need to be told twice and within a week of the father son chat he had set up home in a nice little flat on the Gray's Inn road. It always made Maxi feel smug when he passed the nearby Royal Courts of

Justice in his gleaming BMW series three, that he still hadn't been collared. His sharp mind had kept him out of trouble when most would have been banged up long ago. Where the majority of Yardie's preferred to live in the area that they worked, mostly South London, Maxi had leased a small flat far enough away so as not to be linked. His parents still resided in Camberwell but as he rarely saw them, it posed no problem. Many Yardie's were now moving to the north. Maxi was well aware that a bag of crack which sold here in the smoke for a tenner could make five times more in Leeds or Bradford. He was also aware that new faces made easy targets, especially when it came to the Old Bill. Lenny Layton had become an acquaintance of Maxi's purely by chance. It was a couple of years ago now, when Lenny had just been released from a five stretch for dealing. Propping up the bar at the Kings Head, Lenny had been waiting for Bobby Race. Unlike Maxi, Bobby supplied anything and not only narcotics. If you wanted a young girl, even a boy, then Bobby was your man. Lenny had been out of Her Majesties for only a couple of hours and was starting to climb the walls. The Kings Head was the only place he knew the youngster to frequent and had popped in on the off chance. Unfortunately for Lenny, Bobby was himself doing a two stretch and wouldn't be meeting anyone for the foreseeable future. As Maxi walked in he spotted Lenny and seeing the man's desperation, moved in for the kill. A deal was struck and there and then a mutual understanding began, that had until recently, been moving along just nicely. It was well known that Yardie's targeted heroin users. Persuading them to move onto Crack wasn't difficult and it was so addictive that after a couple of free rocks, they were hooked. Then it was sit back and watch the profits soar. It hadn't been the case with Lenny but with a few free wraps of his preferred drug, he was soon happy to join Maxi's work force. Recently Lenny had been having more and more rocks on account and Maxi had decided enough was enough. Lenny had been selling the crack in order to get cash for heroin but he hadn't handed over the money, well now his time was fast running out. As was standard practice with Yardie's, killing was a Medal worn like a badge of honour and it wouldn't be the first time that Maxi Trueman had completed the circle of someone's life. No, Lenny Layton was going to pay and pay dear at that, or he was going to have to work extra hard for Maxi. Roxy was back where she belonged and enjoying every minute of it. Having not made up with Lenny immediately, she had stayed at Carmel's for a couple of nights but had eventually returned home to her man, tail between her legs so to speak. Lenny had missed her income and had welcomed her with open arms. To Roxy Baxter this was a sign that she was loved and she spent hours at the cooker making them both something nice to eat. Lenny had hurt her feelings by pushing his food around the plate and after a couple of fork full's, he stood up from the makeshift table and told Roxy he needed to go out.

'I need some air girl, this is doing me fucking head in.'

'But I thought we could have a night in babe, make up for the last few days?'

Lenny shook his head as he proceeded to put on his one and only jacket.

'Need a fix, besides shouldn't you be out earning or do you expect me to provide every fucking thing?'

Roxy didn't have any fight left in her to argue. As her man began to trawl the Streets in search of a hit, she began to glam herself up. Most of her clothes were soiled and she made a mental note to go to the launderette. A tiny black T-shirt was all she really had clean but it had short sleeves. Short sleeves and Roxy Baxter were a definite no no. She didn't care how miniscule her skirts were but tops had to be preferably high necked and definitely long sleeved. Rooting through the cardboard box that doubled as a laundry bin, she found a long sleeved grey top that could just about count as passable. Slipping out of her worn dressing gown, she surveyed herself in the cracked mirror that hung on the back of the door. Her arms were almost covered in tiny scars from shoulder to forearm. The sight of all the pink lines made her at once have an overwhelming need to cut herself. It had been a vicious circle of cutting, doctors, therapy and more cutting her whole life. Nothing anyone could say or do made a difference to Roxy and she hated herself for it. Lenny had never bothered about the scars, so she didn't either but if a punter saw them, then that would be any chance of a trick out of the window. They would see her as damaged goods, like she had some kind of disease and then she wouldn't be able to earn for Lenny. The last thing she wanted to do was upset him, not when things had been going so well since she'd returned. Taking in a deep breath, she hurriedly put on the grey top and smoothed down the material over her arms. Staring at her face in the mirror she touched the cut on her lip that Lenny had split open only a few days earlier. It was healing nicely and with extra lippy and gloss it would hardly notice. After applying pale blue eye shadow and dark eyeliner, the look was complete and it was time to go. Closing the front door, she stood on the step and looked out into the road as she spoke. 'If I jumped off a bridge, would anyone miss me at all?' Smiley Cosgrave, named because of the permanent smile a punter had given her years earlier, was entering the flat next door.

'You all right Roxy?'

'Yeh! Fine, why?'

'You was fucking talking to yourself that's why. First fucking sign of madness is talking to yourself.'

Roxy grinned as she began to walk and turning back over her shoulder called out.

'No it's not Smiley, it's when you start answering your bleeding self that you have to worry.'

There was no reply and Roxy doubted that the woman had even heard her. Once again she could feel the total loneliness envelope her. It was cold again tonight and she could see her breath emitting in little white jets as she walked along. There wouldn't be many out tonight and she didn't feel like standing alone. There was nothing for it but to head for Carmel's and hope she was in. Roxy could see as she passed Soho Square that as usual Denzel was out touting for business. Continuing to walk along, she suddenly stopped when something strange crossed her mind. When Denzel saw her coming he hadn't called out, in fact he'd turned to face the other way and she knew it wasn't because he hadn't seen her. Just to make sure, Roxy backtracked and entered the square. Two or three youths milled around and she knew that as soon as she was out of sight, they would be after Denzel for whatever he was selling today. He saw her approaching and was about to make a quick exit, when she called out.

'Hi Denzel! busy tonight?'

Hanging his head, Roxy could only just make out what he was saying.

'Look Rox, I aint got no ruck with you but you need to fuck off and quick. Maxi's on the warpath looking for your man and if he sees me talking to you, then I'm in big

75

trouble.'

Never one to let go of a problem easily and with the added agro that it involved her man, Roxy pushed the weasel standing before her.

'What do you mean, he's after Lenny?'

Denzel was starting to get agitated and suddenly he walked away.

'Denzel! Denzel come back!'

Roxy's words fell on deaf ears and suddenly she felt scared. Rubbing her arms, partly due to the cold and partly due to her fear, she could only think of one person who might be able to help, Carmel. Lenny Layton had scored from Bobby and was making his way back to the flat, when a car pulled up beside him. Glancing into the cars window he saw it was Maxi Trueman. At that moment nothing mattered more than getting away and as old as he was, Lenny could still out run most when pushed. The trouble was that no mans speed could match that of a series three BMW. Putting his foot down hard on the accelerator, Maxi laughed as he chased after his prey. When he finally cornered Lenny just a few feet from the man's flat, he clenched his fists in a euphoric gesture. Lenny Layton was doubled over and panting like a grey hound. In Soho it wouldn't have been a problem getting away but in Berners Mews there were no rat runs. Admitting defeat he held up his hands as Maxi got out of the car.

'Len me old mate! What say we go inside for a chat?'

Lenny was in no position to argue, he couldn't utter a single word and his breathing was raspy and laboured. Placing his key in the lock took several attempts, as his hands were shaking so much. He knew he was in for a beating but that fear was fast becoming superseded by his need for drugs. One look at his face and Maxi knew he was in for an easy ride. Entering the dilapidated room that barely passed for a lounge, Maxi sucked in air between the gap in his teeth.

'How the fuck do you live in a pigsty like this man?' Lenny didn't answer, his hand now inside the pocket of his jeans, caressed the tiny package. He just wished his tormentor would get whatever it was he wanted to do over with and leave him in peace. Maxi moved closer and before Lenny knew what was happening, the man was holding a gun to his temple. The piece wasn't ordinary run of the mill either; no this was a true Yardie signature weapon. A point two two-air pistol converted to take bullets but at a quick glance didn't appear suspicious in the eyes of the law.

'Right you cunt! You've pulled the piss long enough. Now the way I see it there are two roads we can go down.'

'Whatever you say Maxi.'

'Shut the fuck up you cunt. Don't fucking speak until I tell you to.'

Maxi Trueman was fast becoming fed up with the man and he lashed out at Lenny's cheek with the barrel of the gun. Pain seared through Lenny and his face felt as though it was on fire.

'Please Mr Trueman! I'll do whatever you want.'

Again Maxi smashed the gun into the side of his victims face and this time they both heard a tiny crack. Lenny's eyes were wide open and he resembled a frightened rabbit, caught in the headlights of a car. Pressing the tip of the barrel into the damaged skin was more than Lenny could bear and Maxi could see the tears starting to form in his victim's eyes.

'Now where was I? Oh yeh, I can either pull the trigger on this pretty little thing and it'll be over for good or you can pay me what you fucking owe me.'

'I'll pay Mr Trueman, I'll pay but I just need a few days. Me girls out earning as we speak and I know she'd be up for a bit of overtime if I asked her. Please Mr Trueman, I know I've taken liberties but it won't happen again, I swear to you.'

'Fucking right it won't cunt because if I come looking for you again there aint going to be no conversation. You've got twenty-four hours then its judgment day and don't think the cash is the end of it, because it aint. You're going to work your skinny white arse off for me in the way of an apology.'

For good measure Maxi poked the man's face one last time before he left. Lenny screamed out and Maxi laughed.

'Na don't be getting any daft ideas like runnin' away cause me hunt ya down like de mad dag dat ya is.'

Lenny Layton hated the way blacks reverted back to a language that wasn't native to them but somehow made them feel superior. He waited until he heard the front door slam, and then removed the tiny package from his pocket. The pain in his cheek was throbbing and he knew that a visit to the hospital should be his main priority. Trouble was if he didn't sort himself out and soon, then he'd never make it to the end of the road let alone the hospital. After he had staggered and fumbled his way into the bedroom, he once more began to arrange the paraphernalia required to carry out the ritual which ruled his life.

Roxy's mind was going in all directions as she hurried along and she decided to take the long route to Carmel's. On Greek Street she turned into Bateman and then onto Dean Street. All the roads were full with revellers and trying to find Lenny was like looking for a needle in a

78

haystack. Entering Brewer Street was like a Moonie meeting, she hadn't seen so many people in a long time. This wasn't an area she came to much and if she did, it was mostly in the daytime when things were quiet. A healthy queue of diners was beginning to form outside Aldo Zilli's fish restaurant and Roxy imagined that if she had a load of money then that would be the place she'd like to go. Turning into Windmill and passing Soho parish school, she shook her head. The building was flanked by sex shops and even to Roxy that didn't seem right. How did you explain to a five year old exactly what the things on display were? Crossing Shaftesbury Avenue, she finally made it to Gerrard Street and entered The Kings Head. It wasn't a pub Lenny took her to; he didn't take her anywhere except bed and even that wasn't exciting. He would never blame himself and told her if she didn't enjoy it, then it was her fault. One of his favourite sayings was "If you worked in a butchers, then you wouldn't want steak for tea". No one in the place acknowledged her, even though they knew she was Lenny's piece of skirt. Walking round the bar, she scanned every corner and realized he wasn't there. Panic again began to build inside her and she was almost run over as she fled the pub and rushed back over Shaftesbury Avenue. Five minutes later, she was banging as hard as she could on Carmel's door. It was an age before anyone answered and Roxy thought her mate must already be out at work. About to descend the stairs, she at last heard the door being unlooked. Carmel's appearance told Roxy that her friend had been asleep and she knew what a grumpy mare Carmel could be when she was woken prematurely.

'Sorry Carm, only I didn't know where else to go. Well to tell the truth I was on my way out and then I bump into

Denzel. Well not really bump into exactly and.'
Carmel Jones put up her hand and showed Roxy the palm.
'Woooo! Hold on there a minute girl. I can't understand a fucking word you're on about. Come inside and we'll have a drink and you can tell me all about it.'
'Carm I aint got time I've got to find.....'
Again the older of the two woman stopped Roxy mid sentence.
'Whatever's happened it won't be any the worse for waiting a few more minutes. Now come on in.'
Roxy Baxter did as she was asked and gratefully accepted the vodka when it was handed to her. Eventually she told her friend what had happened and about walking the Streets trying to find her man.
'What should I do Carm?'
'Well I don't think you should be thinking about work tonight, do you? Probably best if you get home and wait it out. Maybe Lenny will come back home before he sees Maxi and then you can warn him.'
The advice was good and without a goodbye, Roxy ran from the flat and made it home in record time. The place was in darkness and fear started to rise as she entered. Running straight to the bedroom, Roxy switched on the light and gave a huge sigh of relief when she saw Lenny asleep on the bed. A tear slipped down her cheek as she walked over to where he lay. It wasn't until she was level with him that she saw the state of his face. It had doubled in size on one side and she knew Maxi had already gotten to him. Her one consolation was the fact that he had allowed him to live. In time his face would heal and then they would be back to normal again. Quietly undressing, she slipped in beside him and gently cuddled up. Roxy fell fast asleep blissfully unaware of what was about to

happen in just a few hours time.

CHAPTER NINE

After their briefing with Chief Inspector Windsor, Tess thought things would change immediately but she was wrong. Joe continued to shuffle papers and when he wasn't doing that, would get out a pack of cards and play solitaire. Not one attempt was made on his part, to do any real work. Time was moving on and as yet she hadn't done a thing about finding her long lost sister. Deciding that she might as well begin her own investigation, she opened up her computer and started the ball rolling. Playing around at first, she entered a few names into the machine to see what came up. After typing in the Chiefs name, a striking photograph popped up onto the screen along with a brief career history. Next she tried Joe's name but no matter how many attempts she made, the screen remained blank. Tess was confused and looking over at the man, who had dropped off to sleep at his desk and was now snoring softly, she shook her head in amazement. Not being able to get any info on him didn't matter to her that much, she knew that things always had a way of coming out in the wash. Pressing the keys to spell out her own name, she smiled at the wording. It was obvious that Sophie had played a hand in typing her history, due to her use of the Queens English and partly due to the over embellishment of Tess's involvement in the paedophile case. Anyone else reading this would have thought Tess had solved the case single-handed and the least she deserved was to be made commander. She laughed out loud but when Joe stirred, she cut short her glee, so as not to wake him. After a few more attempts she was now confident to try the criminal records. Ever since she'd found out about her sister, she'd been dying to search through the database. While she was still in Spalding, to have put any London names in the system would have aroused suspicion to say the least. Tony in IT was able to cover his tracks but she hadn't actually seen the wording for herself. His brief was limited and she hadn't dared push him too far, or he may have started to ask questions. The force didn't look kindly on its employees using information for personal gain. Now here she was in the very place where her sister lived, or so she hoped and everything was at her fingertips. Nervously she typed in the name Sally Sayers and sat back in her chair waiting for something to appear. Five minutes later and the screen was still blank. Tess wanted to kick herself, what had possessed her to think that her sister even had a criminal record. For all she knew, Sally was married now with a couple of kids. She decided that tomorrow she would take the day off and make inquires at the public records office. If Sally had married, then that would be the best place to begin. The thought that she may be an aunt by now hadn't crossed her mind but she liked the idea of it all the same. Knowing that Layton was her only link at the moment, she typed in a name she'd been dying to find out more about. Immediately the screen flashed up with her first piece of evidence, Lenny Layton's criminal history.

Born 13/4/1959. Walthamstow. East London. Previous. Conviction for manslaughter 1984. (Time served five years) Conviction for supply of class A drug. 1996. (Time served five years). Last known address 15 Moxon Street. Marylebone. Known associates. Maxi Trueman. - Drug dealer. Bobby Race. - Drug dealer. Harry Marsh. - Handling stolen goods. Terry Westland. - Armed robbery. Denzel Howard. - Drug dealer.

The list was endless and Tess was so taken back with what was coming up, that she began to shake. Pressing the print key, she waited for the information on this low life of a man to vomit itself from the machine. Checking the time by her watch, Tess knew she had at least another hour before Joe would wake and want to go for his obligatory end of shift drink. Scanning the list she chose the name of Maxi Trueman as a starting point. The information that filled the screen was electric and she thought that maybe it was possible to nail two birds with one stone. Although Trueman had never been charged, there were too many associates and too many failed attempts to prosecute, for him not to be guilty of something. It looked like Trueman had nine lives but Tess believed in justice and Maxi Truman's time was fast running out. Annette Windsor wanted the Streets cleaned up and what better way to start, than with information on local dealers. Drugs weren't something Tess had any real experience of and she didn't quite know where to begin but having to start somewhere, she continued with the names of Bobby Race and Denzel Howard. Just as the last piece of paper was printed, Joe finally woke.
'What are you up to?'
Closing down the file, she logged out and turned to her boss.
'Nothing much, just trying to find my way around the system.'
'Waste of time if you ask me. If you need machines to do police work, then we're all doomed.'
'Oh don't be so old fashioned Joe. It's about time you moved into the twenty first century. Ready for a drink or are you staying there all night? Stupid question really, you've probably taken up root.'

Standing up Joe Reynolds held his back, which was aching like mad as he tried to stretch out.

'You're getting a cheeky cow Davey!'

'I know, now are you coming or not?'

As was becoming the custom, the two made their way out of the station and headed towards the Ship and Shovel. Joe had been smitten with his new recruit from day one. It wasn't her looks that was for sure but there was something genuine about the girl. It was a trait that was seldom seen these days and one that Joe Reynolds liked. The following morning, Tess slept late. Having cleared it with her new boss at a cost of two large scotches, she'd decided to have a little time to herself. Pulling on her dressing gown, she grinned at the knock on the door.

'Come in Agi.'

'Morning sweetie! wondered if you was a little under the weather?'

'No I'm fine, just a day off that's all.'

'That's good, only Mr Seaman and me were a bit worried about you. You aint been down to breakfast for a couple of days. Nothing wrong with the grub, is there?'

'Nothing at all Agi. Give me a few minutes to get ready and I'll show you just how good your catering is. I'm famished.'

Agi Goldstein almost skipped from the room. She loved having guests and loved cooking for them even more. People may have said that her over the top spreads were wasteful and too extravagant but then they hadn't been in Germany in nineteen forty four. It wasn't something she would discuss with anyone, not even Geoffrey but no one would ever leave her house hungry and that was a promise. Tess sat down to a small helping of bacon and egg followed by, at Agi's insistence, a large bowl of porridge. Smiling Tess began to spoon the glutinous

85

mixture into her mouth. When Agi went to freshen up the pot, she poured the remainder of her breakfast back into the serving dish, just as Geoffrey Seaman came into the room.

'Morning Tess.'

'Hello Geoffrey, hope you're hungry!'

The two were having a private giggle just as Agatha re entered the room. Tess held her stomach in a gesture of fullness.

'Well Agi, that was fantastic as usual but I really need to make a move. I have a few places to go to and times getting on.'

'Hold on a second and I'll get me coat sweetie, I could do with a breath of fresh air.'

Tess gritted her teeth, this was all she needed. Luckily for her she was saved by the kind Geoffrey Seaman.

'For goodness sake Agatha! The young woman probably has private business to attend to and she doesn't want a silly old woman tagging along.'

Glad of the rescue, Tess still felt guilty when she saw the hurt in Agatha's eyes.

'I'm so sorry my dear, I didn't think. Perhaps when you don't have so much to do we can have a day out shopping together?'

'I would love that Agi, now I really do need to hurry along. Bye!'

Not until he heard the front door close, did Geoffrey Seaman take Agatha into his arms.

'Come here you silly woman and give me a kiss.'

Agi began to act coy and tried to shy away from the aging man.

'You'll have to catch me first!'

After hailing a cab, Tess reached Charring Cross station.

From there she boarded a train to Orpington. Lying
awake last night thinking, she decided that maybe the
public records office wasn't the best place to start
looking; maybe there was somewhere far better. The
journey lasted less than half an hour and when she caught
the number 353 bus to Ramsden Estate she was
beginning to enjoy the trip. Her dad used to take her on
the buses and for once it brought back happy memories.
The estate was clean and tidy and she imagined it was a
nice place to grow up in. What had made her sister want
to leave and follow a low life like Lenny Layton?
Number ten was a typical eighties end of terrace, in a row
of four. The front garden was neat and the nets a pristine
white. Nervously Tess rang the bell and waited. A tall
rather distinguished looking gentleman answered the door
and after Tess explained who she was, the man invited
her inside. A rounded homely woman emerged from the
kitchen, complete with farmhouse style apron, which
strained to cover her ample bosoms. Robert Parsons
informed his wife in a dictatorial tone as to who their
guest was. Mavis Parsons nodded her hello then
immediately disappeared back into the kitchen. Entering
the living
room, Tess was struck by its bareness. Apart from a sofa
and one hard chair, there was nothing in the room. A
large crucifix took pride of place above the mantle and all
at once she began to understand why Sally had left.
'So Miss Davey, how can I help?'
Smiling her thanks, Tess accepted the offer of a seat that
had been pointed to by her host.
'I'm not really sure Mr Parsons. It's a shot in the dark
but I just wondered if maybe there was anything you may
have forgotten that could help me find Sally? It doesn't
matter how tiny a detail, it's just that I'm not having a lot

of luck tracking her down.'

Suddenly the man became agitated, as if she had said something that the family were so very desperately trying to keep hidden.

'Miss Davey! I have told you all that I can. Sally stayed with us for a few years before running off with a man many years older than herself. The girl was nothing but trouble and broke my wife's heart. Now if there is nothing else, I would appreciate it if you left.'

Obviously Tess had touched a raw nerve but she knew the man would divulge nothing more. Making her way back towards the bus stop, she hadn't got more than a few hundred yards, when she heard her name being called. Turning round she saw a red faced Mavis Parsons running towards her. She was still dressed in the ridiculous apron and her breasts flew in all directions as she moved. The woman must have used every bit of energy she had and was puffing and panting profusely when she reached Tess's side.

'Miss Davey I'm sorry for my husband's ungracious behaviour.'

'It wasn't anything I didn't expect Mrs Parsons. It must be painful to have all this raked up again.'

Mavis Parson shook her head.

'Without going into detail, well let's just say my husband isn't the easiest person in the world to live with.'

Suddenly the woman thrust her hand inside the pocket of her apron. She pulled out a well-worn photograph and handed it to Tess.

'I don't suppose this will be of any help but it's the only one I have. Mr Parsons doesn't know I have it. My husband doesn't believe in the frivolity of keepsakes. If you find Sally will you tell her that I miss her?'

'Of course I will and thank you, thank you so much.'

Slowly the woman turned round and began to walk towards her house. Tess could see how down trodden she was and understood that if the man had treated her sister like that, then the girl would have had no reason to stay. Ironically it was the same kind of upbringing she herself had experienced, only with the parental roles reversed.

Within the hour Tess was once more in Charring Cross. Her first steps hadn't gone according to plan, so she decided to visit Layton's last known address. It was a fair way to Marylebone and Tess didn't fancy fighting her way across the capitol on the underground. Opting to treat herself, she hailed another cab. Number fifteen was in a small block of privately owned flats and as the ground floor accommodation was large, she hoped that it was owner occupied. A grossly overweight man in a stained string vest answered the door and she could tell straight away that he wasn't happy at being disturbed. Flashing her warrant card, Tess asked if the man could recall a Lenny Layton living at that address.

'Oh, that bastard! 'Course I can. Wasn't here long but left owing me a month's rent. He had a pretty young girl with him though, I think she'd been around the block a few times, you can tell cant you?'

The man's words pierced Tess's heart and she wondered just what kind of life her sister was living.

'How do you mean?'

'Nothing I could put my finger on but I've been alive long enough to know when someone's up to no good! Mind you I wouldn't have said no if it had been offered, know what I mean?'

Tess's skin began to crawl but she didn't let the man see her distaste. Passing him her card for inspection, she asked if he knew Lenny's whereabouts and when he shook his head, asked him to call if anything else came up. Slowly she began the long walk home. Instead of going back to Agi's, Tess continued her journey and ended up in the heart of Soho. Enjoying the cosmopolitan atmosphere, she stopped for a coffee at one of the small cafes. Choosing a table by the window, she sat and people watched for the best part of an hour. It was now early afternoon and the place was starting to come alive with a mixture of human beings, in fact any nationality you cared to mention. Tess saw every colour and creed as she stared through the window, leisurely sipping at her coffee. The bustling Street markets, up and running by six am every morning, sold just about anything you could name. Men and women alike, called out in strong cockney accents to anyone who cared to listen 'Five for a tenner. Come on ladies get your best fillet steak, five for a tenner.'

Behind the glass façade of the coffee shop Tess couldn't smell the ripe aromas of fish mingled with vegetables and it was just as well. Higher-class shops flanked the stalls on either side but the two seemed to marry along nicely. Paying for her drink she once more emerged onto the Street. The place had a unique identity, even if it was fading fast. Rising rents and theme bars owned by large conglomerates had begun to push out many of the more colourful characters that had resided here all their lives. It was a sad thought but one Tess knew could never be halted. Somehow she had ended up on Windmill Street and Raymond's Review bar stood out with its neon lights, even in broad daylight. Soho life was lived at a different pace and the best and worst of people inhabited it. Everyone who lived here seemed to tolerate any kind of life style, no matter how sad or depraved. Tess found the area exciting but at the same time didn't know if it was somewhere she could stay long term. She felt a chill run

90

down her spine and decided it was time to go back to Agi's for a little comfort. After the day she'd had, there was nothing better to look forward to, than the warm welcome she could expect to receive from her landlady. Silently she said a prayer to her sister and hoped with all her heart that Sally was living in the same conditions as she was. To imagine anything else was unbearable and she whispered the words 'Hold on Sis, I'm trying as fast as I can to find you.'

CHAPTER TEN

While Tess had been out and about by ten o'clock that morning, Roxy Baxter was just waking up. Sleepily stretching out, she felt across the bed for Lenny and could feel that the empty space was still warm. Dragging herself from the cosy place that she could willingly have spent all day in, she made her way to the kitchen. Placing the kettle on the stove, she was rummaging in a drawer for matches when she sensed him behind her. Turning round, Roxy was shocked at the look on his face and it wasn't anything to do with his injury. At that precise moment he wore an expression of pure hatred and for the life of her she didn't know why. Walking towards him with arms open wide, she wanted to embrace him but he remained like a statue.

'I know what's happened Len! I saw Denzel on the way out and he told me Maxi was after you. What's going on?'

'Never mind what's fucking going on bitch, where's your cash.'

'What cash? I aint got any.'

'I sent you out there last night remember. Now unless you're fucking giving it away for free there should be a nice wedge here somewhere.'

Roxy turned her back to him and began trying to light the stove again. Tears stung her eyes but she wouldn't allow him the pleasure of seeing her hurt. Instead she carried on as if nothing had happened and after getting the mugs from the cupboard, continued to prepare the tea.

'Are you fucking deaf or what? Where's the fucking money?'

Roxy was now losing her temper and as she swivelled

92

round to face him, knocked the carton of milk off the unit.

'Now look what you've made me do! For the last time Lenny, I aint got none. Yes I was out and about to go on the earn but then I saw Denzel and I couldn't think about anything but you. I ran round to the Kings Head and when I couldn't find you, went on to Carmel's. She said I should come back home and wait for you, so that's what I did.'

Lenny took a step closer to her and Roxy could see that he was in pain. She wanted to stop arguing and just hold him but she knew Lenny and today wasn't going to be good.

'That fucking bitch has interfered in my business once too often, where the fuck does she get off telling you what to do?'

'Lenny don't talk about Carmel like that. She's been a good friend to me and at times I don't know what I would have done without her.'

Another step and Lenny was level with her. Roxy could smell his sour breath on her face and she turned away from him. The next thing she knew she was being swung round by her hair and then suddenly being let go. It felt like she was spinning across the room and as she smacked into the fridge, Roxy fell to the floor. Having felt the wrath of Lenny's anger many times over the last couple of years and no more so than just recently, she curled into a tight ball. Each kick felt as if her insides were being torn out and she cried out in pain as he continued dishing out her punishment in an almost state of frenzy. A few seconds later, although to Roxy it seemed like much longer, Lenny Layton finally stopped. While Roxy lay writhing in agony on the dirty kitchen floor, he took a seat at the table, calmly lighting a cigarette as he did so.

'Roxy, Roxy, Roxy, why do you have to be so bleeding lippy all the time. If you weren't so fucking cocky and spoke to me with a bit of respect, we wouldn't have to keep going through all this.'

Lenny stood up and walked over to where she still lay in the foetal position and placed his hand on her head. Roxy flinched at his touch and he smiled at the respect he commanded.

'Now I want you to listen, are you listening Rox?'

She knew better than to ignore him and although she couldn't speak, nodded her head vigorously.

'Good girl. Now I owe Maxi Trueman big time and naturally he wants his money. When you've got yourself cleaned up I want you back out on the street selling your arse like never before. I need a grand by the end of the day and another tomorrow. Think you can manage that?'

Again she nodded and received another smile for agreeing.

'Right then let's not waste time. Get in that shithouse and sort yourself out. By the way, Maxi wants me to work for him, so we could be on the fucking up in a few months.'

Roxy staggered to her feet and used the fridge to support herself.

'Get a fucking move on then times ticking away tick tock tick tock!'

He playfully slapped her behind as she passed, it was as if he was oblivious to the events of only a few seconds ago. This time his words didn't require a reply and for Roxy, the fight had been knocked out of her and she just wanted to curl up and die. The bathroom was barren and cold. They'd been without heating for months and even though she earned good money, there was never any to pay bills with. Lenny was so fond of getting high that he didn't care about heating. Filling the basin with cold water, she splashed her face and shrank back from the porcelain as waves of pain washed through her. Wiping her hand across the cabinet mirror, she peered at her reflection. He'd really done it this time! Roxy's left eye was beginning to close and the split lip from earlier in the week had reopened. The urge to cut was beginning to build up inside her but for once she was able to contain it, the pain was so bad that she doubted she'd have the strength anyway. It was hurting her to breath and she guess that he'd probably cracked one of her ribs. Gently patting her face dry with the only towel they possessed, she shuffled to the bedroom. As she tentatively slipped from her dressing gown she slowly began to put on the clothes of last night. The top was beginning to smell and she liberally sprayed herself with cheap perfume that she'd brought down the market for a fiver a go. Dressing took twice as long as normal and she worried he would come after her and dish out some more, just because she was taking so long. Pulling the top over her head she caught sight of her torso in the mirror. Large purple bruises were beginning to form on her skin and by tomorrow Roxy knew she would look a right state. Not bothering with makeup, she pulled on her coat and picked up her handbag. The front door was in sight and the only thing Roxy wanted, was to get as far away from Lenny as possible. Thinking that her prayers were going to be answered, she was about to turn the handle when she heard him behind her.

'Not trying to sneak off were you? Only if you were thinking of going on the trot you can think again. You know I'll always find you.'

He was directly behind her now and she could feel her

whole body begin to tense. The restriction to her ribs caused more pain and she wanted to cry out. Instead she turned round and tried with all her might to smile.

'Why do you beat me Lenny? I sell my body for you and you get all the money, aint that enough?'

She knew her words were like a red rag to a bull but somehow she couldn't stop herself. Lenny raised his hand and was about to bring it sharply across her face, when she was saved by a knock at the door.

'Fuck off and earn some money and don't come back until you have what I need.'

Roxy was out of the door and charging by Maxie Trueman so fast that she didn't even notice him in the doorway. Maxi did a double take when he saw her. Secretly he'd always had a thing for Roxy but today he could hardly recognise her. It had never ceased to amaze him that she'd given Lenny the time of day let alone sleep with him.

'Poor bitch! got done over by a punter or what?'

Lenny smirked at his handy work.

'Nah, just getting a bit lippy that's all. I have to put her in her place now and again, let her know whose boss like. Cunts like Roxy are only good for one thing and believe me, she aint all that. Anyway come on in and have a drink.'

Maxi could remember the state of the place from last night and instantly declined the offer.

'I'll wait in the car.'

Lenny fetched his leather jacket and was soon sitting beside the Jamaican in his gleaming BMW. Maxi started the engine but before pulling out, turned to Lenny.

'You got me money?'

'Bit of a problem there mate, the bitch didn't earn last night but after I explained everything this morning, she's gone out to earn it now. By tomorrow you should be fully paid up.'

'Yad beata bwoy or ya know wa it'll be.'

He was back using the patois again and Lenny hated it. He was also feeling scared and knew that the darky always kept to his word. Facing straight ahead, he didn't look at Maxis face and the two drove off in silence. The drive to Camberwell took thirty minutes due to the heavy traffic. Lenny didn't get out of his own manor much and was enjoying the change of scenery. He didn't have a clue where they were going and in all honesty he didn't care. Right at this moment he felt as though things were possibly on the up and that feeling was enough to make him happy. They pulled up in Cold Harbour Lane, a tiny side Street that had another road running horizontally across its top. Maxi, with the engine still running, pointed to a small coffee shop further along.

'You'll find a bloke called Drayton he's expecting you and will give you a package. Don't speak to no one or ask any stupid fucking questions, do you hear?'

Lenny was about to get out of the car, when he felt Maxi's hand on his arm.

'Take this.'

Pressing a twenty-pound note into Lenny's hand, Maxi put the car in gear.

'What's that for?'

'Are you planning on fucking walking back or what?'

Suddenly the penny dropped and Lenny knew he was a mule, pure and simple.

'Fuck me Maxi! When you said about working for you, I didn't think you meant fucking running.'

Maxi Trueman instantly lost his temper and slammed his hands on the staring wheel.

'You're nothing but a cunt Layton, do you really think

97

I'd give you anything decent to do. You will fucking mule for me or any other thing I fucking ask of you. Unless you'd rather have your punishment over in one fell swoop?'

Lenny knew what the man meant and decided that this way was the better of two evils.

Closing the car door, he didn't make any further attempt at conversation and Maxi Trueman roared off into the distance. The café had a pungent smell of ganja and although he was used to dealing with all sorts of low life, Lenny now felt scared. There wasn't a white man to be seen and all eyes were on him as he entered. Drayton Livingston was a Yardie through and through, unlike Maxi, who used his roots only when it benefited him. Drayton hated whites with a vengeance and was going to enjoy toying with the man who had just walked in.

Lenny scanned the café and when he spotted the large dread locked man holding court at the rear, knew this was the person he was supposed to see. In his best hard man image he swaggered to the fixed table and introduced himself.

'Hi! I'm Lenny. Maxi said you have something for me.'

Drayton Livingston eyed up the man standing before him and grinned, showing a mouthful of yellowing teeth.

'So da mang's sent a bwoy ta do is job?'

Lenny realised this pick up wasn't going to be easy. All he wanted was to collect the gear and get back to Soho but he knew this wasn't going to be the case. For some reason the man in front of him was hell bent on making things difficult. Deciding that he could either stand there and be made to look a fool or front up to the black bastard and see what happens, he chose the latter.

'I aint looking for any trouble man. I'm just trying to do the job I've been paid for. Now if you have a fucking

98

problem with that, I suggest you take it up with Mr
Trueman.'

Drayton respected this honkey's balls. There weren't
many white's who would show a good face when put up
against a room full of blacks. Slowly nodding and
smiling slyly as he did so, Drayton motioned to one of the
numerous men that were milling about. With a gentle
hand movement he gestured for Lenny to accept the
parcel being offered to him. Drayton made it a policy
never to personally handle the goods, therefore never
incriminating himself.

'Tak dat ta da broder. Tell 'im Dray sez hi.'

Lenny didn't wait for any further instruction and placing
the package inside his jacket, got out of the place as quick
as he could. Not happy until he was back over the water,
Lenny at last phoned Maxi on his mobile. Nearly out of
credit, he was glad to hear his new boss's voice.

Carrying enough crack to send him down for a lengthy
stretch, Lenny was eager to get rid of the gear as soon as
possible. Maxi arranged for them to meet up in Soho
Square at twelve thirty, then curtly hung up, Lenny was a
happy man.

Roxy Baxter had been standing outside Kings Cross
station for over an hour. A few coins in the bottom of her
bag had enabled her to get the bus one way. Pain seared
through her entire body and she knew that doing any
business would be almost impossible. Even if she hadn't
resembled one of the living dead, her pain wouldn't have
allowed her body to be abused. Spying a pay phone, she
dialled the operator and asked to reverse the charges to
Carmel's number. Carmel Jones hadn't been awake long
and was enjoying a cup of strong coffee while she
watched Trisha on the television when the phone rang.
Snatching up the receiver she shouted into the

mouthpiece.

'Yesssss!'

'I have a Roxy Baxter on the line, will you accept the charges?'

This wasn't something Roxy had done before and Carmel knew the girl must be in trouble.

'Yes, yes now for fucks sake put her on.'

Instantly the call was transferred but all Carmel could hear was the soft sound of sobbing.

'Roxy? is that you girl?'

'Help me Carm, I hurt so much!'

Carmel Jones put her hand to her mouth and suppressed the curses she wanted to shout out.

'Get a cab babe and come straight over.'

Roxy was crying more than ever now and even a hardened pro like Carmel, felt as though her heart would break.

'I aint got a bean Carm!'

'Don't worry about that sweetheart; I'll pay when you get here.'

Roxy hung up and staggered out of the kiosk in search of a black cab. They were numerous at this time of day but one look at their fare and the cabbies drove off straight away. Finally she managed to find one who was feeling charitable. Every bump in the road made her feel as though she would pass out and by the time they entered Old Compton Street, Roxy thought she was going to die. Carmel had dressed quickly and was standing outside the flat when the black hackney pulled up. Paying the driver, she helped her friend to the front door, though she didn't think Roxy would make it up the stairs.

'Babe I think we need to get you to a fucking hospital and sharpish.'

Roxy became almost hysterical at the suggestion and

Carmel could see that the girl was scared to death.

'No, no I'll be fine when I've had a lay down.'

She wasn't convincing by any means but Carmel knew when to shut up. Tenderly she helped her friend with every step and a few minutes later they were inside and away from prying eyes. Leading Roxy into the bedroom, she slowly undressed her friend and grimaced when she saw the state of the girl's body. Over the years Carmel Jones had experienced more than one punter cutting up rough with her but this was something entirely different. It looked as if Lenny had actually enjoyed beating her. Almost every inch of her torso was covered in purple bruising.

'That cunt!'

'It's not that bad Carm and besides you don't know the whole story.'

'The whole story! Aint no story deserves the likes of this. You can try telling me but I warn you there aint no reason on this fucking earth that you can give me to explain this.'

Roxy began to tell her friend all that had gone on in the last twenty four hours and somehow when she told Carmel about Maxi Trueman, she tried to justify what Lenny had done to her. Carmel shook her head in despair.

'So now what? You aint seriously thinking of going fucking back? Oh please Rox don't do it love.'

'He'll be fine by the time I get home, you know Lenny he don't hold a grudge for long.'

'Roxy if you go home with no money, he'll kill you. We aint talking about enough for a hit here! it's two fucking grand. Fuck me! if he owes Maxi Trueman and don't pay, well let's just say Lenny Layton will cease to exist.'

Carmel pulled her coat from the wardrobe and walked

towards the door.

'Where you going?'

'Never mind about that, you just lay there and get some rest.'

Roxy closed her eyes. Too tired to resist, she fell asleep before her friend was half way up the road. Three hours later, she woke to find Carmel sitting at the bottom of the bed watching her. Turning her head towards the clock, Roxy saw the time and struggled to get up.

Instantly Carmel was by her side, gently pushing her back onto the bed.

'Carm I have to go, I have to get the money somehow.'

Carmel placed a brown envelope on Roxy's chest.

'There's two grand and as much as it gall's me to give it to that fucking low life, I will on one condition. You let me take it round and you madam, promise to stay here for at least a couple of weeks.'

Roxy knew she had no choice and in all honesty, knew her body couldn't cope with another beating so soon. As the tears trickled down her cheek, she nodded. Carmel again put on her coat and tucked the envelope deep inside her shop lifting pocket. Soho was a dodgy place at the best of times and if anyone knew you had a couple a grand on you, well in all honesty it didn't bare thinking about. Not wanting to risk crossing the square, Carmel took the long way round. It was still early but already a few undesirables were starting to gather on the Street corners. With the collar of her coat pulled up tightly around her neck, she walked to Berners Mews. Carmel stood outside the flat for several minutes, before she at last plucked up the courage to knock on the door. Years of living by her wits had taught her never to trust anyone and Lenny Layton was as bad as they came. Several knocks later and she was about to walk away when the door at last opened.

'What the fuck do you want, you interfering old cow?'

'Hello Len, nice to see you as well. I've got that poor little cow Roxy at mine and a fine state she's in too.'

Patting the bulging pocket of her coat, she stared straight into his cold eyes.

'I know what's going on and I wouldn't want to be in your fucking shoes for all the tea in china.'

'Come to fucking gloat have you, is that how a shrivelled up old cow like you gets her kicks?'

'No Lenny that's not why I'm here. I've got a proposition for you.'

'A fucking proposition! You daft old bat!'

Carmel couldn't for the life of her understand what Roxy saw in this animal. He was nothing to look at and years older than her but still the stupid girl kept going back for more.

'I've got the two grand on me that you so desperately need. Poor Roxy's lying at mine with her guts kicked in and you still tried to send her out to work. Your nothing but fucking scum Lenny Layton and sooner or later you are going to get what's coming to you.'

Lenny wasn't about to take any shit from this old bag and was about to shut the door when an image of Maxi entered his head. He knew he only had until tomorrow so there was little choice but to listen to the old girl.

'Change of heart have you, or are you fucking shitting yourself thinking about what that black bastards going to do to you. Now this money is from me and I'm giving it to you as a favour to Roxy. You can have it and get out of the scrape that you're in but you leave the girl alone for a couple of weeks and give her time to heal.'

'Yeah, yeah, yeah whatever you say.'

'I mean it Lenny. I still know a few faces and if you

103

think Maxis worth worrying about, then these blokes will certainly do the business if I ask.'

Lenny knew that she was speaking the truth, which was the only reason he'd never given her a hiding before. There weren't many men who'd put up with a woman meddling in their lives like she'd done in his.

'Fine!'

Handing over the envelope, Carmel stepped back sharply. She didn't trust him an inch and wasn't prepared to give him the satisfaction of landing one on her. Turning to walk away, she cringed at his final sentence.

'Get her all fixed up and looking pretty before you send her back.'

'You really are a prize piece of shit Lenny.'

If she'd had a knife, Carmel knew that there and then she would have stabbed him. She hadn't, so there was no point in wishing. Upping her step, she got away from the flat fast and made her way home as quickly as she could to Roxy.

CHAPTER ELEVEN

Chief Inspector Annette Windsor had been in residence at Agar Street police station for just over a week. Her initial meeting with the stations officers had proved fruitless. Drumming the top of her desk, she knew it was time to take some action. Either the criminals in this neck of the woods were extremely clever, or her words had fallen on deaf ears. Worse still, they had been completely ignored altogether. If there was one thing Annette couldn't stand, it was being taken for a fool. Pressing the intercom on her desk, she summoned Elaine through to her office. Elaine Dillinger had been secretary to Chief Bateson for three years and working at the station for the last eight. As with everyone else, Elaine had become lazy and was used to spending her mornings doing the Suns crossword. The Chief had seldom been at the station so Elaine had little to do most of the time which suited her. Suddenly all hell had broke loose and now she was expected to work, the change didn't come easily. Tapping on the door, she waited to be invited inside. Annette Windsor eyed the grubby looking woman over the top of her designer spectacles.

'Sit down I want you to take a letter Elaine. Tell me, has there been any response since the meeting last week?'
Elaine Dillinger shrugged her shoulders as if in a silent reply.
'For goodness sake woman, have the courtesy to speak when you are spoken to.'
Her seniors harsh tone made Elaine sit upright in her chair.
'I'm sorry Ma'am. No there have been no arrests or feedback since you spoke to everyone.'

'In that case make it a memo. Tell everyone to be in the conference room this afternoon at two. If you are met with any negativity or excuses, inform the parties that they will answer directly to me if they are a no show.'
'Yes Ma'am.'
Elaine stood up to leave but didn't manage to reach the door before her boss spoke the word she'd been dreading. 'Elaine, it would be appreciated if you smartened up your appearance. This is a police station in case you've forgotten and not a Street café. Smart suit and comfortable shoes will be the order of the day as from tomorrow.'
'Yes Ma'am.'
Annette Windsor was livid at the blank wall she had come up against. What no one realised and something she was glad of, was the fact that this wasn't the first time she'd taken on a dysfunctional station and brought it up to speed. God help them all if they imagined that they could get one over on her. If it took every last breath in her body she would bring them all into line, no matter what it took.
After drawing a blank regarding Lenny Layton, Tess didn't know what her next step should be. Naively she'd assumed finding Susan was going to be a damn sight easier than it had been finding out Layton's address. The Parsons were hiding something but Tess didn't think it was anything that would help with her own investigations. If Joe would just get off of his backside and pull in a few dealers, then maybe she might get a little further along. Tess guessed that if Layton had already served a five for dealing, then the chances were he was still involved and active in the area. If she had been back in Spalding, then she'd have gone out and felt a few collars herself, with or without back up.

The trouble was, she wasn't in Spalding she was here in London and she knew no one, especially any of the criminal fraternity. Just at that moment as if her prayers had been answered, Elaine Dillinger walked in with the chief's memo. Shoving Joes feet from the table, the angry looking woman slammed the paper onto his desk. Elaine was pissed off big time and it showed. Joe wasn't happy at being pushed about but he smiled all the same to see Elaine's simmering anger. The pair had fallen out within a couple of weeks of the woman joining the force. Elaine had heard Joe refer to her as Feline Dillinger and she was never one to forget a personal slight made against her, no matter how small.

'Ooooh! and who's shit in your path?'

'Fuck off Reynolds! I'm getting enough grief from that jumped up bitch without a wanker like you adding your two penneth.'

Slamming the door behind her, Elaine stormed onto the next office to hand out her message of doom.

'Whatever was all that about Sir?'

Picking up the memo from the Chief, Joe shrugged his shoulders as he began to read. Tess didn't interrupt; she had a hunch that it wouldn't be good news. At last Joe lay down the white paper but he didn't resume his laid back position of before.

'Seems, you were right Detective.'

'About what Sir?'

Joe handed her the note then walked over to where his dilapidated excuse for a jacket hung.

'About Windsor coming here to do a cleanup. Well if she wants a few collars to keep her happy, then that's what she'll have. Come on!'

Joe was out of the door before Tess had chance to grab her bag. Never having seen him in such an urgent state

107

made a pleasant surprise and she ran as fast as she could to where he waited beside a parked car.

'Can you drive?'

'Of course I can drive Sir, is there anyone who can't nowadays! Why?'

Throwing Tess a bunch of keys, Joe got into the passenger's side and lit a cigarette. Driving in the city wasn't something she was looking forward to. Tess hoped that even if he wouldn't drive, the least he would do was navigate. It was eleven in the morning and as usual cars were backed up bumper to bumper.

'Where are we going?'

'You'll find out when we get there, now just concentrate on your driving will you!'

Nothing was moving and she knew that they weren't going anywhere in a hurry.

'Sir you seem a little uptight, I hope it wasn't my remark about driving?'

'Tess there's a lot of things you don't know about me.'

'Then why don't you tell me, I mean it's not as if we're flying along. By the looks of things were going to be here for quite a while yet.'

He turned to her and she could tell he was feeling uncomfortable.

'Ok. I don't really know you and yet I feel as if I do, so I'm going to trust you Miss Davey. Believe me that's an honour in my book and something I don't do lightly.'

Loosening his tie, Joe Reynolds began to tell his story.

Paul Lewis had a brilliant career in the police force, but a six-month secondment to Newcastle had brought his career to a premature halt. Paul was the head of a team of crack detectives on the drug squad and the notorious gang in question had been extremely difficult to catch. As the only one who wasn't local, Paul had offered to go undercover. Unluckily for him, the gang, led by Tracey Woods a feared Tyneside villain, was warned via a tip off from a single bent policeman. A high-speed car chase had resulted in Paul almost losing his leg and being forced into hiding. Tracey had sworn on his son's life, to track Paul down and kill him. It wasn't a threat that had been taken lightly and on the orders from above, Paul Lewis became Joe Reynolds overnight. It wasn't something he enjoyed and many times over the last couple of years he'd been desperate to get out on the Street and do what he loved most.

'Wow! no wonder I couldn't find any of your records.'

'Been checking up on me have we?'

Tess was suddenly embarrassed, she realised how it must look and she was mortified.

'No it's not a case of that Sir! I was bored one day so I decided to get to know the system. For a laugh I decided to put in a few names, mine included I might add.'

He didn't comment and finally the traffic began to move.

'Take a right onto Charring Cross road, Tess then turned left into Lisle Street.'

A few minutes later they pulled up outside The Kings Head. The doors were open and Tess could see from the interior that it wouldn't be a pub of her choice. They didn't resemble typical Old Bill but unlike the Ship and Shovel, they wouldn't be taken for city types either.

'So what's this place Sir?'

Joe was about to open the door when he stopped and turned towards her.

'I may not have been active but I've still kept me ear to the ground. This is a haunt for low life's and none more so than Bobby Race.'

Removing a picture from inside his jacket, he proceeded to show it to her.

109

'Familiarise yourself with it, we may be in for a long wait. If you hadn't noticed, there are several exits. Perfect fucking villains' pub if you ask me. I'm going in one side and you the other. If that scum bag Race appears, I'll tip you the wink but be warned, he may try to do a runner.'

Tess could feel her heart start to pump and she knew the adrenalin was beginning to kick in. This was what she'd missed, what she joined up for in the first place. Two hours later and they were still sitting in their separate seats, when the door nearest to Joe opened. Tess had started to get anxious when she saw that it was coming up to one thirty. She didn't want to be late for the Chiefs meeting and this exercise was proving a waste of time. Suddenly Joe winked at her and she knew the man entering must be their target. Bobby Race reached the bar but one look from the Landlord told him to run. Joe was up in a second but he wasn't fast enough. As Bobby passed Tess's stool, she deliberately stuck out her leg and their suspect landed neatly at her feet. Joe Reynolds, in hot pursuit, roared with laughter as he knelt beside the man and placed him in handcuffs. Close enough so that Bobby could feel his breath but no one else could hear, Joe whispered in his ear.

'You're going down Racey and this time they are going to throw away the fucking key!'

Hauling the man to his feet, Joe grabbed hold of Bobby's shoulder and pushed him from the building. As with all his arrests, Bobby was full of bravado and attitude.

'You aint got shit on me copper! I'll be home before me old woman's had time to watch neighbours.'

Tess got into the driver's seat and Joe, still biding his time, placed Bobby in the back and climbed in beside him.

110

'You're right sonny we aint got nothing on you.'
Joe removed a bag from his inside pocket that contained a brownish looking powder. He waved it in front of Bobby Race's face.
'But when did that stop Old Bill getting a collar if they really wanted one.'
The entire colour drained from Bobby's face and he could feel sweat beginning to form on his forehead. The amount of gear contained in the bag was enough to send him down for a long time and he was only just starting to enjoy his freedom again. He turned to Joe.
'So what's all this about guv'nor, what you want from me?'
Tess had been silent as she concentrated on her driving but her ears were picking up every word that was said. Now the man in the back wanted to sing and she smiled to herself at Joe's unorthodox methods. Unorthodox or not, they seemed to get results and wasn't that really what this line of work was about.
'We have a new boss at our nick and she's a real tidy lady. Seems she wants to do a bit of domestic work round this shit hole and clean a few dealers off the Streets. You seemed as good a place to start as any.'
'Oh fuck me governor! I aint been out long myself. Give a bloke a break for fucks sake!'
'Sorry son no can do; now we're nearly there so you should be back inside by teatime. It's normally fish on Fridays, so you've got a real treat to look forward to.'
By now the sweat was running down Bobby's face and he turned his cheek towards his shoulder and tried desperately to wipe it away. Looking out of the window at all the passing cars, he searched for a means of escape but it was futile. Realising how hopeless the situation was, Bobby accepted there was only one alternative left

111

open to him.

'Suppose I give you a couple of names as a trade? after all two collars are better than one aint they?'

Joe smacked his lips, making a tutting sound.

'I don't know about that son, it'd have to be good and besides I have a partner up front. Maybe she don't do trades'

Suddenly Tess could feel Bobby's eyes boring into the back of her head, as he began to plead.

'Please!!! Mrs help me out here I promise I aint bull shutting you honest. I can give you one name of a real top bloke. What you say?'

Tess wanted to laugh again, Joe really was a bastard. Deciding too at last put the man out of his misery, she spoke for the first time since their journey began.

'I'm not having anything to do with it. This is entirely up to you Joe.'

Minutes later and nowhere near Agar Street nick, they dropped Bobby Race off. He had, to both of their amazements, furnished them with the names of Maxi Trueman and Lenny Layton. The name Bobby race hadn't meant much to Tess at first but when she wrote down Maxi's name, alarm bells started to ring. When he mentioned Layton, she had almost jumped out of her skin. Doing her best to hide her feelings, she continued to drive until they reached the stations car park. With the engine turned off, she undid her seat belt and turned to her boss.

'Is that the normal way you interrogate a suspect and just what is that stuff inside your jacket?'

Joe Reynolds scratched his head.

'Tess you get nowhere with these low life's unless you put the fear of god into them.

As for this, it's talc and a little gravy powder but looks a lot like smack wouldn't you say?'

'I suppose so but that isn't really the point is it. If our methods are so close to those of the criminals, oh I don't know it just doesn't seem right somehow.'

'Tess you don't have to like it but if it gets results, then that's all I'm concerned with.'

'So, now what?'

'We go after this Layton bloke but he's not the one I'm really interested in. Trueman on the other hand has a reputation for dealing coke and crack and if there's one drug in the world I hate, its crack. When I was in Newcastle, it was all that bastard Woods dealt in and you wouldn't believe the heartache it causes.'

Tess had been staring out of the window while he talked but now she faced him again.

'I understand that Boss and I know that my experience with drugs is limited. What I don't understand is why after so long, you're interested in getting involved again?'

Joe Reynolds glanced at his watch, it was almost two o'clock. If he hoped to bring in Layton and then possibly Trueman, then there was no way they would make the briefing.

'Tess I've sat in that fucking office for far too long. I was ordered not to get involved with anything and being lazy became a way of life for me. Windsor turning up has changed all that. Do you know that the drug industry in Britain is worth over eight billion a year and that forty percent of British kids have dabbled in the stuff before they reach sixteen?'

'No I didn't know that Sir but I can't see how putting yourself about and risking word getting back to Tracey Woods, is worth catching a few dealers for.'

Joe pointed to the ignition.

'Start her up again, were going after Layton. I'm tired Tess, tired of doing nothing. If I get bumped off tomorrow, then so be it but at least I'll go doing what I love most.'

She didn't know how to reply to his last statement and decided it was better not to try.

'We're heading for Berners Mews it's at the back of Soho Square.'

Tess once more pulled out into the heavy traffic and looking at the overhead digital clock, knew they wouldn't be seeing Chief Windsor until much later in the day. For once she wasn't bothered about her superiors, who they were about to meet was far more interesting. Joe told her to stop the car fifty yards from the address. He didn't want to risk Layton seeing them approach as druggies seemed to have an inbuilt alarm for the police. Slowly they walked towards the flat and Tess could feel her heart begin to race once again.

'I aint had any dealings with this one Tess but be careful because they are all the fucking same, slippery bastards each and every one of them.'

'Sir if you're not that interested in this bloke, then why are we even bothering coming here?'

'Oh Tess! You've got so much to learn still. Look, Layton's a little fish and the Met aint interested in tiddler's they are only after the whales. If this scumbag, can give us anything on Trueman, then the trips been worth it.'

Tess stood back as Joe rapped on the front door. The place looked disgusting and she wasn't relishing going inside. Slowly the door opened just enough for one beady eye to be seen and Joe Reynolds didn't waste the opportunity of showing his warrant card. Lenny's acrid breath could be smelt through the gap and Tess instinctively put her hand over her nose. As soon as Lenny saw the card, he slammed the door shut and walked back to the bedroom to begin his ritual of jacking up.

'Come on Lenny open up, we need to ask you a few questions.'

There was no reply and the door remained tightly closed. Joe knew they weren't going to get inside and as they didn't have a warrant, he didn't fancy having to answer to Windsor if he forced an entry.

'Tess lets go back to the car and wait a while. He'll be out and about soon enough and when he shows his ugly face we'll nab him.'

An hour later and they were still seated in the car. Tess began to think about the bollocking they were in for on their return to Agar Street. As desperate as she was for information on her sister, right now she just wanted to go back to the station and get it over with. As always she sat back and did as she was told. Joe was her boss and if he said they had to wait, then wait they would.

CHAPTER TWELVE

Roxy was enjoying her stay at Carmel's. The woman fussed around her like an old mother hen and it was nice to have three square meals a day. Carmel spent all day with her guest and only slipped out to do a few tricks when Roxy was tucked up in bed. It had always been Carmel's dream to be part of a family but without the babies, she hated crying kids more than anything. Unlike many of the girls on the Street, she hadn't been stupid enough to get caught by a punter. So many of the children in Soho and Kings Cross were the result of a one-night stand and often the families of brasses would be multi coloured. The desire to be part of a family unit was probably the reason Carmel had helped out so many waifs and strays over the years. For the short time that a young girl who was in trouble, entered her life, Carmel became the good Samaritan. She wouldn't hear a word said against them and they would, over night became her family, until they robbed her or even beat her up. It had happened on several occasions but it never stopped her being there when someone was in need and at this precise moment in time it was Roxy Baxter's turn. Roxy needed fresh clothes and had given Carmel her keys. It wasn't something Carmel wanted to do but she couldn't afford to kit the girl out with new gear. She'd been warned by Roxy that everything was dirty and decided to call in at the launderette on her way back. It was a bright afternoon and really quite pleasant walking through the square. It didn't take on its seedy appearance until after dusk and then it was a place Carmel Jones wouldn't venture into, not unless she really had to. Carmel was Streetwise and she knew that the druggies, who frequented the square, would slit a parson's throat for a few quid. Oxford Street was bustling with shoppers as usual and no one paid her any attention as she crossed into Berners Street. The Mews were a little further down and she always laughed when the name was mentioned. It sounded like some posh little area that you found down a quiet Street off Kensington. In reality, it was three or four small purpose built blocks of corporation flats. Carmel imagined that whoever named them was either pissed at the time, or was having a laugh at the borough's expense. Hoping that Lenny wasn't home, she slipped the key into the lock and called out as she entered. With her mind set on getting in and out as quickly as possible, Carmel hadn't noticed the two people sitting in the car a few feet away. Normally she was alert to anything out of the ordinary and could not only see Old Bill but smell them before they had a chance to get within spitting distance. The flat was silent and she walked through to the bedroom. Removing a black plastic bag from her coat pocket, Carmel opened up the ageing wardrobe and began to remove Roxy's clothes. A groan came from the other side of the room and she spun round to see Lenny coming down from one of his highs. Speeding up her work, she quietly closed the door and made a hasty retreat from the flat.

In the car that Carmel didn't see, Joe Reynolds narrowed his eyes when he saw the woman enter and leave the flat. His interest hadn't gone unnoticed by Tess and she was intrigued.

'Who's that Sir?'

'A face I aint seen for over a decade! I didn't even know she was still in the area. That Detective Davey is Carmel Jones, one of the legendary old breed of Soho's brasses. Carmel and me have had many a run in over the years but still managed to maintain a mutual understanding and if only slight, an admiration for each other.'

'Admire a prostitute? they're dirty and continually break the law!'

Joe again pointed to the ignition, signalling to her that they should leave. Tess started up the engine and pulled out onto the Street. It was a couple of minutes before he continued with the conversation.

'Tess for someone who's been in the force for several years, you don't seem to have much real experience. If a woman lasts a year or two in the sex industry she's doing well. Carmel Jones has been on the game for over forty. Story goes that she was the bastard of a brass and put on the game by the time she was twelve. Now to last that long, you have to be sharp and Carmel Jones is one of the sharpest I know. What I don't understand is why she's knocking around with a low life like Layton.'

The car turned into the station car park and Tess looked up to see Chief Windsor staring down at them from her office.

'Aren't they all low life's Joe?'

'Don't ever make assumptions Tess. Lenny Layton and the likes would slit your throat for a bag of scagg. On the other hand, Carmel Jones would go to the ends of the earth to help you. There's a big difference.'

'I think we've got more to worry about than some old brass at the moment! The Chief's been boring a hole in my forehead.'

Joe laughed and Tess couldn't think for the life of her what was so funny. Tommy Radcliff was on desk duty in reception as they walked in. He signalled to Joe, who went over to where the man was trying to deal with a drunk wanting to report a theft.

'Lady Windsor aint best pleased with you pal. Sent a

message down, that you're both to report to her office as soon as you set foot in here.'

Tommy couldn't understand why his mate didn't seem fazed at the command and was glad he was just a lowly sergeant dealing with stupid Joe public, like the one standing before him.

'Look mate, if some winos pinched your sherry that's tough fucking luck. Now piss off out of my station, before you make it stink more than it already does.'

Doing as he'd been told, the old boy exited the station but not before he'd left the present of a yellow puddle on the floor. Sighing heavily, Tommy Radcliff switched on the light to the store cupboard in search of a mop. Tess and Joe climbed the stairs and knocked on the Chiefs door. After they heard the command to enter, Tess walked in behind Joe. Annette Windsor was standing at the window and Tess could see from the look on her face that they were in for a dressing down. When she was promptly excused from the meeting, she thought that as her senior, it must be Joe who was in for a roasting and made her way back to their office to wait. With the door to the Chiefs office firmly closed, Joe walked over to his boss and cupping her face in his hands, kissed her tenderly. Seconds later and the woman pushed his hands away.

'You take liberties with me Paul.'

'I know but you love me and don't call me Paul. I've gotten used to Joe and to be honest I prefer it now. I couldn't believe it when you walked into that briefing Annie, you really have risen in the ranks girl!'

'I had no choice! You'd gone and all I had left was my work. Why didn't you ever get in touch again when you got back to the smoke?'

As he held her tightly, never wanting to let go of her

119

again, he spoke.

'I couldn't take the risk. You don't know how many times I have picked up that phone and dialled half of your number.'

'Half's no good Joe, it needed to be all and that was something you were never prepared to give me was you?' He didn't reply but she could see longing in his eyes, eyes that she had loved for more years than she cared to recall. 'And now? Is it too late, or are you just not interested anymore?'

'Annie I'm a wanted man and I always will be. There's bound to come a day when Woods finds out where I am and I'll be on the run again. I can't put you at risk. When I get the call telling me that he's dead, well that'll be the day I can start again. Until then sweetheart, we can be no more than friends.'

Joe kissed her again tenderly and wiped away the tears that had silently fallen onto her cheeks. She didn't question him about not being at the meeting. Annette Windsor loved him with all her heart and if he'd told her he was on the golf course, she would have forgiven him. Joe Reynolds could do as he liked and she would forgive him over and over again, her heart wouldn't let her do anything else.

Tess was busy surfing the internet when her boss walked in. If Chief Windsor had berated him, then it didn't show. Joe Reynolds peered at the screen and was interested at the site she'd found.

'I see you're swatting up on the drug industry?'

Tess switched off the screen and turned towards her boss. 'I didn't realise how ill informed I was and to be honest, slightly ignorant. I know we have basic training in substance misuse but if it isn't much of a problem in your area, then you don't get any hands on experience. That

120

seems to be changing fast now and I want to be able to stand my ground.'

Joe was already seated at his own desk but had turned his swivel chair forward, so that it was now facing his new partner.

'That's commendable Tess but something's been nagging away at me ever since you turned up. If the world of drugs wasn't your primary reason for coming to the smoke, then what was?'

Tess hadn't bargained on this question and was hesitant with her answer. She knew she could bluff it out and give some weak reply but after he had been so frank with her earlier, she owed him the truth.

'My father died recently.'

'I'm sorry!'

'No it's Ok but I then found out from my bitch of a mother, who turned out not to be my mother at all, that I was adopted. After a little digging, I learned I had a twin sister.'

'Did you find her?'

'Not yet but I have a feeling I'm getting closer.'

Joe pushed on his feet and his chair glided across the floor on its own. Suddenly he was on the opposite side of Tess's desk and staring directly at her.

'This is intriguing, tell me more!'

A similar conversation to the one she'd had with Sophie followed but when she reached the part about Lenny Layton, Joes eyes opened wide.

'So Tess! We really do need to bring the bastard in and have a word.'

'You mean you'll help me Sir?'

'I'd like nothing better and this is one mystery I'm sure we'll solve. Have you thought how you'll cope if things go tits up?'

121

'Go wrong you mean? What's to go wrong?'
'Babe, the likes of Layton aint nice men. If a parsons been in his company for a period of time, then you can bet your last quid that they aint as white as the proverbial driven.'
Tess had felt a warm feeling inside when he'd referred to her as babe, she didn't realise it was a term, along with darling and several other corny names, that Londoners used to address anyone. Now after his last comment she wanted to reach over the desk and slap his face.
'My sister isn't a low life and anyway, I've already put her name through the system and drew a blank.'
'Tess that don't mean diddly squat and you know it. I can see you're desperate to find her and I understand that but from what you've told me, she's led a totally different life. The chances are she doesn't even go by the name of Susan?'
'Sayers, its Susan Sayers!'
'All right! Calm down. Look I don't want to put the mockers on things but I want you to be prepared, that's all.'
Tess could feel her face begin to flush red with embarrassment as she watched her boss walk over to his jacket.
'I know you do and I'm sorry I snapped. I'm trying to stay positive because I dare not think about the alternative. If I do, then I know I won't have the guts to continue and all this will have been a waste.'
'Yes you will, now are you coming or do I have to go it alone?'
'Where to?'
'The Ship and Shovel, where else! This calls for a celebration and then first thing in the morning we are going to get things moving.'

'How's that then?'

'By bringing in Layton, that's if you're still up for it?'

Suddenly things didn't seem so bleak and a wide smile spread across her face.

'Too right I am!'

Seconds later Tess was grabbing her coat and bag and running from the room. The feeling of excitement was so strong that she thought she'd burst any second.

CHAPTER THIRTEEN

Roxy was still safely installed at Carmel's and although money was scarce, she didn't want to leave her houseguest and only went out for a couple of hours a day. Over the last few years it had become more and more difficult for her to earn a living and now with the extra mouth to feed, it made the money side of things even tighter. Carmel's looks had never been that of a stunner and as she aged and her lifestyle took its toll, she was starting to resemble a dock rat that even the drunkest of punters wouldn't give a second glance to. Only three years away from drawing her pension, Carmel didn't know how she would manage in the nearing future. The rent on her flat was more per week than the state handed out and she'd never been one to save for a rainy day. Even when times had been good and they were few and far between nowadays, she would be down the market the next day and spend and spend until there was nothing left. The box room at her flat was small but she decided that after Roxy left, she would have to move into it and let out her own room to survive. There was always the possibility of becoming a maid but it was something that had never appealed to her. Oh, there were benefits no doubt but the hours were long and Carmel really didn't fancy cleaning up after another brass and having to cater to her every whim. The reality of life had started to play on her mind but it was something she didn't want the girl to see. For as long as Roxy Baxter needed her, there'd be a warm bed, food and no pressure. It had been raining all night and even now it was still drizzling. Soho was drab enough during the day but when it rained it was dismal. Carmel had been staring out of the window and was contemplating her future, when Roxy emerged from the bedroom.

'You're deep in thought Carm! anything wrong?'

Carmel turned round and as if seeing for the first time, noticed just how beautiful Roxy was. She smiled.

'No darling just watching the world go by. Soho's like two separate places that are a million miles apart.'

'How do you mean?'

Carmel again pulled back the greying nets and peered out onto the Street.

'Well, by night it's alive and vibrant. Full of people all really wanting and having a good time.'

'Yeah and?'

'And by day its dead, almost like a morgue.'

'You're just down because it's raining. If the sun came out you'd be as right as nine pence.'

Carmel Jones grinned at the girl's words and tried to lift her own spirits.

'You're probably right. Ready for a bit of breakie?'

'Please, I'm fucking famished. I reckon I could chase the horse and eat the jockey.'

'And I bet you have before now, you dirty cow'

The two women laughed and once again the atmosphere was one of happiness, if only temporarily. Carmel cooked them both a hearty breakfast but halfway through their egg and bacon, Roxy began to speak.

'I thought I'd go out later Carm.'

Suddenly Carmel Jones felt afraid. She knew what was coming but it was something she couldn't stop. Placing her fork on the table, she looked long and hard into Roxy Baxter's eyes.

'Where to?'

'Well I aint seen Lenny for a while and I'd like to check on him. Don't look so worried I aint going home to stay.'

125

That was a lie and Carmel knew it, they both knew it. She wanted to grab the girl and shake her but it was pointless. If Roxy set her mind on something, then there was no stopping her, no matter how daft the idea. When the dishes were cleared away and Roxy had gotten dressed, she pulled on her jacket and kissed the older woman on the cheek.

'Don't look so worried Carm! I'll be back in an hour or so I promise.'

Carmel Jones watched from the window, as Roxy walked slowly down the road. Her ribs were a long way off mending and Carmel wondered what state she'd return in. That's if she returned at all.

Joe Reynolds and Tess Davey drove out of the station car park, only this time Tess needed no directions. As if on autopilot, she turned onto Charing Cross road. Before she knew it they had pulled up a few feet from Lenny's flat.

'Fuck me! that was quick.'

'Traffics a lot lighter Sir, besides I knew where to come didn't I?'

Joe didn't answer and was already out of the car and walking towards the flat. Knocking as hard as he could on the door, they stood waiting when Roxy walked up.

'Who the fuck are you two and what are you doing outside my gaff?'

Joe held up his warrant card and Roxy sighed deeply.

'Look I aint done nothing. I aint even bleeding living here at the moment.'

Tess stepped forward and couldn't stop herself from asking a question.

'What's your name Miss?'

Roxy narrowed her eyes at the stuck up cow in front of her. Old Bill were all the same, didn't think their shit stunk and all that.

'None of your fucking business, now mind out me way.'
Pushing past them, she opened the door and was about to
slam it behind her, when Joe put out his foot. She began
to scream and curse and the commotion woke Lenny,
who staggered from the bedroom.

'What's all the bleeding row about? Cant a bloke get a
bit a peace round here?'
Rubbing his eyes hard, he realised who it was.
Hi ya Roxy babe, how you doing?'
Lenny had calmed down in the short space of time she'd
been away and his opinion of that bitch Carmel, had
slightly softened.

'Has the old tart been looking after you?'
Roxy was about to reply, when Lenny looked past her
and saw Joe and Tess at the end of the hall. Immediately
he recognised the Old Bill and raised his hand towards
Roxy's face.

'I wouldn't do that Layton, if I were you.'
Clenching his fist, Lenny thought better of it and placed
his hand inside his trouser pocket.

'What you doing bringing the filth around?'
Tess took a step forward but was stopped by Joe's
forearm. He gave her a look that told her in no uncertain
terms he was taking charge of this one.

'If you mean us Lenny, the girl didn't bring us here; it's
you we need to have a word with. Now you can come
down the station and we do this the easy way, or I can
arrest you here and now and probably get you banged up
for the night'
Lenny knew he didn't have a chance and winked at Roxy
as he passed. Holding out his wrists, he waited to be
handcuffed and was surprised when Joe told him there'd
be no need for that.

127

'It's only an informal chat Lenny and at the moment you're not under arrest.'

Roxy stood on the doorstep as they led her man away. It was a scene she was used to and she didn't feel unduly worried. After checking that the cooker and lights were off, she pulled the door closed and began he walk back to Carmel's. Tess held the top of Lenny's head as he got into the car. The last thing they wanted was a claim for damages because they hadn't taken due care and attention. Especially as at this moment, he was only helping with enquiries. No one spoke on the way back, even though Tess was burning up in side with frustration. She wondered about the girl but quickly dismissed any notion that she could be Sally. Agar Street nick was a hub of activity. It was an everyday occurrence now and something Tess enjoyed. Entering through the back, Joe saw that it was Sergeant Radcliff who was booking in arrests that day. Four or five dodgy looking people were sitting on the bench waiting to be processed and Joe could sense that the sergeant was stressed.

'Hi Tommy! Looks like you've got your hands full?'

'You can say that again mate, I aint even had time for a fag yet. I suppose you've brought me another one?'

'No not this time you'll be pleased to hear. Just someone come in to help us out a bit with our inquiries. Has the Chief rolled up yet?'

Tommy checked the last piece of the prisoner's belongings into a plastic bag and ticked a box on his clipboard.

'About ten minutes ago.'

Joe nodded and led Lenny Layton along a short corridor, to the first in a line of interview rooms.

'Take a seat and we'll try not to keep you. I just need a few minutes with my colleague here and then we'll get

128

started. Can I get you a tea?'

Lenny wasn't used to this kind of treatment and decided to make the most of it.

'Yeh, two sugars and a few smokes wouldn't go a miss either.'

'I'll see what I can do.'

Tess left the room a few seconds ahead of Joe and he could see she wasn't happy. He didn't speak until they were outside and far enough away, for Lenny not to have a chance of hearing.

'I can see you're pissed off with me and.......'

Tess didn't allow him to finish. She began to pace the floor and her rage was building to such a crescendo, that her face became a darker shade of red with ever step that she took.

'Pissed off with you is an understatement. First you stop me asking any questions and when we finally get back here, you're as nice as pie to a bag of shit. What's going on Sir?'

'Tess! we've got no real reason to have hauled Layton in here. By treading carefully we may find out where your sister is. If we go in with all guns blazing, we'll come up against a brick wall and end up with a big fat zero.'

Tess began to walk back towards the interview room but was stopped by her boss.

'Just hold on there a minute girlie! you need to calm down and take another look at the situation.'

'I've told you before, don't call me girlie.'

'All right I'm sorry but let me have a word with him on my own. Please Tess! You go and get him a drink and some fags.'

Inwardly she counted to ten and decided not to argue. Doing as she was asked, she made her way to the canteen. When Joe Reynolds re-entered the room, Lenny

129

was sitting comfortably and had his feet up on the table. He'd sussed out the situation and was going to play it cool. Joe Reynolds first question knocked him for six.

'Where's Sally Sayers?'

Lenny placed his feet on the floor and sat back in his chair. He didn't answer straight away and tried to weigh up Joe by staring directly into his eyes. When all he got in return was a look of contempt, he turned his face towards the blank wall.

'Never heard of her.'

'Lenny we know you took her away from her foster parents. What we don't know is why and where she is now.'

Tess came back into the room and she could tell that her boss hadn't got very far. Placing the hot drink in front of Lenny, she handed him a cigarette. The room was silent and she waited apprehensively to see who spoke first. It was Joe Reynolds.

'Right let's move on shall we? What can you tell me about Maxi Trueman?'

Suddenly Lenny was up on his feet and pacing the floor. Joe had hit the nail on the head and he wasn't going to stop now.

'Maxi's one of the main men on the Street and you work for him.'

Lenny's nerves started to get the better of him and a child hood stutter that had been absent for years, returned with a vengeance.

'No, no I don't. I know hu hu who he is, who don't? but you're not g g g g going to bring me in on something I know n n n nothing about. I want a brief and I aint s s s saying n n n n nothing more until I get one.'

It wasn't going to plan and suddenly Lenny felt scared. If Maxi got wind that he'd even had eye contact with Old

130

Bill, then he was a dead man. Joe Reynolds smiled and
motioned with his head for Tess to join him outside.
Once in the corridor, he leant against the radiator and
folded his arms.

'He's bricking it Tess, he knows a lot more about
Trueman than he's letting on.'

'I thought we brought him in to find out about my sister?'

'We did but there's no harm in killing two birds with one
stone, now is there? We have to let him go now but I
think a couple more visits will scare him shitless and he'll
tell us whatever we want to know. I'll give him a few
minutes to stew, and then tell him he's free to go. A
smack head like Layton won't know what to make of it
and I guarantee he keeps his head down for a bit.'

For the third time that day, Tess wasn't happy. As much
as she wanted to take control, the decision as to the way
forward had been made and there was nothing she could
do to change things.

Roxy didn't make it back to Carmel's. After walking
through the square she'd seen Denzel coming towards
her. When he did a quick right turn and disappeared into
Sutton Row, she knew there was something bad going
down. Denzel Howard had seen Lenny being driven off
earlier that morning and as with most of the criminal
fraternity, could also smell Old Bill. Now as Roxy
approached, he wanted to become invisible and fast. The
last thing he needed was for Maxi to get a whiff that he
was involved. All the pleading in the world wouldn't
make a shits worth of difference as far as that nutter was
concerned. Thinking he'd got away with it, Denzel
almost jumped out of his skin when he heard her call out.

'Denz! Denzel hang on a minute mate. I want a word.'

His pace quickened and she soon lost sight of him.
Roxy's high boots had stopped her chasing after him and

she didn't have the first idea where he'd be hiding out.
She decided to head back to the flat and prayed that
Lenny would be home soon. Two hour later and she
heard his key in the lock; silently she made a sign of the
cross over her chest.

'Thank fuck you're back, oh Lenny I've been so
worried.'

He didn't speak and flopped down into one of the
dilapidated chairs, as if all the life had been sucked out of
him. Gently Roxy sat on the arm and ran her fingers
through his hair.

'What's going on Len? only I saw Denzel a while ago
and he couldn't get away fast enough!'

Lenny had a habit of biting on his top lip if anything was
bothering him. Roxy noticed him doing it in an almost
state of frenzy.

'Hey, hey! Babe! come on whatever's the matter?'

Instantly Lenny stood up and the chair toppled over.
Roxy fell to the floor and when she looked up, Lenny was
standing over her.

'What the fuck have you been up to girl and don't give
me any of your fucking bullshit? They wanted to know
about Sally Sayers, now where do you suppose that's
come from?'

'Honest Len! I aint got no idea.'

Lenny knew her so well that he could always tell when
she was trying to spin a tale. The look on her face told
him, she hadn't got a clue what he was on about.

Suddenly and out of character, he knelt on the floor and
cradled her in his arms. The two rocked back and forth
for what to Roxy seemed like and age. At that moment,
she had never felt closer to another human being in her
entire life. Sadly she heard Lenny breath in deeply and
knew the show of affection was coming to an end.

'You'd best get back to Carmel's now.'

'But I want to stay here Lenny; I need to be with you!'

Roughly he grabbed her by her arms and she knew it was time to obey.

'Old Bill was asking about fucking Maxi Trueman. If he's in bother, then the shit will really hit the fan. Fucking Denzel Howard must be in on it somewhere but I'll tell you something for nothing Rox, I aint taking all the fucking flack. Now get your coat and I'll come and get you when things are a bit calmer.'

Roxy did as she was told and after kissing him tenderly, once again set off for Carmel's. Her journey back was uneventful and she wouldn't have noticed if it had been any different. Her mind was full of what Lenny had said and the name Sally Sayers kept whirling through her mind.

CHAPTER FOURTEEN

Of late, Joe Reynolds had begun to arrive at work much earlier. Doing nothing in the office had stopped and he had smartened up his appearance. No one in the station was aware of his past history with Annette Windsor and he wanted it to stay that way. It was assumed by all of his fellow officers that Tess was the focus of his attentions and he didn't bother putting them right on the subject. Living close by the station on Martlett Court meant that he was able to walk to work and no one ever understood why he'd begun to sleep at the station in the first place. His flat was small but tastefully furnished and the area was one of wealth. Never one to waste money, Joe had purchased the property early on in his career and with the house market booming, he was set for a comfortable retirement. The Royal opera house was situated dead opposite and Joe frequented it as often as he could. His passion was a well-kept secret and no one would have believed that this ruff and tumbled looking man loved nothing more than to watch Madam Butterfly in all its glory. Joe was a loner. For most of his career, he'd been known as a tough nut but since the trouble with Tracey Woods he'd become scared. It wasn't something Joe would ever admit to anyone and sleeping at the station had been a comfort to him, when only thoughts of the villain had filled his dreams. He didn't know why but over the last week he'd felt the old confidence start to come back, an almost arrogant confidence that had been part of his make up when he was known as Paul Lewis. With the arrival of Annette, Joe could imagine again being the detective he once was. The rota for the week dictated that Joe and Tess's shift should start at eight am but by seven Joe was walking to work. The station car park was empty but for a lone squad car and Annette Windsor's Audi. Glancing up at her window, he saw her watching him and when she waved her hand and beckoned for him to come up, he quickened his pace. Not bothering to knock, he walked straight in.

'A bit keen aren't you Joe?'

Dressed in one of her trade mark navy suits and with her hair piled high, she was stunning and the vision reminded him of why he'd fallen for her in the first place.

'I couldn't wait to see your smiling face that's all.'

'Detective you're so full of crap but I like it all the same. Coffee?'

'Mmm!!! please. Annie, there's something been niggling away at me. Why are you here?'

'You know why, to get this station moving again

'You're lying, I can tell. You always twitch your nose when you're telling a porky and you're doing it now. There's no way, the top brass would send a fast tracker like you to Agar Street nick, not without good reason anyway.'

Annette Windsor placed the coffees on her desk and beckoned for him to take a seat.

'Joe, this stations been under observation for quite some time. I don't need to tell you that several of its detectives are rotten through and through, present company excluded of course. It's not just vice we're talking about here but hard drugs. It hasn't been possible to prosecute anyone, as we can't seem to get any hard proof, that's why I'm here. What we do know, is that there are three main men, a small amount of plods are involved but they are small fry and not who we're really interested in at the moment.'

'How corrupt are we talking here Annie?'

'From what we can gather, large amounts of heroin and cocaine are flooding the area and our boys make sure there's no hassle. Our informant even told us that the station was used on one particular night to store the stuff before it was divided up between the local dealers! Can you believe that?'

She didn't give Joe the chance to reply before she carried on talking.

'The officers in question take possession from a main dealer, and then hand over the drugs to several smaller ones. Quite clever really! I mean who'd give Met detectives a second thought if they were seen calling at a dealers home?'

'Who's the snout?'

'Honestly Joe? I don't know. The information we have is very limited and has whittled its way down from above. What I do know is that it's come from the top and I do mean the top! At the moment there's a massive drive to clean up the Mets image and this is only the beginning.'

'Well you can tell me who the bent coppers are at least.'

'Derek Masters, George Abbey and Simon Franks.'

'Fuck me Annie, George Abbey has been on the force for over twenty years.'

'That means nothing Joe but I wonder for just how many of those years he's been involved in all of this. Anyway, are you really telling me that you didn't have an inkling about what's been going on?'

'Do you really have to ask that?'

'Sorry!'

'I may have been a bit of a bastard in my time Annie but a bent copper, never! I don't mix with any of the others and I'm only on nodding terms with the majority. Remember I came here to keep my head low, not sign up for the Agar Street Social Club.'

Opening her desk drawer, Annette took out a packet of
silk cut cigarettes and removing one, reached for the gold
Cartier lighter that Joe had given to her on their first
Christmas together.

'I thought you'd quit?'

'I did but I'm under so much pressure to bring this to a
conclusion, that I started again two weeks ago. Now
then, let's get back to all the trouble here. Marsters and
Franks have been frequently seen with a Maxi Trueman.
He's one of the Yardie bunch but hasn't set foot on
Jamaican soil since he was a tiny child. Using the Yardie
badge gives him credibility and to be honest, I think he
likes the notoriety that goes with it. Intelligence tells us
that the nearest he's come to the Caribbean since the real
Yardie invasion, is via his old mums jerk chicken.'
Annette carried on talking but stopped when she saw the
expression on Joes face.

'What's up?'

Joe didn't reply immediately. Taking a few seconds, he
weighed up in his mind if revealing what Tess had
confided to him would be of any benefit. Deciding that
he had no option Joe began to speak. After sharing all of
Tess's secrets with his superior, he waited for her to tell
him that Maxi Trueman was a no go area. He was
surprised with what she said next.

'Carry on! Pay him a visit. You can use the ruse of
asking some informal questions about the missing girl.
Get a feel for the place, where he lives and the
conditions. That should tell us a thing or two about the
man. We've had no reason to bring him in before and we
were advised not to hassle him, as he's the type to scream
police harassment. As you are both in the process of
investigating a missing person, so to speak, going to
interview Mr Trueman in connection with that, is a

perfectly legitimate reason to go door knocking. If you get no joy, then try leaning on any known associates.'

Joe did feel a small amount of guilt at revealing personal information about a colleague but he also knew only too well what could occur if he interrupted a surveillance team. Joe left Annette's office but not before kissing her tenderly. The woman was like a drug to him, he was fine if he didn't see her but as soon as he did, then he had to take her in his arms. Joe didn't have a clue where all this was going and to be truthful he didn't care. For the moment, she was back in his life and that was all that mattered.

Tess was up at the crack of dawn. Things were finally beginning to move and she had a real gut feeling that they would soon find Sally. Her anticipation was so strong that she had no appetite, something that had started to worry Agi Goldstein. The woman had tried to catch Tess but she was either at work, or asleep in her room. Today was no exception and Tess had left the house before her landlady was even awake. Joe had been waiting in the office for a good half an hour and when Tess walked in, he didn't give her chance to take her coat off.

'Don't bother getting settled, we're out of here!'

'Where to? Are we bringing Layton in again?'

'Not for now Tess, there's bigger fish to fry at the moment. When we get in the car and away from prying ears, I'll tell you all I know.'

Joe trusted Tess, over the years he'd come to recognise good and bad and she was definitely a good one. He didn't like to admit that he hadn't seen the signs with Marsters, Abbey or Franks but then to be honest, he hadn't stepped out of his office much. At least he hadn't until Tess had set foot in the place. Once they were on their way, he relayed all that Chief Windsor had told him.

'So looking for my sister goes out the window?'

'No not at all. The Chief wants us to go see Maxi Trueman. He's one of the bigger fish but also connected to Layton. If he doesn't know anything about Sally, we can at least use him as a threat to Layton if we need to.'

'Where are we heading then?'

'The last known address we have for Trueman, though I doubt very much if he still lives there. Just let me get the map out and I'll give you directions. Right here we are, head for Waterloo Bridge and then for Camberwell. It's a fair trot and I bet we're going to have trouble finding the Brandon estate once we get there.'

Tess hated driving in the city and the outer boroughs were even worse. Biting her lip, she didn't complain and instead manoeuvred the car through the heavy traffic. Surprisingly the Brandon Estate turned out to be easily found. A deprived run down area, it wasn't the sort of place where you could go out alone after dark and feel safe. The Trueman family had been listed as living at flat two two one block B. As expected the lift was out of order and Joe and Tess had three flights of stinking stairs to climb. Each return on the stairwell stank of urine and was littered with used condoms and fast food packaging. When they located their destination they both gave each other a look of surprise. The walkway on either side of the flat was painted in a cherry red high gloss, the windows shone and the nets were a pristine white. As usual Lady Trueman had gone out to her cleaning job and Joe was pleased about that fact. Maxi's file stated that his mother was always unhelpful and wouldn't give the police one piece of information regarding her son. As luck would have it, Solomon Trueman was at home from work with a bad cold. Tess rang the doorbell and waited. A large portly man, who stood over six feet tall, answered

139

the door. With greying hair and a beautiful chocolate brown complexion, he revealed perfect white teeth as he smiled. Solomon invited them into his home and they were even more surprised at what they found inside. Every inch of the place gleamed and the furniture and fittings were of the highest standard. Solomon Trueman had worked hard and both he and his wife were both overly house proud.

'Me can sees ya shock wi me howes. Me Lady keep it jus nace don't ya tink?'

Joe smiled at the aging man and wondered how, a decent human being like the one standing before him, could ever have spawned a bastard like Maxi. Tess decided to try and appeal to the man's fatherly side and spoke in a hushed almost childlike tone.

'We won't keep you long Mr Trueman. It's just that we're trying to locate your son and this is the last known address for him. Solomon grinned to again reveal the most amazing set of gleaming white teeth that Tess had ever seen.

'Tell me darlin' whas a priddy ting lak yuh wana be doing workin' fa de police?'

'I'm trying to make the world a better place Mr Trueman.'

Solomon smiled sagely and this time nodded his head.

'Sure ye arr darlin'. I tell yuh whe me bwoy is an make a betta place too if yuh knaw wha a men.'

Winking at Tess, Solomon continued to give out Maxis Truman's Grays Inn road address. Back outside, Joe was flabbergasted at how easy it had all gone. For years it had been almost impossible to locate where Maxi lived and here they were, within ten minutes of arriving and they knew not only the road but the flat number to boot. Deciding not to waste any time, he told Tess they would

go straight to the address and do a touch of surveillance.
'Do you think we'll have any trouble Sir?'
'Don't know but we're about to find out. Now let's get a move on before the little fucker goes out for the day.'
Greys Inn Mansion was a large contemporary building and the name said much more about it, than its modern architecture. The foyer was lush with suede sofas and exotic palms. Waiting for the lift, Tess glanced around and couldn't help but be impressed.
'Who says crime doesn't pay, Sir?'
Joe ignored the remark and walked through the now open stainless doors. It was only a short ride to the third floor and Maxis door was directly opposite the lifts entrance. Gently tapping on the wood, as if it was a request from a neighbour, Joe then pushed Tess so that she stood right in front of the spy hole. A handsome man of Caribbean decent opened the door several seconds later. Maxi Trueman waited for her to ask something and when all Tess did was stare, he tried to slam the door closed. Joe Reynolds had anticipated the move and pushed the flat of his palm against the polished surface.
'Come on now Maxi! you're about due for a pull. In fact I'd say it's long overdue, wouldn't you?'
Realising there was no point in resisting, Maxi swaggered into his lounge and both Tess and Joe followed. The room was a stark white, from the carpet, to the walls and the ceiling. Three large white leather sofas filled most of the wall space and a fifty inch plasma television dominated one end.
'My my Maxi! and haven't we done well for ourselves. It's amazing what you can do with the money the dole pays.'
Maxi sucked air in between his teeth in a gesture of pure contempt. When he stared into Tess's face, she turned

141

away. No villain had every scared her but this one was different. Maxi's eyes were cold and she sensed evil through and through. Joe took a seat on one of the sofas and he could see that his action upset Maxi big time.

'Don't mind do you? Only I'm a bit knackered see, been working too hard trying to catch criminals! Now we'd like to have a few words with you, here or down at the station, your choice?'

Maxi didn't bother trying to use his well-practiced patois, he was too wound up.

'So what's all this about?'

'We're looking into the case of a missing girl. Her names Sally Sayers and we have reason to believe you may know of her.'

'Never fucking heard the name in my life, now am I under arrest or what?'

'No lad it's just an informal chat that's all.'

'Well in that case copper you can fuck off because I don't ever fucking speak to the filth about anything!'

Maxi Trueman had been in the game long enough to know they had nothing on him. If they had, it would have been armed response surrounding him, instead of some washed up looking filth with a mousy haired plod in tow for company. Joe knew he had no real reason to take in the man, so decided to leave things as they were for the moment. Luckily for them, word on the Street hadn't reached the main man and Maxi had no idea that Lenny Layton had been interviewed. It at least brought them some time to dig a little deeper.

'Well thanks for your cooperation Mr Trueman; I'm sure we'll see each other real soon. You take care now.'

Tess followed her boss like a lamb, never before had she been so pleased to be out of a building. Joe marched ten to the dozen and she had trouble keeping up. When they

142

reached the car, her boss was wrenching at the handle and she struggled to get the keys out of her pocket.

'Calm down Sir, whatever's got you so rattled?'

'It's cunts like him, pardon my French. They play the game all their lives and hardly ever pay the piper. Well I'm going to make sure that bastard gets his comeuppance.'

'And I thought I was the naive one! Surely you didn't think it was going to be easy.'

'I didn't expect any different to what we got, I just hate the fucking Maxi Truman's of this world with a vengeance. Drive over to Layton's, I think it's about time we paid him another visit.'

Lenny had let the flat get into a worse state than normal. Food containers, which were mostly burger cartons picked up from one of the late night vendors, littered the floor. The ashtrays were all overflowing and upturned beer cans had spilled the remainder of their contents onto the rug. Lenny was oblivious to the scene and the only one who cared was Roxy. Now that she wasn't here, it didn't matter and in any case Lenny knew she'd sort it out, once she was back where she belonged. The knock at the door woke Lenny, who'd been gently coming down from his last hit. The time scale was getting shorter by the week and he knew that soon his habit would be out of control. Until recently he'd been able to handle it, or so he'd thought. Now his body craved opium every hour of the day. With as much enthusiasm as he could muster, Lenny pulled himself up from the armchair and slowly walked to the door. If it was kids messing around or some scumbag salesman, then he was going to give them a mouthful the likes of which they'd never heard before. Seeing Joe Reynolds and his colleague on the doorstep, Lenny nervously ran his fingers through his hair.

'Not you bastards again! Why can't you fucking leave me alone. Look, I'm only providing a service, just a bit here and a bit there. Enough to keep me going, that's all. I'm trying to earn a living same as everyone else but you want to fucking crucify me for some reason. What you should be doing is getting out there catching the real villains, not harassing the likes of me.'

Joe Reynolds pushed pass the poor excuse for a man and walked along the hall into the lounge. Deciding not to take a seat, he glanced around at the carnage that was Lenny Layton's life.

'Lenny you are a villain, albeit small time. The system loses track of you so easily that most fucking dealers and users are on the same treatment programme. Easy way to pass on gear I suppose but then you're too fucking thick to think of something like that. The likes of Maxi Trueman wouldn't be, well that's if he ever got his fucking hands dirty but he uses soft twats like you for that, don't he?'

Lenny hung his head. He wasn't feeling too good and the last thing he wanted was to get into a conversation about his new boss, especially with Old Bill.

'Right Lenny! Its cards on the table time now. We're not interested in a wanker like you, only your supplier.'

'Oh fuck off! I aint no grass and besides I'd be dead by this time tomorrow.'

Tess had walked over to a small melamine storage unit that had a couple of small framed photographs on top. One was of Lenny and a few other men and Tess guessed by their attire, they we're friends from his lengthy sentence. The other one was of the girl who was here at the flat the other day. Long dark hair cascaded from her shoulders and how totally different she appeared from the rough and solemn person she had met earlier. All the

144

while Tess looked around; she still kept her ears open and was listening to the conversation between the two men. 'I need Maxi Trueman badly and you're going to help me. If you do, we'll leave you well alone and out of all this. If you don't, then I'll just have to tell Maxi it was you who grassed. Either way I'll get a result, maybe for his drug dealing or maybe for topping you but a result all the same.'

Lenny could feel his mouth open but no sound emitted. It was deep trouble this time and there was no way he could worm his way out. Once more he started to run his fingers through his greasy hair, while stalling for time to think. His next sentence came out full of vengeance. With each word, a shower of fine spittle sprayed into the air and Joe knew he had Lenny just where he wanted him. 'Listen cunt! The chain is long and I'm at the bottom. Old Bill aint daft, one dealer down and there are ten more to replace him. What's stopping me telling you a load of fucking shit then pissing off? You wouldn't know the difference.'

Joe Reynolds calmly walked over to Lenny and without a second thought, punched the man firmly on the jaw. His injuries from Maxi hadn't healed and the pain was now intense. Lenny fell to the floor at the same time as Joe Reynolds shoe made contact with his ribs. Lenny Layton was good at dishing out punishment to women but when it came to himself, his pain threshold was non-existent. All the while Tess watched with concern, it was certainly different from the way things were done in Spalding. 'Because Mr Layton, I would make it my life's work to track you down. The C.P.S would fast track you through the courts and Maxi would have you fucking done over before your bed was made up. Now I know there are a couple of bent coppers mixed up with Maxi and we aim

145

to get them all. Are you going to give me the information
or shall I just take you in now and fucking charge you?'
'Charge me with what?'
Once more Joe removed the talc and gravy powder that
had so scared Bobby Race and waved it in front of
Lenny.
'There's enough here to get you a five stretch at least! So
what's it to be?'
Joe raised his foot again but before he had chance to land
a kick, Lenny put up his hand in submission.
'I don't know nothing about no bent coppers. Maxi uses
me to collect the gear, that way the cunt keeps his hands
clean. I overheard him on his mobile the other day that's
all I can tell you.'
'And?'
'A large amount of crack is coming in tomorrow and he
needs a safe haven to hide it. I heard him arranging to
meet some blokes at the Bleeding Heart Tavern tomorrow
night at ten.'
'What over in Farringdon?'
'Yeah and apart from that, I know nothing. Now will you
fuck off and leave me in peace!'
'Sure we will Lenny! now it weren't that fucking hard
was it?'
His last sentence was spoken as Joe headed towards the
front door. This was the information Joe Reynolds had
been waiting for and he was desperate to relay it to the
chief. Running to the car, he was again impatient as Tess
searched through her bag for the keys.
'Why the fuck don't you keep them in your pocket?'
She didn't reply and squeezed the remote to let them both
in. All the way back to the station Joe scribbled furiously
in his not book, smiling smugly at the same time.
Suddenly he had come alive and it wasn't a sight Tess

was familiar with. The traffic was light for the time of day and their return journey didn't take long. Joe had not given Tess a second thought and was so excited at the prospect of banging up so many bent coppers, that her silence passed unnoticed. He could feel the adrenalin start to run through his veins and it was a feeling he liked.

CHAPTER FIFTEEN

On their return, Joe flew up the stairs and almost ran into the Chiefs office. Tess followed but her enthusiasm was waning, since all efforts on her boss's part to find Sally had disappeared. Closing the door quietly, she stood silently at the back of the room as Joe revealed all to Annette Windsor.

'Good work you two but we now need to move swiftly. I don't want either of you speaking about this outside of this office. I can arrange a team from Paddington to give us a hand. I've worked with them all before and unlike here, they are as straight as they come.'

Joe nodded his agreement but out of the corner of her eye, Annette could see something was troubling Tess.

'So detective Davey, how did you enjoy today?'

'It was good Ma'am.'

'Good! You've just gathered information that could nail a large scale drug dealer. Not to mention several bent officers and you say "It was good".'

'I'm sorry Ma'am; it's just that I'm a little preoccupied at the moment.'

Annette Windsor walked around her desk and over to where Tess stood near the door. For several seconds the Chief studied the girl before smiling.

'Is it to do with your sister?'

For a moment Tess was stunned but a feeling of betrayal quickly followed this. In no uncertain terms she gave Joe a look that cut him to the core. Everything she'd shared with him had been private and now she found that he'd told other officers. For all she knew it was now the gossip of the station.

'In a way Ma'am. I originally came to London to find

my twin as I imagine D.C.I. Reynolds has informed you. It now seems that my investigations have been put on hold due to Maxi Trueman and a few others.'

'Detective! In case you'd forgotten, you are employed to do a job of work. Anything personal must be carried out in your own time and not the Met's. Do I make myself clear?'

Tess's cheeks flushed with embarrassment.

'Yes Ma'am and I'm sorry. I just thought the force was a place where we all looked out for each other and gave help when it was needed.'

Joe Reynolds could see that he'd really upset her and felt momentarily guilty. Butting in before the Chief had chance to comment on Tess's last statement, he too now stood in front of her.

'Tess, I told you I would help you and I will. For now Maxi and the likes have to take centre stage but once they're dealt with, it'll be back to the search for Sally and that's a promise. Hopefully your sister is safe and warm somewhere and still will be when we finally track her down. The Maxi Truman's of this world can disappear overnight, so they have to take priority.'

Tess sighed. She knew what she was hearing was right but she was so desperate to find her sister that all thoughts of real police work had flown out of the window.

'I know Sir and I'm grateful, truly I am.'

Annette Windsor couldn't believe what she was hearing and her voice jumped several octaves with her next sentence.

'Excuse me but isn't your main priority catching villains, or did what I just said go in one ear and out the other? While I sympathise with you Tess, I will not have this kind of behaviour in my Nick! Now for the last time, is that understood?'

Neither Joe nor Tess replied and Annette Windsor wasn't used to being ignored.

'Well! is it?'

It was Tess who answered first but only with a nod of her head. Joe sighed deeply and after several seconds he too motioned his agreement. Annette could see that the pair would have a good working relationship and it pleased her. Not one to normally give explanations, today she reasoned this was a different situation.

'Tess. Please don't think that D.C.I. Reynolds has been telling everyone about your private affairs. Joe and I go back many years and anything he's felt the need to share with me, I can assure you has remained strictly between the two of us.'

Tess nodded and her superior could see that she had taken on board the semi apology. Now turning to face Joe Reynolds, Chief Windsor once more got down to business.

'As soon as I have any news I'll contact you but I suggest for now, you both take the rest of the day off, loose lips and all that!'

Joe nodded his agreement and together he and Tess left the office.

'Ship and Shovel?'

'Thanks Sir but I've left something in the office and after that I have a bit of shopping to do, if that's Ok?'

'Fine but make sure you keep your mobile on. When it's time to move I want everything to run smoothly.'

Tess watched as he headed for the front reception and when she was happy that he wouldn't return she slowly walked back to their joint office. In the solitude of the room, Tess switched on her computer and waited for the monitor to burst into life. She had acknowledged and also accepted all that the Chief and Joe had said but her heart was now ruling her head and she couldn't wait any longer for their help. Racking her brain for all the snippets of information she'd gathered in the last few days, her thoughts stopped at Carmel Jones. Joe had said she was a good sort and if she knew Lenny Layton, then she possibly knew Sally too. Tapping in the name, she waited for a file to appear. It didn't take long and what a file it was. There were numerous charges for soliciting, some resulting in only a fine and a few ending with weeks spent in Holloway prison. The list seemed to go on forever and Tess scanned the screen for known associates. There were none. Next she looked for a last known address and the Old Compton Street abode appeared. Tess decided that as she'd been given the remainder of the day off work, then she would take a leisurely walk home. Old Compton Street was definitely on her way and she wanted to kick herself for not following this up sooner. All the time they'd been after Lenny and this woman was just a stone's throw away from Tess's own digs. Glancing at her watch, she saw that it was three fifteen. After closing down the file and switching off the computer, she made her way out of the station. Fifteen minutes later and Tess Davey turned into the famous Street that could possibly reveal to her all the answers she was desperate for.

Now that Roxy was on the mend, Carmel was back to work every night. It was her usual practice not to rise until around four thirty in the afternoon and today was no exception. The knock at the door not only woke her but also pissed her off big time. Roxy was at the flat less and less and Carmel knew she would have to answer it herself. Pulling on her housecoat, she opened the door and was surprised to find a woman, who was obviously in

151

a different line of work staring back at her.

'Yeah?'

'Carmel Jones?'

'Who wants to know?'

Tess held up her warrant card and saw the expression of horror on Carmel's face.

'Look whatever you're after I aint done it. Fuck me! Cant a girl earn a living nowadays without some snotty bitch from the filth interfering.

Tess smiled. She wanted to laugh at the woman's self-description of being a girl; she was in her late fifties if she was a day.

'It's nothing like that Carmel. We seem to have a mutual friend and I wondered if you could possibly help me with the case of a missing person I'm looking into.'

Carmel instantly relaxed and invited the woman inside. On inspection, the flat wasn't as bad as she was expecting. After Lenny Layton's place, Tess knew that at least this woman had a little pride, albeit tiny. Declining the offer of a glass of Vodka, Tess watched as Carmel Jones drank her own in one, then immediately lit up a cigarette. Inhaling deeply, the woman began to cough uncontrollably. When Carmel doubled over and Tess could hear the throaty phlegm that was trying to escape, she became worried. About to ask if she required help, she was stopped when Carmel held up a hand. A few more coughs and several seconds later, the woman stood upright.

'Ah! that's better, now what can I do for you?'

'I work with Joe Reynolds and he said you may be able to help.'

Tess delved into her coat pocket and withdrew the photograph that Mavis Parsons had given her. It was at least ten years old and badly faded but it was the only

152

image Tess had of her sister. She handed it to her host. Squinting her eyes, Carmel looked at the image and then walked over to the window, in the rouse of needing more light. Instantly she recognised Roxy but her face gave nothing away.

'Who'd you say this was?'

'I didn't but her names Sally Sayers and she's my sister.'

'Runaway is she; see a lot of them in my game. Come to the smoke thinking the Streets are paved with fucking gold and end up on a mortuary slab.'

Carmel didn't think about what she was saying and it wasn't until she glanced in Tess's direction again, that she saw the young woman had a tear in her eye.

'Take no fucking notice of me love, run on half the fucking time and make no sense the rest of it. Are you sure you won't have that drink after all?'

Tess was about to decline a second time when she remembered she was off duty.

'Why not!'

Carmel parted the beaded curtain that separated the kitchenette and pulled another glass from the cabinet.

'Must say it's the first time I've had Old Bill up here socializing. Well I suppose that's not strictly true but best to let sleeping dogs and all that, hey?'

Tess Davey found herself laughing at this ridiculous looking woman. She was a prostitute and a rough one at that. She earned her living illegally but Tess Davey found her to be warm and friendly and the type of person everyone needs in their life at some point.

'Look Miss?'

'Tess, please call me Tess.'

'Well Tess, I don't think I know the woman in this picture but I can ask around a bit. You never know, someone may have seen her or knows of her. Can I keep hold of this?'

The photograph was the only one Tess had and in the last few days had come to treasure it but she also knew that without it, Carmel wouldn't have a chance. She nodded to the older woman that it was ok. As much as she liked the woman, Tess didn't really trust Carmel but realised she had little choice if she ever wanted to find Sally.

Over the next hour the two miss matched females shared a few more drinks and gradually Tess opened up to Carmel. She spoke about her father and mother and about finding out she was adopted. Lastly she told Carmel all that her sister had been through, or at least as much as she knew.

'Well it's a sad story I must admit but nothing compared to some of the tales I could tell you. Make your fucking hair curl and no mistake but I know no one's troubles are as bad as your own, so I'll do what I can. I must say you don't look alike.'

Tess smiled.

'I know it's fuzzy but I think from the picture, my sister dyes her hair. From the records I have, it seemed our whole family were mousy coloured.'

Carmel studied Tess's face. The girl was average, nothing more or less. Straight hair and being slightly overweight, gave her the appearance of being older than her twenty-eight years. In a line up, no one would guess in a million years that beautiful Roxy Baxter could ever be related, let alone the twin, of the woman now seated on Carmel Jones's sofa.

'Well now Tess, it's been really nice meeting you but it's about time this girl started getting herself beautiful and ready for work. We all have a living to make!'

Tess stood up and was embarrassed at how she'd opened up to a complete stranger. Her cheeks were flushed and she knew the vodka had played a large part in helping to loosen her tongue.

'Of course and I'm sorry to have kept you so long.' Carmel placed a hand on Tess's shoulder and guided her towards the door.

'Not at all and if I find out anything I'll be in touch.' Tess walked slowly down the stairs, feeling better than she had in weeks. Maybe it would end up being another dead end, maybe not. She decided that for once she was going to be positive and that soon she would meet her sister and everything would be alright.

At the same time as Tess walked away from Carmel's flat, Roxy was heading towards it. The two passed each other and at first Tess didn't recognise the woman. Suddenly she stopped dead in her tracks and watched as the girl from a couple of days ago, entered the address she herself had just left. There was nothing strange in the fact that Carmel knew this girl; after all, the older one knew Lenny so that was the connection. Just the same it was something Tess couldn't get off her mind for the rest of the evening. While Tess had recognised Roxy, Roxy hadn't given her a second glance. Climbing the stairs two at a time, she let herself in with the key Carmel Jones had given her. The sight as she walked in made her burst out laughing.

'Well fuck my old boots; you look like a fucking zombie.'

Carmel had only just applied the face pack and she was trying her hardest not to speak but with Roxy's incessant cackle, it was proving difficult. Eventually she realised it was a futile exercise and went into the kitchenette to wash of the rapidly setting pack. Patting her face with a less than fresh towel, Carmel re-entered the room.

'I've had a visitor?'

155

'Good earner?'

Carmel lit up another Benson and in haled before she continued.

'Not that sort of visitor you soppy cow I mean a proper one. She was actually asking about you.'

The older woman knew that this would get Roxy's back up and for once she was actually enjoying baiting her.

'Who?'

'Guess.'

'Oh don't fuck about Carm, who the fuck was it?'

Carmel Jones inhaled deeply as she took in another lungful of nicotine. Walking over to the window she watched her friend and knew that if she didn't answer soon, the girl would blow a fuse.

'Your sister.'

'Don't be fucking soft!'

'I aint! I tell you it was your sister and to top it all, she's Old Bill! Must say darling when they was handing out the looks she was at the back of the fucking queue but she's probably been compensated with brains.'

Carmel's attempt at a joke passed unnoticed and Roxy didn't react how Carmel thought she would. Standing up she began to pace the floor, all the time tapping her bottom lip with her index finger.

'For years I dreamed of this but as time passed and she didn't bother to find me I kind of gave up on it.'

'And now?'

'I don't know Carm, I really don't know. I mean fucking hell! a brass and a plod in the same family!'

The two women began to laugh at the absurdity of it but deep down Roxy Baxter was very frightened. If this woman was going to the trouble of interviewing prostitutes, then she wasn't about to let go easily. If Lenny found out about this there'd be a price to pay and

156

right at this minute Roxy was truly broken. Physically, mentally and in just about any other way that was humanly possible. Carmel saw her friend's expression change and knew straight away what she was thinking. Making her way to where the girl stood, Carmel wrapped her arms around Roxy and rocked her back and forth.

'Don't worry I didn't tell her anything. Said I didn't know you but I'd ask about and get back to her.'

Carmel pulled out the old photograph from her housecoat and handed it to Roxy.

'It's old but I knew it was you as soon as I saw it. Only one your sisters got and I could see she treasured it.'

'What's her name?'

'Tess.'

'That's pretty. I suppose her nice family changed it; she's really a Susan. Susan and Sally Sayers that's us! Twins and we've never even met. How sad is that Carm?'

Carmel Jones didn't answer, she didn't know how to, instead she gave her friend another hug.

'Don't worry babe we'll sort it. One way or another I promise, we'll sort it.'

CHAPTER SIXTEEN

Tess hadn't slept a wink all night. Everything that had happened yesterday whirled through her mind. For some reason the girl from Lenny Layton's flat was a constant vision and every time she was about to drift off, would appear before her eyes. Dragging herself from the bed, she washed and dressed in jeans and a pullover. The house was quiet and Tess decided to make herself a light breakfast of toast and coffee. About to open the kitchen door, she was stopped by Agi Goldstein's voice.

'Tess how lovely to see you, come on in and have a bite. Geoffrey and me were just about to sit down but it's much nicer to have three at the table. Better conversation if you know what I mean?'

This was all she needed but Agi was so sweet that Tess couldn't hurt her feelings by declining. As usual the sideboard groaned with enough food to feed a large portion of Africa and the sight alone of so much food, made Tess's stomach begin to churn. Placing a single round of toast on her plate, she spooned a small amount of scrambled egg on top.

'Tess! You've not got enough there to keep a sparrow alive. Why don't you try a couple of the kippers, they're Mr Seaman's favourite.'

Tess looked over to where Geoffrey sat with a plate piled high. He gave her a knowing wink, which made her smile.

'I couldn't Agi really. We had a farewell drinks party yesterday lunchtime and I'm really feeling a little under the weather'

Tess hated lying but knew that if she didn't, the contents of her stomach would reappear within the hour. Agi pulled back a chair and motioned for Tess to sit down. 'Say no more sweetie! I've been there enough times myself over the years.'

Her little white lie had paid off and this time it was her turn to wink in Geoffrey Seaman's direction. The unlikely threesome spent the next hour making idle but enjoyable chitchat. After helping Agi clear away the dishes, Tess made her way back to her room. She was about to put on her coat and set off for the station when her mobile burst into life. Kept on the bedside table during the night, she must have knocked it to the floor and began to panic when she couldn't see it. Finally Tess felt under the valance and her hand snatched up the oblong leather case. As the voice mail was about to launch itself into action she flipped open the receiver. 'Hello?'

'Tess it's Joe. Listen the boss wants us to stay away from the nick today. She's given the go ahead for us to take part in the job tonight but only on the understanding that we keep a low profile. How do you feel about that?'

'Fine by me. I didn't think we'd get within spitting distance to tell the truth.'

'Well as none of this would have been possible without us, Annette felt it was only fair.'

'Ohhhh! Annette is it now?'

'Don't be cheeky Tess. Now be on the corner of Garrick Street at nine tonight. On second thoughts, there's a pub called the Corner House. I'll meet you inside. It's not a pub used by the Met, so we shouldn't be recognised. And Tess....'

'What?'

'For fucks sake don't be late! This operation goes ahead with or without us and I would like a little of the credit.'

'I'm always on time Sir and the phrase 'Pot and kettle'

come to mind, but I won't mention it. See you tonight.'
With that she hung up and putting the phone on the
dressing table where she could keep an eye on it, walked
over to the wardrobe and replaced her coat. Glancing at
her watch she could see that it was only now nine thirty.
Eleven and a half hours was a long time to fill but she
had a feeling she wouldn't find it too difficult.
Roxy was up with the larks and while Carmel was still
snoring softly, she made her way to Lenny's. All night
long her mind had been filled with apprehension about
her sister and she'd still not come to a decision. Roxy
didn't want to talk to Lenny about it but seeing him
always made her feel better and besides it was about time
she went home for good. After placing the few items of
clothing she had with her into another black plastic bag,
Roxy slipped out of the flat. Not writing a note, she
knew that by simply leaving her key, Carmel would know
the score. At just after twelve o'clock, Tess Davey
knocked at the door of Carmel Jones's flat. It was the
same scenario as yesterday and the woman was still
sound asleep in bed. Tess didn't give up and continued to
rap until her knuckles were sore.
'All right! All right I'm fucking coming and you'd better
have the mother of all excuses for getting me out of bed.'
Flicking on the hall light she opened the door. Carmel
rolled her eyes when she saw who it was.
'You've got a fucking good knack of getting people out
of their beds. It's now two days in a row! Well come in
for fucks sake don't stand there wasting me fucking
electric.'
Tess did as she was asked and followed the woman into
the room. The place now seemed so familiar after only
her second visit.
'I'm sorry I woke you! I forget that not everyone works

the same hours as me.'

Carmel was lighting her obligatory first cigarette of the day and peering out of the window at the same time. She knew Roxy wasn't here because her coat had gone from the chair but she was worried the girl might return at any moment.

'Look Tess, I don't mean to seem rude but I've got a lot on today. I said I'd ask about but I aint had a chance yet.'

'No it's not that Carmel, it's about the photograph. I need to have it back.'

Carmel Jones became suspicious and her eyes narrowed as she continued to peer out of the window.

'I don't know where I've put it at the minute. Why don't you come back later after I've had chance to tidy up a bit and look for it.'

Tess knew when she was being given the brush off; she also knew that if she didn't stand her ground then she would lose the battle.

'It's Ok, I'll wait.'

Carmel mouthed the words 'fuck' to herself but turned round smiling to look at Tess.

'As you like. I'll get dressed and have a rummage in the bedroom while I'm at it. Feel free to make a cuppa.'

Walking towards her boudoir, as she liked to call the bedroom, Carmel glanced at the hall table and saw the key. Stopping she picked it up and instantly knew there was no worry of Roxy walking in. The stupid little mare had gone back to that loser for more punishment and the thought of it made Carmel's blood boil. Walking into her room, she picked up the picture from her bedside table and returned to where Tess was still seated on the sofa.

'Here we are, not lost after all. Now if you will excuse me, like I said before I'm really busy today.'

'Sure and thanks Carmel.'

161

Seconds later and Tess was once more outside the flat. Two doors down she found the small coffee shop of a few days earlier. Tess took up a seat near the window and when her cappuccino arrived, she removed the photograph from her pocket and studied it for quite a while. There was no mistaking; it was the girl from Lenny's flat, the girl from yesterday and the girl that Carmel Jones denied knowing. What Tess couldn't fathom out was why the woman had lied. Studying the picture again made Tess smile, she'd at last found Sally and neither of them had known that their paths had crossed on two separate occasions and in as many days. Two hours later Tess still sat in the coffee shop. She'd hoped that Sally would call in to see Carmel Jones but now realised that probably wasn't going to happen. Aware of where her sister was and what she looked like, would have to be enough for now. Not having eaten since breakfast, Tess realised that tonight was going to be a long haul and without food unbearable. Hurrying back to Agi's, she was happy in the knowledge that the woman wouldn't let her leave again, at least not without something hot inside her.

By eight o'clock Tess was changed and fed. A homemade stew and dumplings had more that quelled her hunger but made her feel sleepy too. That didn't make for good policing or as Agi thought, a night out on the town. Pulling on her warmest coat and wrapping a scarf tightly round her head, Tess sat off for the Corner House and her meeting with Joe. It was a fair walk but she'd allowed herself plenty of time and besides, the fresh air would wake her up a bit. The place wasn't hard to find and by the time she arrived it was still quiet. A young couple sat at a side table and three men, none of whom took any notice of Tess, stood at the bar. Ordering a slim line tonic, she took a seat in the corner. It was slightly hidden but still allowed her a good sighting of anyone who came inside. At a quarter to nine the door burst open and as large as life, in walked Carmel Jones. Her dress was a tight silver sparkly number and fought constantly with every curve of her body. The woman either thought she was two sizes smaller than she was, or she'd owned the dress since her teens. Either way, it was terrible and together with her back combed hair and poppy red lipstick, made her look exactly what she was. Tess had never been able to understand why these women dressed the way they did. It wasn't sexy, it was downright cheap and rough looking and she wished someone would give them a lesson in style. Carmel walked up to the bar and was still oblivious to Tess's presence.

'Give us a large Vodka Barry and go easy on the ice. Your fucking spirits are watered down enough as it is.' The three men standing at the bar burst out laughing and Carmel sidled up to them. When they realised she was trying to pull a trick, they all turned their backs.

'Please yourselves, you're all fucking scabby looking cunts anyways.'

Carmel sauntered over to the jukebox, oblivious to how ridiculous she appeared. Placing a pound coin into the slot, she selected three songs. Down Town by Petula Clarke, Delilah by Tom Jones and last but by no means least, her favourite, My Way by Sinatra. As the first tune emitted its opening bars from the overhead speaker Carmel began to sway with the music. The song was almost closing when she finally set eyes on Tess.

'What the fuck are you doing in here?'

Tess beckoned for Carmel to come over; the last thing she wanted was a scene. The woman had only had one

163

drink but she was already far too loud. Still moving to the music, Carmel made her way to the corner. The sight made Tess want to laugh but she bit down hard on her bottom lip. It was a scene that most people would recognise from family weddings and the like. An older relative would have too much to drink and approach everyone in the place, while still trying to move to the music. The only difference here was that Carmel wasn't drunk. Tess would guarantee she was almost stone cold sober. This was Carmel Jones acting as she did everyday of her life.

'Honestly Carmel I didn't know this was a pub you used. I'm being collected here soon, that's all.'

Carmel narrowed her eyes and placing her palms flat on the table, leaned in close until Tess could see the colour of the woman's eyes. Tess wasn't scared but she was embarrassed. Talk in the rest of the bar had reduced to almost a whisper and she knew the others were trying to hear her conversation.

'This aint no Old Bill pub! Fuck me girl if they knew who you were, you'd be out on your fucking ear.'

'Look I don't need any trouble. As I said before, I'll be collected very soon.'

Carmel turned and began walking away when Tess spoke again. She had tried to hold back the words with all her might but her mouth seemed to move without her control.

'Why did you lie about my sister?'

Carmel didn't answer straight away but she did stop dead in her tracks. Finally she turned and walked back to the table.

'I don't know what you're talking about.'

'I'm talking about my sister and the fact that you told me you didn't know her.'

'I don't!'

'Well then whoever went into your flat after I left was doing a damn good impression? She was the same girl I came up against in Lenny Layton's flat a few days ago, the same girl who if you look hard enough, can be seen in the photograph I let you borrow.'

Carmel wanted to kick herself; she should have destroyed the picture when she had the chance.

'So that's why you came round mine, to check it was her?'

'No actually Carmel! It wasn't until after I left your flat that I looked at the photo again, then put two and two together.'

'Look, Roxy's had a rough time of it. That bastard Layton knocks her around and......'

'Roxy?'

Carmel laughed without opening her mouth. The kind of laugh that comes out of the nostrils in short rapid bursts of air.

'Yeah, her names Roxy Baxter now. Or at least that's what she calls herself these days. Sally Sayers don't sound right for a brass somehow.'

Since it was all out in the open, Carmel was enjoying the shock her words were causing this plod.

'Didn't know did you? Roxy's been on the game a few years now and fucking good at it she is too.'

Tess didn't know what to say. Suddenly her dream had turned into a nightmare, one from which she was desperate to escape. Of all the things she'd imagined in the last few weeks, nothing was even remotely close to what she'd just heard. Tess had imagined various scenarios, some happy, some lonely; even one where she'd found out her sister had died. Now a thought entered her brain maybe that might have been a better outcome. She dismissed it at once and turned her

165

attention back to Carmel.

'I can see you are enjoying this Ms Jones but let me give you a word of warning. Have your fun now because in the morning, if I decide to come after you, you'll wish you'd never been fucking born!'

Tess stood up and forcibly pushed the woman to one side. The pub was in total silence now and all eyes were on Tess, as she headed towards the door. Carmel couldn't believe the change in the woman. Yesterday Tess Davey had sat in Carmel's flat, hanging on her every word. Now the woman who'd just walked away, was strong, confident and in charge. What bothered Carmel Jones more than anything was the amount of venom Tess's words had been spoken with. Yesterday she would have laughed at the idea but tonight she was frightened and it took a lot to scare Carmel. Before Tess had time to put her hand on the brass plate, the door opened inwards. Joe Reynolds stuck his head round and motioned for her to hurry up. Carmel didn't do any business that night, she was too uptight. Her big mouth had got her into trouble in the past but she'd never learn. Past dealings had taught her that Reynolds could be a good friend to have but a bastard if you got on the wrong side of him. If that snooty bitch went back to him and asked for help, then she was in for grief. If only for tonight, Carmel decided to try and forget about things. Handing her last tenner over to the barman, she ordered a double vodka.

CHAPTER SEVENTEEN

Maxi Trueman had woken with a massive headache. It was nothing to do with alcohol, he never touched the stuff, and the reason was because today Maxi was planning to carry out one of the biggest deals of his life. If everything went to plan, then he'd have enough money to pack it all in. If it went wrong, well that scenario wasn't even worth thinking about. Recently Maxi had begun to have bad dreams. Dreams that saw him behind bars and he knew that if they ever came true, it was something he wouldn't be able to handle. Every dealer before a big job, said it was going to be their last but deep down knew they would continue their illegal acts, at least until they died or were caught. With Maxi, he actually believed his words. Walking through the apartment that he'd called home for the last couple of years, Maxi surveyed all that he had achieved. A state of the art sound system, that would take the average family years to pay for, filled a large cabinet. The plasma television, which was Maxis pride and joy, gleamed in the light of the early morning sun. Walking over to the sofas which had set him back over ten grand, he gently caressed the white calf skin. If the man from up north came through for him, then trinkets like these would seem like a poor man's dream. Maxis eyes sparkled at the thought of all that he could have and have it he would, he was determined about that. After entering the pristine kitchen he opened up the fridge and pulled out a jug of iced water. Pouring himself a glass, Maxi drank quickly. The cold liquid seemed to hit every sense he possessed and the pain in his head was excruciating. Seconds later and he'd achieved what he was after, the pain and headache were gone. Running a hot bath, he slipped into the soapy water and tried to relax. It was hours away from his first meet and he had to chill, either that or they would be the longest hours of his life.

Over in Camberwell, Drayton Livingston wasn't the least bit worried about the forth coming events. True this was his largest deal to date and must score at least a seven on a scale of one to ten but if all went well, he was going to become far bigger than he'd ever thought possible. There was a saying back in Kingston and it was one he liked "Lickle we lickle but we tallawah" deciphered it meant we're small but robust. Drayton smoked so much ganja that he thought himself invincible. It was a trait Maxi hated in the man and something that worried him constantly. Drayton Livingston was the epitome of a Yardie. He wore his dreads with pride and spoke in patois whenever he was in a position to make someone feel small. Many of the up and coming youths had difficulty in mastering the slang and he enjoyed the embarrassment it caused, when they couldn't understand him. Young boys who dreamed of joining the brotherhood, though who in reality understood nothing of its violence and would listen on in wonderment as Drayton erupted with a barrage of Jamaican Patois. Drayton had become an acquaintance of Maxis back in school, when they'd both strived to be the daddy of their year. Drayton had been the brawn and Maxi the brains and together they had become a formidable force in the corridors of their comprehensive. On leaving school they had seen less and less of each other and their reunion had happened by accident. Brixton Academy on the Stockwell road, had become a regular place for Maxi to sell E's. Entering under the front of wanting to see the new leading edge bands, he was then free to deal to his heart's content. It was small time but lucrative for a sixteen year old. It was only six months into his new line of business that Drayton Livingston had turned up. Drayton had the same idea as Maxi but was just that much slower than his counterpart. Harsh words had ended with a fight in the clubs back alley but at the same time a solution had been found. Drayton agreed to supply the tabs and Maxi would sell them. The profits would be split fifty fifty and everyone was happy. The arrangement had worked well for just over a year but when Maxi was continually asked for Charlie, he realised bigger and better things were on the horizon. It was impossible to deal Coke openly at the academy but with a list of willing punters growing daily, he didn't worry. A small black leather bound book was now the only thing he needed to carry and all entries were written in code. Drayton continued to supply the merchandise but now the profits weren't shared. Maxi figured that he was taking the bigger risk and told his friend that it had to be a flat fee, payable on collection. Drayton Livingston was not put out by the new arrangement, in fact it suited him. Within a few months, Maxi Trueman wasn't his only buyer and he began to carry out business in the Camberwell coffee shop. By the end of their second year of trading, he had forced the owner to sell him the property at a knock down price. Installing a couple of decks in the shop, he carried out business under the ruse of providing a venue for up and coming D.J's to showcase. Drayton now surrounded himself daily with a small posse of young men, all eager to be known as a Yardie. Although dark skinned, most were not from the "back yard" but it didn't bother Drayton. As long as they fell over themselves to help him, they could dream of being wannabe gangsters for all he cared. A small room at the rear of the coffee shop was where the real action took place. After buying the cocaine, Drayton would divide it into two. Half would be for his more disconcerting clientele and obviously Maxi Trueman. The other half would be washed with ammonia or bicarbonate and then baked in the microwave. This produced the rocks that were so hungrily sought out by the crack addicts and brought in Drayton's biggest profits. Coke was more expensive but the sheer volume of crack he sold, meant that the costlier drug couldn't compete with its lower class relative.

At four o'clock that afternoon, Maxi was hyped up and ready to do the collection. As far as he could see this was the most dangerous part of the deal. The weather was chilly and overcast and Maxi tried hard not to take it as an omen. Dressed in one of the several Armani suits he owned, Maxi pulled his cashmere overcoat tightly together. It wasn't overly cold but he had a chill running down his spine all the same. Getting into the car, he didn't bother to turn on the music. He needed to concentrate and didn't want to do anything that would draw attention to himself. His clothes told any onlooker that he resembled a young successful business man, rather than the low life dealer that he was. It had become the norm for Maxi to use a mule and recently that mule was Lenny Layton. However this deal was the exception to the rule and too large to let that scum bag anywhere near. This deal had to be done in person and at a location away from Camberwell. Choosing a disused warehouse on the Copleston Road in Peckham had been a good idea. By five o'clock the estate traffic had almost disappeared, as most people had finished work for the day and were heading home to their families. Maxi pulled into the overgrown car park and drove round to the rear. A large roller shutter, which had been broken for years, was half pulled up and Maxi could see Drayton's Discovery parked inside. He switched on the cars headlights and the place became a little easier to see into. When he spotted the lights, Drayton Livingston got out of his vehicle and walked round to the back. Opening the rear door, he felt around until his hand touched the baseball bat that he kept for emergencies. The cold metal nestled in his palm and reassured him at the same time. A large holdall took up most of the space, so after closing the tailgate, Drayton leant against the bumper. His nerves began to get the better of him and he became jumpy. When the car pulled inside and he saw that it was his old pal, he relaxed immediately. Maxi glanced all round, it wasn't that he didn't trust his associate in crime but he wasn't about to get tucked up either. Drayton knew the score, he also knew Maxi Trueman well enough to know that he would be just as nervous himself. It was one thing dealing coke to well heeled white honkey's, who made their money in the city and partied hard after dark but this kind of deal was a step higher and a big one at that. Unlike Maxi, Drayton Livingston wasn't a sharp dresser. Where Maxi preferred well cut suits his friend wore trainer bottoms and hoodie's. His outfit would always be topped off with a long black leather coat with his hoodie pulled out at the back. Grinning widely and showing a mouth full of yellow teeth, he stood up and walked over to the BMW. Maxi got out and Drayton offered his hand. The two men shook before walking back to the discovery, where Drayton proceeded to remove his cargo. Conversation was none existent as both men concentrated hard on the task in hand. Gently Maxi Trueman unzipped the holdall and removed one of the tightly wrapped parcels. From his jacket pocket he took out a small pen

171

knife and plunged it into the packet. Retracting the blade, he licked its point and after rubbing his gums with the tip of his tongue, he smiled.

'Good gear Dray, knew you wouldn't let me down.'

'Anytin' for a broder but aint ya forgettin' sometink?'

Maxi laughed out loud and told Drayton to drive the Discovery over to his car, so they could swap merchandise. As thorough as Maxi had been, Drayton was even more meticulous. The cash he was collecting was sniffed, felt, held up towards the light and lastly a few notes were picked out at random and held under a portable ultra violet light. Finally satisfied that things were as they should be, the pair shook hands again and Maxi was about to leave when his friend spoke.

'Good luck mang me tinks ya ma be needin' it.'

'Thanks mate I really wanted to hear that. I mean it's not as if I aint fucking bricking it enough already!'

Drayton Livingston began to laugh and Maxi shook his head in disgust as he climbed back inside his car. Desperate to get home, he kept to the speed limit but only just. When he pulled up once more on The Grays Inn road, Maxi sighed in relief. It had been a dilemma when deciding where to stash the bag but the only sensible solution, had been his flat. Now having a feeling that Drayton may have had him watched, he knew that to leave it in the car would be a stupid mistake. He trusted no one and with this amount of gear, he had no alternative but to take it home. It was a golden rule that he'd never broken before and having to go against it, made him feel more than a little uneasy. As far as Maxi Trueman was concerned, tonight couldn't come soon enough.

CHAPTER EIGHTEEN

Getting from Garrick Street to Farringdon took less than fifteen minutes. Joe Reynolds's was so hyped up that Tess could actually feel the tension and expectation. His excitement was such, that he hadn't noticed anything unusual at The Corner House. She was glad, the last thing she needed tonight was a telling off by a senior officer. Carmel's revelations ran through her mind and the mental images she imagined, whirled so fast in her head that she felt dizzy. Seedy pictures flashed before her eyes of all the bad things that happened in the dark hours of Soho. Tess saw her sister laying in a gutter battered and bruised. Next she saw a man getting his money's worth up against a wall down some dark alley. She shook her head so violently, that Joe turned his eyes from the road to look at her.

'You alright?'

Tess realised that she had to pull herself together. Tonight was a big shout, probably one of the biggest of her career and she had to put all thoughts of Sally to the back of her mind.

'Fine! Just a bit of a muzzy head that's all.'

Joe didn't reply and a few minutes later they pulled in behind a parked car on Greville Street. The Bleeding Heart was a trendy, slightly up market place and much to Joe's annoyance, very busy. He slammed his palm onto the steering wheel.

'Fuck it! It's going to be harder than ever to catch this lot in the act with a pub full of punters fooling around and acting pissed.'

The Mondeo car they were in was unmarked and still registered to Joes step dad. Harry Maxwell had passed away over three years ago but Joe hadn't got round to changing the documents. Keeping the car hidden in a small garage he rented, Joe had always thought it would come in handy and for tonight's operation, it was just the job. When the back door opened, both Joe and Tess spun round in their seats. Annette Windsor wore a dark wig and spectacles and for a second neither recognised her.

'You didn't think I was going to miss out on all the fun did you? Its years since I've been on a bust.'

This was all Joe needed. It was bad enough having Tess Davey here, now he had his boss to contend with. Joe didn't think of himself as a chauvinist but he admitted to feeling women had a place and it wasn't here in a dangerous situation.

'I can see what you're thinking Joe and believe me I know how volatile the situation might get.'

'Yeah well it might have helped if the place wasn't so fucking busy.'

'Nothing we can do about that I'm afraid, anyway it's an ideal set up for Maxi to conclude his business so I wouldn't worry about it. There's close circuit television in most of Farringdon's Streets now and I have an officer watching to see who is entering and leaving. To get the bastards all in the same place at the same time is something, so we shouldn't push our luck.'

Joe turned to face her and she could see the concern on his face. His poor face looked so tired and she wanted to wrap her arms around his neck and kiss all the stress away. Making herself return to reality, she spoke in a sharp tone.

'Joe, there are over twenty SO19 officers in the shops and doorways of this road. Even the observers inside are SO7 and you're fucking worrying?'

'Alright Annette calm down! It's been a long time since

174

I've been involved in a major collar and I just want everything to go well and to get the results we need.'
'You and me both Joe!'
All this time Tess had sat quietly listening. She now felt more than a little dim regarding what she was about to ask. Directing her question towards the Chief, she spoke in a timid voice.
'Ma'am I know this sounds a bit daft but could you remind me again who SO19 and 7 are? I know they are terms used all the time in the Met but not where I come from. It's been a long time since training school and I'm a bit rusty to say the least.'
Annette Windsor gave a little laugh but it wasn't sarcastic in any way shape or form.
'Tess SO19 is the specialist firearms unit and SO7 are the serious and organised crime group, also known as the flying squad.'
It was now Joe's turn to ask a question.
'Bit fucking heavy for this aint it?'
Annette began to reply but all the time she stared ahead, not wanting to miss the action once it started.
'Maxi Trueman is known to carry a gun and if push comes to shove he wouldn't hesitate to use it. Plus I had to be sure the men used were trustworthy and these have been handpicked.'
Just as she finished her statement, her mobile burst into life.
'Chief Windsor here.'
Annette listened intently for several seconds before hanging up.
'Trueman has just left his flat. Seems Marsters, Abbey and Franks have been inside for over an hour. All we have to do now is give it a few minutes and then move into our position.

175

Maxi Trueman carried a large holdall filled with Coke and Crack. It was heavy and he had to put in real effort when he lifted it into the boot of the car. Glancing round every few seconds, he could feel his nerves getting the better of him. Maxi wasn't a man who scared easily but even he was aware that getting caught with this amount of gear would result in years at her majesties pleasure. When he was happy that the coast was clear, he pulled the BMW away from the curb and began the short journey to Farringdon. He drove slowly down Greville Street looking for anything unusual. When he saw nothing suspect he turned around on Hill Shoe Lane and re entered Greville. Maxi took no notice of the old empty Mondeo. Joe, Tess and Annette were now sitting inside a surveillance van that was situated two Streets away in Baldwins Gardens. Maxi parked his car as near to The Bleeding Heart as he could and after checking the road several more times, removed his precious cargo. Pushing open the front door of the pub, Maxi Trueman entered and felt relief when he spied Derek Marsters, George Abbey and Simon Franks, sitting at the far end. The bar area was full and people milled around trying to chat and having to shout above the sound of the music. The pubs interior had been decorated with an American theme and high backed booths encased the outer walls. The booth next door to the corrupt officers seated Louis Stebbings and Charlie Draper. Both men were highly regarded detectives and if their time was added together, it amounted to over fifteen years in the flying squad. Louis wore a tweed jacket and heavy spectacles and Charlie was dressed in similar attire. With a pile of folders on the table, the two resembled high brow academics and on inspection posed no threat to the men seated nearby. SO11 or better known as the Directorate of Intelligence,

176

provided state of the art recording equipment and the two men could clearly hear every word of the ensuing conversation. Derek Marsters was the most outgoing member of the bent trio. He usually made the decisions and the others meekly followed along. George Abbey was due to retire in a few months and he needed as much cash as possible to finalise his villa in Majorca. Simon Franks was a yes man who'd fallen into bad company purely by chance. Originally a stickler for the rules, it hadn't taken long for him to be overwhelmed with the serious amounts of cash that was on offer. It was Derek who spotted Maxi and waved for him to join them. Never one to tolerate any ethnic minority, he had made Maxi an exception to the rule early on. Maxi hated all three of the men with a vengeance but with him, the end always justified the means. This meeting along with many in the past had gone a long way to making him a rich man. For that reason and that reason alone, he always appeared happy and glad to see his accomplices in crime.

'Take a seat my friend, what do you want to drink? George go and fetch Maxi a scotch'.

George Abbey did as he was told. On his way he didn't bother to seek out any potential problems. The three had been carrying out business like this for so long now, that they had all become too complacent. It was this complacency that would be their downfall.

'So what cargo are we looking after this time?'

Maxi Trueman leant forward and in hushed tones, informed Derek that it was the largest amount to date and was made up of both Charlie and rocks. Derek Masters now seized the opportunity to squeeze more money out of the pot and furrowed his brow.

'I don't know about that Maxi. Until now it's only been

177

coke but crack? Fucking nasty stuff that, how about another five percent for our trouble?'

Maxi could feel his blood begin to boil, though no one looking on would ever have guessed.

'In your fucking dreams my friend. Before you had to do several drops, this time there's only one.'

Derek didn't push the question of more money any further. He was well aware how Maxi Trueman operated and if they stepped over the line, he'd just walk away and that would be their bankroll finished.

'How come?'

'Branching out my friend, that's all. I've given a business associate of mine your personal number and he'll be contacting you tomorrow.'

Derek Masters couldn't believe what he'd just heard.

'You've given out my private number to a fucking villain!'

'What did you want me to do get him to call you at the fucking station? By the way a word of warning Derek don't ever call Tracy a villain to his face.'

'Fuckin Tracey! What is he a fucking he she or what?'

Maxi stared at the man and a feeling of hatred filled him up. He would have loved to have punched Derek Masters but instead he just smiled sarcastically.

'Tracey Woods is the hardest bastard I've ever come across and if you want to live long enough to spend your money, then I suggest you show him plenty of respect.'

Derek rubbed his palm roughly across his mouth several times. The goal posts had been moved and he didn't like it, he didn't like it one bit.

'Ok! ok! Maxi but I aint happy with it.'

'You aint got to be, just make sure it goes down and we'll all be happy.'

Annette Windsor had listened to every word and the

178

mention of a big time face on her patch changed everything. Via several mobile phone calls, she alerted all units involved to allow the suspects to leave the premises. Once they were on their way, then it was all systems go to arrest Maxi Trueman. A few minutes later, saw Derek Masters leave carrying the holdall that Maxi had brought in. George Abbey and Simon Franks followed closely behind, leaving Maxi sitting alone in the booth. As luck would have it the fire arms unit weren't needed. As soon as they were given the go ahead, Louis Stebbings and Charlie Draper stood up and walked to where Maxi sat. Before he knew what was happening, two police issue pistols were pointing directly at him. Louis aimed for the head and Charlie for the groin area. The smoothness and calm manner of both detectives, told Maxi he'd been done bang to rights. His only words as he was handcuffed were 'Fuckin hell, fucking hell' over and over again. Back at New Scotland yard, Tess and Joe were at a loss as to what had occurred. When Annette Windsor entered the room and placed a tape in the machine, Joe looked bewildered. Chief Windsor motioned for them both to take a seat; while she remained perched on the corner of her desk.

'Something surprising came up at The Bleeding Heart but I'll go into that in a minute. Now, Masters, Abbey and Franks have been allowed to go for the time being. As far as they are aware the deal went down as sweet as a nut. Maxi Trueman will be kept at the yard indefinitely, until this whole mess has been cleared up at least. There's no way the others will find out he's banged up, so we've brought ourselves some time. Now listen to this.'

Switching on the tape, she watched both of their faces as they heard the conversation that had taken place earlier in

179

the pub. When Tracey Woods's name was mentioned, Joe began to break out in a sweat and rubbed at his leg furiously, it wasn't the reaction that Annette was expecting and the sight shocked her.

'You alright Joe?'

'Yeah fine! It's just a name I'd hoped not to hear again.'

Walking to where he sat, Annette placed a hand on his shoulder and squeezed down hard.

'I know but don't you see, this way he can be out of your life for good.'

Joe Reynolds didn't reply and for a second the room was eerily silent.

'Right! I've got an investigation team looking into Derek Masters personal records at this very moment. Shortly we will have his mobile number and permission to tap the line. When Tracey Woods calls, we will be one step ahead of him and be there to greet them all at the rendezvous. I want you both to go home now but be back at Agar Street by eight tomorrow morning. We have to be ready to move at a moment's notice.'

Tess was the first to stand, while it had all been exciting stuff she hadn't been able to get Sally out of her thoughts. It would be good to get home and clear her head. Joe remained seated and stared ahead as if in a kind of daze.

'Joe! are you coming?'

Standing up he walked to the door and followed Tess out of the room. He didn't bother to say goodnight to his boss, in fact he didn't even speak to Tess on the journey back. When she got out of the car close to Agi's house, Tess said goodbye but he didn't utter a single word. Tess was too caught up in her own problems to really give him a second thought and besides she reasoned he was big enough and had been through enough to look after himself. While Tess Davey slept soundly, Joe Reynolds relived every second of his time in Newcastle. When his alarm burst into song at six thirty, he was already laying there staring at the ceiling. The bed sheets resembled world war three and Joe's hair was plastered to his brow with sweat. Today was the day he'd dreaded for the last three years, it was also the day that he would put his demons to bed once and for all. Showering as fast as he could, Joe arrived at the station long before the required time. Tommy Radcliff was standing in for the jailer and was surprised when he saw Joe.

'What's up mate?'

'Tommy, who's the jailer at Scotland Yard?'

'It's Freddie Lemmings, why?'

'I can't say at the moment but do you know him well?'

'Well! we've played snooker with him every Tuesday night for the last ten years. Why?'

'Like I said I can't say but thanks Tommy.'

'You're welcome mate.'

Joe didn't hear the man's last words as he was already on his way out of the station. Pulling onto the Strand, Joe turned left at Trafalgar square and continued along Whitehall. Reaching Parliament square, he took another left into Victoria Street and his destination quickly came into sight. Arriving at New Scotland Yard was an experience all on its own. He was asked for his warrant card and after providing identification, was instructed to wait in a side room. Simon Garrett, a detective of small stature entered soon after and inquired what his business was. Joe informed the man, that he had been told to have a brief word with the suspect on the orders of Chief Windsor. When Garrett told Joe Reynolds that he would have to check with the Chief, inwardly Joe began to panic.

'Ok by me pal but I warn you, she don't like to be

181

challenged. It's your neck on the line not mine.'
Somehow Joe's words penetrated the jobs worth of a man
and he decided against doing the checks. Ordering one of
the plods to escort Joe to the cells, Garrett then left the
room. Joe Reynolds let out a huge sigh of relief. If
Annette ever found out he'd even been here, she'd have
his balls, let alone anything else. Ten minutes later and
he was standing in the custody suite. It made Agar Street
look like a toy box and he began to perspire. Everything
was high tech and cameras glared down from every
angle. Joe knew that if he was caught out, then his career
was on the line but right at this minute he didn't care.
The only thing on his mind was Tracey Woods and
finding out why he was moving south to do business, or
if in fact Joe was the main reason. The custody sergeant
showed Joe to the cell and after unlocking the door, stood
outside. He'd been on the force long enough to know
what the set up was and allowed the man a few minutes
with the arrested villain. With his head in his hands Maxi
sat on the concrete plinth that also doubled as a bed. He
didn't look up when Joe entered.
'Hi Maxi, how you doing?'
Still with his head in his hands he spoke in a quiet voice.
'Fuck off copper. Whatever you want to know I aint
fucking telling.'
With two large steps, Joe was standing directly in front of
Maxi and he grabbed a handful of the man's hair with as
much force as he could muster. Yanking Maxis head
upwards until their eyes met, Joe stared long and hard
into a face that wore no expression.
'What's Tracey Woods doing trading in the smoke?'
Maxi didn't reply and Joe knew he had to use the only
weapon he had.
'I know Tracey from way back and when he's brought in

and I tell him it was you who grassed, what do you think his reaction will be?'

It may have been Joe's only weapon but it was a good one and Maxi soon began to speak, though they were not the words Joe wanted to hear.

'I don't give a flying fuck whether you say I was a grass or not! I'll tell you something for nothing, Tracey Woods will cut you're fucking head off and shit in it, you jumped up little cunt!'

Joe swiftly pushed his forearm against Maxis throat and pressed hard.

'Ok! ok man, cant we cut a deal here?'

'Fuck a deal, what's his reason for being in London?'

'How the fuck would I know! He did say he had a few old scores to settle though.'

They were the only words Joe needed to hear. If the bust went tits up then he was a dead man. He knew one day Woods would come looking for him but he'd hoped it would be a bit further down the line than now. Walking out of the cell, Joe felt a total feeling of emptiness. He'd been waiting for it for the last couple of years but now that it was here, he was lost. Nodding to the sergeant, Joe left the Yard and headed back to his own station. He couldn't talk to Annette about this, as she'd blow a gasket if she found out where he'd been. After letting Tess down over the last couple of days, he was sure she wouldn't be interested and besides she was nowhere to be seen and in all honesty, would have been of little use anyway. No Joe Reynolds would have to deal with his own turmoil and just pray to god that nothing went wrong.

CHAPTER NINETEEN

As Joe Reynolds desperately fought with his inner demons, Roxy Baxter was on cloud nine. Lenny had been overly nice to her last night and he'd even made her stay home instead of going out on the earn. Waking early she'd decided to visit Carmel. She hadn't seen her old friend for a day or so and as Lenny would be away with the fairies for at least a couple more hours, she knew that now was a perfect time. It was only eight thirty and Carmel would still be in bed. There'd be a rumpus when she was forced out of her pit but Roxy was sure that deep down, the woman would be glad to see her. Roxy was crossing Soho square as Tess Davey was walking along Manette Street on her way to work. Unluckily the two women's paths wouldn't cross this day. Tess was eager to arrive at the station and get today over with. The sooner all this corruption business was dealt with, the sooner she could find out more about her sister and try to start building a relationship. Glancing at her watch, she decided there was just enough time to call in at the Silver Spoon and grab a bacon sandwich. Bracing herself for a lengthy conversation with Theo Domingo, she was surprised to find a pretty dark haired girl standing behind the counter.

'Morning, can I have a bacon sandwich to go please.'
The young woman didn't speak but nodded her head.
'No Theo today?'
The young woman, whose name badge spelled out Rosetta in bold black letters, handed Tess her sandwich and shook her head. Her eyes filled with tears and suddenly Tess felt really sorry she'd asked the question. Obviously there was something very wrong with Theo

184

but today of all days; she just didn't have the time to spare inquiring about his health. Laying two pound coins on the counter, she picked up her sandwich and left the shop as quickly as possible. Annette Windsor's car was parked in its allotted space but the station was unusually quiet. Tess made her way up to the shared office and opened the door. Switching on the light she was surprised to see Joe sitting at his desk. If not for the single bulb, the room would have been in darkness. The Venetian blind at the window was tightly closed and Tess walked over and pulled it up to its full height. Suddenly the room was bathed in a glorious light and walking over to the light switch, she flicked it off. Joe hadn't spoken but he stared hard into her face.

'You alright Sir?'

Still he didn't answer and Tess began to feel awkward. Breaking her sandwich in two, she offered Joe half, expecting him to decline. She was a little disappointed when he accepted the breakfast and almost ate it in one bite. When he'd finished, Joe went over to the kettle and made them both a coffee. They sat in silence and Tess didn't know what to do next. She began to ramble on about what she'd seen on late night television, all the time she was aware that he was studying her face. If only she knew how he was feeling inside and Joe wished with all his heart that he could open up to her but it was something his mind wouldn't allow. Years of undercover work had made him hide any emotions so deep, that even he had difficulty in retrieving them. Oh! he'd told her briefly about his past but that was all it was, brief and to the point. Now he had to sit and wait and all the time terrible thoughts of what could happen ran through his mind and he couldn't share them with another living soul. Roxy hammered hard on Carmel's door. She knew the sound would have her friend rushing to answer and she'd curse when she saw who it was.

'Alright! Alright! I'm fucking coming!'

Opening the door, Carmel stood there in the same old housecoat, with mascara smeared down her cheeks and hair standing up on end.

'You leery cow! Why can't you knock sensibly like anyone else, come to that why can't you call round at a decent hour?'

'because I wanted to see how fast you could move. Might as well be hung for a sheep as a lamb or so my old mum used to say.'

'You never knew your fucking mum. Sometimes Rox I don't think you're the full ticket, anyway what you doing up so early. Shit the bed did you?'

Roxy pushed past her friend and went into the small kitchenette. After placing the whistling kettle on the hob, she returned to the living room. Carmel was searching the sofa for her cigarettes and Roxy knew they wouldn't be able to have a sensible conversation until the woman had lit up and half coughed her guts up. Spying the offending packet on the corner of the table, she handed them over.

'Brilliant! Pass me the lighter babe.'

Roxy did as she was asked and then returned to make the tea. By the time she walked back through with two steaming mugs in her hand, Carmel had just about finished hawking and stood in the middle of the room, with a face so scarlet that a stranger would have thought she was choking.

'Those things are going to kill you.'

'Something's got to sweetheart and it might as well be these. Anyway as you never answered me before, I'll ask again. What you doing here so early?'

186

'Nothing, I just wanted to see you that's all. Cant a girl miss her old mukka?'

Carmel lit up her second cigarette but this time her body didn't reject the deep lungful of smoke she inhaled.

'It's that cunt Lenny again, aint it?'

Roxy sighed, this was becoming a regular question and she was fed up with it.

'No it aint. If you must know he's treating me like a queen. I had a great night last night and I woke with the birds, that's all.'

Carmel began to pace the carpet and when she stopped at the window and parted the net to look outside, Roxy knew there was trouble in store. Carmel had a habit of only peering out of the window when she was nervous and she only ever got nervous when it was something serious.

'I can read you like a fucking book Carm, come on spill the beans before you wear a hole in the carpet and send me fucking dizzy.'

Roxy hadn't a clue what to expect but her friends next sentence knocked the wind out of her.

'I saw your sister last night, jumped up fucking cow! She really pissed me off big time Rox. I mean I thought she was following me, turns out she weren't but it was too late then. I mean how was I supposed to know?'

The entire colour drained from Roxy Baxter's face. She still hadn't decided whether to meet her sister and it was a decision she wanted to take her time over.

'Carm tell me you didn't, please!'

'I'm sorry Rox but she sat there so fucking high and mighty and I'd had a bad day and all and it somehow came out that you were on the game. Sorry!'

Roxy covered her face with her hands. If she had decided that she wanted to meet up with her twin, it was now out of the question. Why would a decent woman want anything to do with a brass? Suddenly Roxy felt robbed, robbed of something she'd never had but robbed all the same. Grabbing her bag she ran from the room. Taking the stairs two at a time, she was out on the Street in seconds. Tears streamed down her beautiful face and she tried desperately to wipe them away with the cuff of her jacket. Early morning commuters stared at her but she didn't care and when a Street vendor tried to take her arm in concern at her distress, she shrugged him off and began to run. Normally her boots would have stopped her walking even fast but today she was oblivious to them. Roxy had nowhere to go but still she ran, ran until it felt as though her heart would burst from her chest. She couldn't believe what Carmel had done and there was no way that her spiteful words could ever be taken back. When the clock in the reception of Agar Street police station struck nine forty five, Annette Windsor made her way down the sparse staircase and along the corridor to Joe's office. Walking in without knocking, she saw her two detectives just sitting and staring at each other.

'Come on you two, time to go!'

Tess grabbed her bag and coat and was behind the Chief as she walked out of the door. Joe on the other hand took his time. Wearily he stood up and slowly walked into the corridor. The last twenty four hours had taken its toll and he felt old, too old to be scared out of his wits about what some villain might or might not do to him. Nothing was discussed until all three were inside the Chiefs car and they were on their way to New Scotland Yard.

'Right! The call we've been waiting for came through five minutes ago. Woods and our boys are meeting at the old gas works over in Euston.'

While still holding the wheel in her left hand, Annette

pushed back her designer cuff and glanced at her watch. 'Just under an hour and A unit will be in place and undercover in the next fifteen minutes and then we just have to sit tight until I get the call. I have a crack shot photographer, who should give us a little extra on the evidence front and there'll be enough hardware at the site to stop anyone doing a runner. I think we should get as close as possible, so we're ready to move when it goes down. Nervous?'

Tess grinned and nodded her head. Joe Reynolds didn't reply and Annette didn't push him for an answer. She only had a vague report of what had happened in Newcastle but she knew it was serious enough to have the love of her life running scared. The car park at New Scotland Yard was full and Annette had to pull up on the double yellow lines on Dacre Street. Removing the keys from the ignition, she threw them into Joes lap.

'I've just got to collect a few papers before we go. Don't let one of those daft traffic wardens give me another ticket or worse still, clamp the car! Drive around the block if you have to.'

Luckily they weren't hassled and the Chief was back inside the car in under ten minutes. Placing a bright orange folder on top of the dash board, Annette started the engine and pulled out onto Victoria Street in the direction of Whitehall. When they reached Kings cross, it was as usual very busy and Annette drummed her fingers on the steering wheel in frustration.

'If we miss this and its down to the bastard traffic I'll......'

'You'll what? Calm down Annie, we've got plenty of time.'

Annette Windsor looked across the passenger seat to where Joe sat and noticed that he had small beads of perspiration beginning to form on his brow. She'd been so wrapped up in getting everyone involved, bang to rights, that she hadn't really given him a second thought. Every minute of this must be torture for him; she just hoped that he wouldn't have to come face to face with Woods. Camden Garden Centre situated on Barker drive was close enough so as not to be suspicious but also near enough to be able to get to the gas holders in a matter of minutes. Parking the car, Annette checked her mobile to make sure her signal was good. Satisfied that it was, she unclipped her seatbelt and tried to make herself as comfortable as possible.

Derek Master, George Abbey and Simon Franks were still seated in their office at Agar Street, when Chief Windsor, Tess and Joe left. They hadn't noticed anything unusual and if they had, it probably wouldn't have registered. Derek was so uptight he was like a ticking time bomb that was ready to blow at any second. At ten fifteen he stood up and the others did likewise. At discreet intervals they all left the station but once outside, got into the same Vauxhall car. Even though their route had been shorter than their superior's, they had only just made it in time. Parking to the left of the old black and red cast iron holder, Derek turned the engine off at the same time as a black M class Mercedes pulled up alongside. The vehicles windows were blacked out and this fact alone, made the three policemen feel edgy. They knew they were being watched but not by who or how many. On Derek's command they were told to get a grip and hold their nerve.

'We're not moving a muscle until they do, do you hear?' George and Simon nodded their heads and waited for whatever was going to happen, to happen. Tracey Woods and his heavy Mikey Brewster stared down into the smaller car and laughed.

190

'Look at them wankers Mikey. They're fucking shitting themselves and we aint even shown our faces yet. Come on let's get it over with, I hate dealing with bastard coppers at the best of times, let alone when it's on their home turf.'

The two men got out of the Mercedes and walked round to the front. When Derek saw that they had made the first move, he somehow felt superior and told the other two to follow him. George and Simon stood either side of Derek but two paces behind, giving the image of heavies. Tracey wanted to laugh again, he'd been told by Maxi that they were bent filth but they obviously weren't aware he was privy to that fact.

'Mr Masters! Our mutual friend has told me a lot about you but I'm sure you don't want to waste time with idle chat.'

Gently waving his hand sideways he gestured towards the rear of the M class.

'Shall we get down to business? Mikey if you'd do the honours'.

Mikey Brewster opened up the tailgate door and a large case could be seen. Snapping open the lid, Mikey revealed layer upon layer of crisp banknotes. Derek Masters stepped forward and at random, removed several of the notes from different layers. He scrutinized each note and when he was finally satisfied that they weren't counterfeit, he nodded in Simon Franks direction. Simon walked to the Vauxhall and took a large holdall from its boot. Struggling, he hauled the bag back over to where the other men were standing. Placing the holdall inside the Mercedes boot space, where only seconds earlier the case had stood, he watched as Mikey carried out his own search. Expertly he opened the bag up and removed one of the packages just as Maxi had done earlier. Taking a

191

penknife from his inside pocket, he stabbed at the polythene. Unlike Maxi Trueman, Mikey didn't lick the blade. Mikey was more than a tad partial to coke himself and after wetting his index finger, proceeded to push it inside the package. When he removed it, his skin was coated in a fine white powder. Placing his finger inside his mouth, Mikey rubbed furiously along his gums and instantly smiled to his boss.

'Top stuff Gov. Fucking top stuff!'

Tracey Woods turned to Derek Masters and held out his hand. Reluctantly and only for safety reasons, Derek shook on the deal.

'That concludes our time here gentlemen. I would say it was a pleasure doing business with you but we all know that wouldn't be true.'

Mikey Brewster slammed shut the boot of the Mercedes and headed towards the driver's door. Suddenly the air was filled with the sound of sirens and at least a dozen patrol cars roared onto the gasworks land. Armed response vehicles came from all directions and the men had semi automatic rifles pointed at them before they knew what was happening. At exactly eleven thirty, Annette Windsor's phone burst into life and she swiftly flipped open the receiver. Not speaking a word, she listened intently to what was being said on the other end. Finally the words 'I'm on my way' were uttered and snapping the cover closed, she started up the car's engine.

'Seems like it's all gone down like clockwork. All we have to do now is turn up and bask in all the glory.'

Glancing at Joe and then into the rear view mirror in Tess's direction, she tutted loudly.

'For Christ's sake! You two could both show a little more enthusiasm. This is all going to sit very nicely on both your records, for many years to come.'

Tess was the only one to speak.

'Sorry Ma'am'.

Joe Reynolds didn't give a toss about looking good in the eyes of the force. He'd forgotten any ideas of promotion, when all the trouble had flared up in Newcastle. Now the only thing on his mind was being forced into Tracey wood's company again and having to look into his enemy's eyes. Within minutes Annette Windsor's car pulled up alongside all the other Met vehicles. Getting out, she smoothed down her designer suit and followed by Tess, walked over to where the culprits were stood lined up against the Mercedes. She could visibly see that her three fellow officers were shaking in their boots, though none of them offered a word of defence. Tracey Woods and Mikey Brewster appeared as cool as cucumbers and Annette knew that before the day was out, they would have some high flyer brief, which was held on an obscene retainer, fighting their corner. She smiled in Derek Master's direction as she spoke.

'What a pleasant surprise gentlemen. To have you all here at the same time is about as good as it gets.'

Taking a few steps forward until she stood directly opposite Tracey Woods, Annette Windsor grinned in her most annoying way.

'And you I take it are the infamous Mr Woods? I've heard so much about you, it's going to be a pleasure finding out what's true and what isn't. Take them away boys and no one gets anything, not even a phone call until I give the say so!'

Joe saw the men being led in the direction of the police vans. Shakily he opened the car door and stepped out onto the gravel. Heading towards his boss, he'd hoped that he hadn't been seen but Tracey Woods didn't miss a trick. Even though he was now in handcuffs, it didn't

193

stop him making a run towards where Joe was standing. 'You cunt! Lewis. I knew I should have fucking finished you off when I had the chance.'

Before he got anywhere close to where Joe stood, the butt of a rifle came down hard on the side of Tracey's head. Knocked out cold, he fell to the floor and was carried back to the Met van by four armed policemen.

Suddenly Joe wasn't scared anymore, the only thing he felt was relief. Relief, that Woods was going down for a very long time and relief that he wouldn't have to do this job for much longer. Sitting in the car earlier, he'd had time to evaluate his life and he didn't like what had emerged. Before the bust had even gone down, Joe Reynolds had decided to call it a day. Tomorrow he would hand in his resignation and after serving his notice, would try to find a better life than the one he was living now. As he winked in Annette's direction, he realised she'd be devastated at the news. He didn't care; the only thing he was concerned about was fulfilling his promise to Tess before he left. Now that it was all over, they could begin their hunt in earnest and that hunt would start tomorrow.

CHAPTER TWENTY

The only place Roxy Baxter had left to go was her flat
but she didn't go straight there. She was too upset at what
Carmel had told her and if Lenny saw her in this state,
there was no telling what he'd do. She decided to take a
seat in Soho square and watch the world go by for a
while. Calling at a small coffee shop along the way, she
ordered a cappuccino to take out. Roxy loved the frothy
coffee and would often treat herself to one when she'd
been to visit her friend. Choosing the best location of the
graffiti covered benches; she removed the lid from her
Styrofoam cup and inhaled the aromas. Children were
still on their way to school and held hands with their
mothers or hired nannies as they skipped along. It always
intrigued Roxy when she saw happy families. She didn't
understand how the same people could live and be happy
with each other year upon year. Shrugging her shoulders,
she breathed in deeply and continued to enjoy her
steaming hot drink. Denzel Howard walked by but he
didn't look in her direction and Roxy couldn't be bothered
to call out to him. She had a saying that she was fond of
"Shame me once shame on you, shame me twice, shame
on me". It was something she tried to stick to in her oh
so muddled life and as Denzel had blanked her once, she
wasn't about to give him the opportunity of repeating the
performance. With only dregs now left in the bottom of
her cup, Roxy placed it under the bench. She glanced at
her trendy watch, a gift from Carmel from the local
market. Seeing that it was now almost midday, she
thought that Lenny would just about be getting up now.
Roxy couldn't believe that she'd sat in the square for so
long, the hours had passed like minutes and she hoped

195

he wouldn't be mad with her. After crossing Oxford Street, she soon turned into Berners Mews and her tiny flat came into sight. Opening the door, Roxy called out but there was no reply. Approaching the bedroom, she could see through a crack in the frame that the bed was empty. When she reached the living room, she called out once more but there was still no answer. Shrugging her shoulders she thought to herself that Lenny must have gone out already and decided to make a nice cup of tea. The cappuccino had left a sharp taste in her mouth and there was nothing like a cup of rosy to put things back to how they should be. It had always made her feel better in the past but deep down she now doubted that anything was going to cheer her up today. Walking over to the oven, Roxy didn't notice Lenny standing behind the door. The kitchen window was slightly open and when a breeze blew the nets, she felt a shiver run down her spine. Feeling as if there was an invisible presence in the room, she scolded herself for being so stupid but still the tingling sensation continued. When she felt a sharp pain as he grabbed a handful of her hair, Roxy screamed out as she tried desperately to turn around. Her nose touched against the sleeve of his jumper and immediately she knew it was Lenny. His smell was distinct and one Roxy would recognise anywhere.

'Please babe! don't hurt me. Whatever have I done?' Lenny mimicked her voice in a whinny tone, which made her skin want to crawl.

'Whatever have I done? I'll fucking tell you what you've done. Maxi Truman's been arrested and its all down to you'.

Still with the best part of her scalp held in a vice like grip, Roxy struggled to continue.

'I aint done nothing, honest'.

'Fuckin honest, you wouldn't know honest if it fucking jumped up and bit you on the arse'.

His grip tightened and she could feel herself being pushed towards the floor. Images of last night flashed through her mind as she tried to think of a reason for why this was happening. Nothing was forthcoming but then it didn't need to. This wasn't the first time Lenny had turned on her for no reason and she would bet it wouldn't be the last.

'I've just had that bastard Denzel Howard round here. One of his girls picked up a punter coming off night duty from Scotland Yard. Guess, which name came up in conversation? Maxi fucking Truman's no less'.

Lenny held his index finger so close to her face that Roxy thought at any minute he was going to poke out her eye. 'Considering you are the only one to have any links with Old Bill, stands to reason it must be fucking you'.

'I aint got a clue what you're on about, honest!'

'Fucking liar!!!!. Old Bill was asking me about Sally Sayers and we both know who she is now don't we?' Everything seemed to happen in slow motion and the cold feeling of the lino on her cheek was somehow comforting. Knowing that there was no way out, she tried to brace herself for what was to come by tightly wrapping her arms around her head. The first few blows were always the worst and when Lenny's foot complete with work boot made contact with her stomach, Roxy felt the hot drink of a few minutes ago, begin to rise from within. The liquid erupted from her mouth and nostrils as she desperately tried to hold it inside.

'You fucking dirty bitch, look at the mess you've made!' Pity wasn't even in Lenny Layton's vocabulary as he kicked ferociously at her sides and face. Roxy felt her lip split in exactly the same place as before and she tried to

197

lick at the blood as it trickled down her chin. One of her front teeth felt loose and this for some reason bothered her more than the beating she was receiving. Suddenly the assault stopped and for once Roxy felt she'd possibly got off lightly. It may have been wishful thinking but her wish wasn't about to come true. With one eyelid still partially open, she could just about make out Lenny standing at the sink unit. The kitchen was filthy and as Roxy scanned the room, she realised just how low she had sunk. Even the care homes had been cleaner than this place and the sight made her feel totally and utterly ashamed. Like a surgeon carefully deciding on which piece of equipment to use, he opted for a cast iron frying pan. Roxy knew what was coming next but still she saw a glimpse of humour in the situation. That pan had been used last night to cook a meal that Lenny said was the best he'd ever had. Now it seemed that same pan was about to dish out the best hiding she had ever had. Roxy still wore the slight glimmer of a grin as the pan made contact with the side of her face. After that there was only blackness and a kind of peace she'd never experienced before. Lenny stood upright and panted loudly. It had taken a lot out of him to dish out such a thrashing and he knew he was beginning to show signs of his age. The thought did nothing to mellow his mood and he kicked out at Roxy one last time in frustration. Even in her semiconscious state, she groaned out loud with the pain but there was no one to hear, no one except her attacker. Taking a seat at the kitchen table, Lenny rolled a joint and surveyed the carnage lying on the floor in front of him. He realised that he'd probably overstepped the mark but she always had to fucking push him. Deciding it was best to lay low for a few days; he grabbed some clothes and stuffed them into a carrier bag.

He'd give it forty eight hours and then come back and see if she'd survived. If she had, then it was business as usual. If she hadn't, then Lenny decided it would be time to try his hand elsewhere. Tess and Joe were back at Agar Street but neither of them were in the mood for conversation. With all that had happened, they were both now at a loose end and Annette Windsor seemed to be dealing with things perfectly well on her own. Tess could see how the Chief had risen to such a high position in such a short time. Even though it was Joe's information that had nailed the guilty parties, it seemed she was out to grab all the glory. Tess thought Joe would be bothered by that but he wasn't, he just sat back in his chair, put his feet on the desk and closed his eyes. After an hour of silence she couldn't stand it any longer.

'Are you just going to sit there all day or what?'

Joe Reynolds didn't move a muscle. With his eyelids still firmly shut he began to speak.

'Tess you have a lot to learn.'

'How so?'

'There are people in this world that thrive on glory and need to feel that pat on the proverbial back. Then there are people like you and me. Let me rephrase that, there are people like me. I don't give a flying fuck about what went down today. That said it don't mean I aint still glad that Woods was tucked up and all. Let the Chief have the collar, she needs it much more than me. To tell you the truth, I made a life changing decision today!'

Tess couldn't for the life of her understand his attitude but she was interested in the last thing he had said. He didn't continue with his revelation until prompted and it pissed her off big time, having to force whatever it was, out of him.

'Well?'

199

Opening his eyes, Joe placed his feet on the floor and turned the swivel chair to face her.

'I'm leaving the force.'

'Pardon?'

'You heard! I've had enough Tess. I'm fed up with being scared. Do you know it's been over three years since I was in Newcastle and every day has been a complete nightmare. Well not anymore! I'm handing in my resignation and when I've worked my notice, I'm off.'

Tess knew that she didn't need him anymore, well not in regard to finding her sister anyway but she did need his support. About to voice her opinion, she was stunned at what he said next.

'That should give us enough time to find what you came to the smoke in search of.'

'You really mean that don't you?'

'I may be a lot of things Tess, even done a lot of things I'm not proud of but going back on a promise isn't one of them. Now I'm off to the Ship and Shovel, want to join me?'

Tess shook her head; the last thing she wanted today was to drink with Joe and his cronies and pretend to be a high flyer in the world of computers.

'Suit yourself but be here early tomorrow, we've got a lot to get through.'

With that Joe picked up his jacket that was hanging on the back of the chair and left the office. A few minutes later Tess signed off duty. Deciding to walk home, she took her time and window shopped in all the places that she passed on the Charing Cross road. It was just before three thirty when she arrived back at the Manette Street house. Slipping inside was easy, Agi wasn't expecting her so early and she made her way upstairs without being noticed. Lying on the bed, she ran through all that had happened in the last twenty four hours. Tess skipped through the bust; it held no interest for her. There were only two things that played heavy on her mind. Everything that Carmel had revealed last night and wondering what her sister was doing right at this very moment. All the old fears emerged as she slowly drifted off to sleep but this time her fears were ten times worse. The face of Carmel Jones repeatedly trespassed into her dreams, only this time it was oversized and grotesque and with makeup which was plastered so thick, it resembled a clown. The image reappeared over and over again and repeated the words Tess had heard last night "She a brass, she's a brass, she's a brass".

Tess woke with a start and reaching over to the bedside cabinet, picked up her alarm clock. The luminous dial read four thirty am and she dropped the ticking timepiece onto the covers beside her. It was far too early to get up but at the same time she was afraid of going back to sleep. She had little choice and drifted back off immediately. Sleep was on her side, the type of sleep where you get into bed and the next minute you wake, feeling like you haven't been in bed for more than five minutes. Tess Davey was exhausted but at least she was thankful that her nightmare had disappeared. Again she glanced at the clock and on seeing that it was now seven am, decided to get up. Today of all days she couldn't stomach the idea of having to face Agi and make idle chit chat about the weather. As quiet as a mouse, Tess grabbed her coat from the hallstand and silently slipped outside. By eight thirty she was entering the rear reception of Agar Street. As usual Tommy Radcliff was on duty and he had a cheery smile for her, as she pressed her security code into the box on the wall. Instantly the inner door clicked open and she walked inside. Tess expected the office to be empty and was surprised when she saw Joe sitting at his desk.

'My! You're early Sir.'.

As I said last night Tess, we have a lot to get through'.

Knowing she had to come clean about what she already knew, made Tess feel nothing but shame. Joe Reynolds could see there was something on her mind but waited for her to offer the information willingly. Taking off her coat, Tess clicked on the kettle and proceeded to make them both a coffee. As she busied herself with the mugs and sugar, she began to talk.

'I have a confession to make. I already know who my sister is, although I haven't been formally introduced yet.'

Joe sat bolt upright in his chair and a smile began to form on his lips.

'That's brilliant news.'

'Please Sir, I haven't finished. She's living with Lenny Layton.'

'What the fucks she doing with that twat?'

'Pleeeease! Just let me continue. If I don't tell you now, then I don't think I will ever tell anyone. He's her pimp Joe. My sister, my flesh and blood is a common prostitute'.

With her back facing towards her boss, Tess poured the boiling water into the cups and as she waited for a response, tears trickled down her cheeks.

'Are you sure? That was a fucking stupid thing to ask, how'd you find all this out?'

'Carmel Jones told me. Seems the girl we met at Lenny's flat, her names Roxy Baxter by the way, well according to Carmel she's none other than my sister Sally. Only she doesn't call herself that anymore, not really a glitzy enough name for a brass!'

202

Joe accepted the drink as she passed it over and studying her face, could see that she'd had little or no sleep last night. It bothered him even more, when he noticed the tears.

'So what do you want to do about it?'

Tess took a sip from her mug and then clasping it in both hands held it close to her chest as if she was freezing cold.

'What can I do?'

'Well you can go and see her, find out if she's Ok at least. You never know, when she meets you, well maybe you can get her away from Layton.'

'I suppose it's worth a try but I'm not getting my hopes up.'

Joe placed his mug on the desk and standing up, took Tess's out of her hands.

'No time like the present then.'

In silence they drove over to Soho and unusually it was Joe at the wheel. The area was quiet, residents were already at work and the crowds of last night were probably tucked up in their beds in the cities more up market districts. Parking outside Lenny's flat, Tess began to get a tightening in her chest. This wasn't how it was supposed to be, this wasn't what she'd dreamed it would be like when she'd first found out about Sally. Joe switched off the engine and turned to face her. The look in Tess's eyes was one of pleading and his heart went out to her. He knew if he suggested driving off and forgetting this idea, then she would agree with him readily. He also knew that she had to do this, if only to save her own sanity.

'Come on girl get a grip. The sooner we start, the sooner it will be over with.'

She nodded, understanding that she couldn't back out

now. Slowly they walked to the front door and Joe tapped lightly on the glass pane. Several seconds later and after no reply, he knocked harder.

'Perhaps there's no one home Sir, we could call back a little later.'

'Tess you know as well as I do, that if we leave this now then you won't be coming back. Besides have you ever heard of a brass up and about at this hour?'

As soon as the words were out of his mouth, he wanted to bite his tongue off. Her faced showed so much pain, that he might as well have called her a whore.

'I'm sorry Tess, I didn't think.'

'It's Ok Sir. I'll have a walk round the building and see if there's any movement elsewhere.'

It was only a few feet to the first window and Tess guessed it must be the kitchen. Placing her hand on her forehead in an almost salute, she peered through the dirty pane and scanned the room. What she saw next sent a shiver through her spine. Roxy had obviously tried to make her way into the hall and had failed dismally. Only her feet and calves were visible and Tess tried to scream out in horror. No words came out, or at least she didn't hear any but seconds later Joe was by her side. When he saw what was inside, he ran round to the front door and broke it down like a man possessed. Tess was only seconds behind her boss and running into the hall, knelt down beside her sister and cradled Roxy's head in her lap. Joe felt for a pulse and when he found one, albeit very faint, he let out a huge sigh.

'She's alive Tess! Thank god she's alive.'

Searching in his jacket, he brought out his mobile and called for an ambulance. In situations like this it was normal for the police to be involved but as they already were, Joe was able to keep any fuss to a minimum.

The paramedics arrived in a matter of minutes. A tall good looking man in a green issue uniform, gently moved Tess to one side.

'Please Miss, just stand over here. It will make our job much easier if you stay out of the way.'

Ignoring the words of advice, Tess was instantly back by Roxy's side and it was Joe who gently pulled her away.

'You must allow the crew to do their job Tess, I know you're hurting but you won't help her by getting in the way.'

All that now entered her head was, how had it all come to this. She couldn't bear the thought of now losing her sister, not before she'd even had the chance to meet her properly. Finally they were able to stabilise Roxy enough to move her to hospital. With sirens blaring, they wasted no time in leaving and Tess and Joe followed on behind. For the entire journey, tears streamed down Tess Davey's face.

CHAPTER TWENTY ONE

Mortimer Street ran horizontally across the top of Berners Mews. Situated directly opposite was The Middlesex hospital, so luckily it would only be a couple of minutes drive. As Joe Reynolds car pulled up outside the emergency department, Roxy was already being wheeled inside. Tess held onto Joes arm, scared out of her wits that someone was about to come and tell them that her sister was dead. The receptionist led them through to the relative's room and took down as many details as Tess was able to tell them. She didn't know much but could at least give Sally's real name, along with her alias and age. Left in the small room with a cup of tea and too much time to think, Tess and Joe didn't know what to say to each other. After what seemed like hours but was in reality only forty five minutes, the door opened and a woman doctor entered the room.

'Miss Sayers I have some news, albeit limited, on your sisters condition.'

Tess didn't try to explain that her name was no longer Sayers, it would have only complicate matters and nothing would be gained from it. She listened intently as the doctor informed her that Roxy had two broken ribs, a very mild fracture to her skull and facial cuts and bruises. 'It really looks much worse than it is; your sister was a very lucky girl. There is a slight problem that's concerning us though. The x-ray showed us that the broken ribs were already fractured and that the fractures are recent, at least within the last two weeks. It's Obvious that whoever did this to her, undid the work her body had been trying to repair.'

Tess's mouth went dry as she remembered the

conversation she'd had with Carmel about the abusive Roxy had suffered.

'I'm sorry doctor but I can't shed any light on her injuries, we don't have that much to do with each other you see.'

The doctor nodded her understanding, as if by looking at Roxy she'd been able to see what kind of life she led. Now in the company of Tess, it was obvious the two women were poles apart.

'You can see her now if you'd like to but we've sedated her, so it may be best if you come back in a few hours.'

'If I could just look in on her, I promise I won't disturb her.'

The doctor motioned with her hand and escorted Tess towards a side room. The door was half glazed and Tess didn't enter. Instead she peered through the glass and saw Roxy asleep on the bed. The tears of earlier once more emerged and at that moment in time, she hated Lenny Layton with a vengeance. Wiping the back of her hand across her cheeks, she vowed there and then, that if it was the last thing she did on this earth, then it would be to make him pay for what he'd done to her sister. Tess re-entered the relative's room and smiled thinly. All the while Joe studied her face for some kind of clue as to what she was thinking but it was difficult. After drinking the last of her tea, Tess placed her cup on the table and gave him a look that said let's get out of here. Together they walked out into the morning sunshine and Tess inhaled a large lungful of air. Immediately she wobbled on her feet just as Joe grabbed her arms.

'Come on let's get you to the car, it's the shock coming out.'

Tenderly he led her to where they had parked and unlocking the door, gently held her head as she got inside. He was expecting her to want to go home, so what came next stunned him totally.

'I want to go and see Carmel Jones, then look for that bastard Layton.'

'Tess! even if we found him we wouldn't be able to do anything. He's not going to admit doing this and Roxy wont lay any blame. I know it's hard but it's a scenario I've seen a thousand times. For some reason these girls hero worship their pimps.'

He saw that he'd hurt her again with his words but this time he didn't feel guilty.

'It's no good looking at me like that Tess. She's a brass and you have to accept that fact. Lenny Layton has a hold over her that you will never be able to understand but at least take it on board and try to accept it. Now I agree with you about seeing Carmel and then we'll take things from there Ok?'

Carmel Jones was still deep in the land of nod and dreaming of a life she knew she'd never lead, when the first series of knocks came at her door. She groaned in annoyance and turned over in the bed. If it was Roxy again, then she could just piss off. As the banging became louder and louder, Carmel knew it wasn't her friend. Slowly she pulled herself from the warm but grubby sheets and reaching for her housecoat, padded her way along the hall.

'Alright! all fucking right! I'm coming. I don't know what a girl has to do to get some sleep in this god forsaken place but whatever it is, I wish some cunt would tell me!'

Normally Tess would have cringed at such language but not today. Today something inside her had changed and she knew it had begun with seeing her sister lying unconscious on a cold dirty floor. As soon as Carmel opened the door wide enough to see who it was, she tried desperately to close it again. Joe was used to dealing with brasses and knowing what she would do, was one step ahead of her. Already prepared, he had his foot wedged firmly against the frame.

'Now come on Carmel, you know the procedure. We only want to talk but if you're going to be fucking difficult then we can carry on with this down at the nick.' Experience had taught him that those words usually did the trick. Brasses hated the stations, on account of spending so much of their time there. Carmel didn't invite them in; she just walked off in the direction of the sitting room. It was now Tess and Joe's turn to stand and witness her cigarette ritual. As normal when she'd finished coughing and her face had turned a frightening shade of purple, she was ready to deal with the world.

'So what are you doing bringing this bitch into me home Joe?'

He didn't answer Carmel's question and walked over to the table at the window and took a seat. Tess herself looked around for somewhere to sit and remembering the disgusting state of the sofa, decided to remain standing. Staring coldly into Carmel's eyes, she began to speak.

'I want you to tell me all you know about my sister, Miss Jones!'

Carmel laughed out loud, she hadn't been called a Miss in years and it sounded ridiculous.

'You can go fuck yourself. You pissed me off big time the other night and because of you, me and Roxy had a major blow up.'

'So was it you who hurt her?'

'Hurt her? What the fuck is she on about?'

Carmel was now staring daggers at Joe Reynolds and he could see real fear in the woman. As he spoke, he casually stared out of the window, as if what he was saying was no big deal.

'Seems our Roxy's pissed someone off big time and we wondered if that person was you. On second thoughts looking at the state of you, you couldn't fight your way out of a fucking paper bag. Come on Tess let's get out of this flea pit she calls a home, I'm beginning to feel itchy.' Tess turned towards the hall as Joe made his way across the sitting rooms matted carpet.

Silently inside his head he began to count and he didn't reach six before Carmel Jones began to rant and rave.

'Are you going to fucking tell me about Rox or did you just come round to fucking wind me up? I bet that cunt Lenny's been up to his old tricks again. If I told her once, I told her a thousand times to leave that bastard and move in here with me. Would she listen, would she fuck! Where is she?'

It was Tess's turn to speak and her words came out like venom.

'You mean he's done this before?'

'Are you thick or what! I told you the other night, the trouble with you lot is you don't fucking listen, that or you think we're all liars. Now are you going to tell me where she is or not!'

'The Middlesex but don't even dream about going there. I mean Carmel, just take a look at yourself! Do you really think you're a good influence, come to that can you really help her in anyway? Of course you can't and by bothering her, you'll just cause her more pain. If you feel anything for my sister, you'll stay well away.'

Tess's words were like a red rag to a bull and if Joe hadn't stepped in between the two women, then he was sure blood would have been spilt. As Carmel lunged forward, he was quick enough to grab the collar of her

210

housecoat. The material strained against the force of her body and the housecoat parted to reveal the body of an old woman. Carmel Jones was no spring chicken but the years of abuse and neglect, had left her with the physique of an eighty year old. Realising that she was showing her nakedness, she clutched at the thin fabric and tried desperately to cover herself. All the time her mouth was still going ten to the dozen.

'Feel anything for her? I love the poor little mare as if she was my own.'

'But that's just it Carmel, she isn't! She's my sister and it's me she needs, not a worn out old pro like you.'

With her dignity once more intact, Carmel again tried to punch out at Tess but Joe managed to get hold of her arm, before she was able to make contact.

'You fucking leery bitch! Who do you think you are? Where were you when he'd beat her in the past hey? I was the only one that cleaned her up and gave her a bed for as long as she needed it. You were nowhere to be seen, probably too busy shagging your way up the ladder for a promotion.'

Instantly Tess became angry and pushed forward, almost toppling Joe over as she did. It had turned personal now and he could see the only thing to be done, was to get Tess out of the flat as quickly as possible. Turning his back on Carmel he grabbed Tess by both of her wrists and glared into her face. The look was enough to tell her to stop and he physically turned her body to face the door. In a second Carmel had moved in for the kill and now held a handful of Tess's hair in her hand. Yanking her arm swiftly back, Tess screamed out in pain. Joe Reynolds took hold of Carmel's hand and gripped it so tightly that the women were now in stalemate.

'You let go right now, or I'll have you down the nick for

assault and believe me Carmel, Old Bill don't look kindly on anyone who hurts one of their own.'

She didn't need to be told twice and a second later Tess, stood holding her head in pain.

'You just messed with the wrong fucking person Carmel!'

Her words shocked him. It was the first time he'd ever heard Tess swear and that alone made him realise just how angry she was. Joe knew the only way to stop the two killing each other was to leave. Almost pushing Tess out of the door, he held onto her shoulder as they both descended the stairs and didn't let go until they were out and onto the street. Carmel now had a chance to run through everything in her own mind and Tess would bet money on the fact that the woman wouldn't stay away from the hospital, in fact she was banking on it. When Carmel saw the state Roxy was in, maybe she'd be a bit more forthcoming as to Lenny Layton's whereabouts. Outside in the cool morning air, Joe leant against the brickwork and lit up a cigarette. He'd tried time and again to give up but over the last couple of days, stress had got to him big time.

'What the fuck was all that about?'

'That old bag just got to me, that's all.'

'Tess if people like Carmel Jones can wind you up so easily; well I suggest you should maybe rethink your career.'

She knew he was right and up until now, no one in her entire time in the force had been able to penetrate the guard she'd built up around herself. Trouble was, this time it was different. This time it was her flesh and blood and she guessed that somewhere deep down inside she blamed Carmel Jones and any other women on the game for the way things had turned out. As if reading her thoughts, Joe commented on a statement that she hadn't yet made.

'It's not Carmel's fault you know. Roxy had a choice in what she did or didn't do.'

'Joe she was sixteen for god's sake. How could she ever have had a choice?'

He placed his arm around her shoulder and guided her towards the car.

'I know sweetheart, come on let's get out of here.'

Joe was adamant that he was taking Tess home even though she protested that she'd rather walk.

'Joe it's only round the corner and the fresh air will do me good.'

'Sorry Tess but I wouldn't feel happy unless you let me drive you and I make sure you get back ok.'

She laughed and doing as she was told, got into the car. Agi Goldstein was taking in the milk when they pulled up. She must have decided to have a lay in with Mr Seaman and Tess smiled to herself at the idea of what had gone on. With or without that thought, she was glad to be home. Joe said he'd call later that day or as soon as he had any news and Tess said she'd do likewise if she heard anything from the hospital. Agi Goldstein didn't know what had happened and she wasn't one to pry but the look on her lodgers face, told her things weren't right.

'Come on in sweets, I've just made a brew and by the look of you, you could do with one.'

Ten minutes later and Joe Reynolds got out of his car and walked towards the rear entrance of Agar Street police station. He was so deep in thought regarding all that had happened in the last two hours, he didn't notice Annette Windsor staring down at him from her first floor window. Tommy Radcliff was still on the desk but unlike his usual smile, his face was deadly serious as Joe entered.

'Big Chief wants to see you Joe and she aint a happy bunny.'

Joe Reynolds laughed out loud, he knew what Annette's problem was and he was ready to deal with her, just like he was now ready to deal with the rest of his life. Slowly he closed his eyes and nodded in Tommy's direction. Nothing more was said between the two men. Tommy knew from past history, that Joe was more than capable of taking care of himself, whatever the situation. Without any rush, he slowly made his way up to her office and as usual he didn't knock. Annette Windsor was waiting and a woman scorned didn't even enter two on her Richter scale. As the door opened, Joe's resignation came flying across the room. She didn't give him chance to close the door, before she erupted in an explosion of questions and accusations.

'What the fuck is this? no don't tell me, let me guess. You need a break, time to make a life changing decision. Or is it that you've had a better offer elsewhere? Let's face it, it didn't take you long to forget about me in the past. Well did it?'

Joe didn't try to answer straight away and instead walked over to where she stood. He didn't know what it was but for some reason, today he was destined to a fate of calming down the fairer sex.

'It's got nothing to do with any of what you've said, well maybe the bit about a life changing decision.'

'I knew it, you don't give a toss. All you care about is........'

Placing his index finger on her lips, Joe halted her mid sentence and being stopped in mid flow wasn't something Annette Windsor was used to.

'Will you give me a few minutes to explain or are you just going to carry on ranting and fucking raving woman?'

Annette was angry but no so angry that she couldn't see sense. Not speaking, she stared into Joes eyes in a pleading way that told him to carry on.

'Annie I love you but I've spent the last few years living in fear, well no more! I'm due a good pension and let's face it; this job aint what it used to be. I was going to ask you to come with me but I didn't for one minute think you would. Your jobs to important to you and I respect that.'

'Come where?'

'I don't know wherever the fancy takes us'.

Annette closed her eyes and right there and then, Joe had his answer. He wasn't heartbroken, it wasn't any more than he was expecting. Taking her in his arms, he held her close as she began to softly cry.

'Hush babe, come on now don't do this. If we're being honest, we both knew this was dead in the water three years ago. I guess it's just a case of knowing when to let go.'

Annette looked up into his eyes and she could see the pools of tears beginning to form.

'I can't get used to calling you Joe. To me you will always be Paul, my Paul and I've never stopped loving you.'

'I know you haven't but darling sometimes it's better to end things while its good instead of hanging in there until we end up hating each other because neither of us had the guts to just let it go.'

'So what will you do now?'

'I'm not sure to be honest, always quite fancied the south of France but who knows. I have made myself a promise though.'

Annette Windsor was looking into his face long and hard,

desperately trying to spot any kind of chink in his armour.

'What's that?'

'Before my time is up, I want to help Tess Davey sort out her personal life. After the result I've given you, I thought that was the least you owed me?'

Lifting her head up, Annette gently kissed Joe on the lips before speaking.

'I owe you everything Joe Reynolds and what you're asking is the least I can do. Take as much time as you or should I say Tess, need. Let's face it I'm losing one brilliant officer, I don't want to lose two.'

CHAPTER TWENTY TWO

After spending only an hour in Agi's company, Tess couldn't wait any longer and after making a feeble excuse, set off for the hospital. The walk would take a good fifteen minutes if not longer but it was time she would use to run over in her mind, all the latest events in the saga of finding her sister. She was sure that by now Carmel Jones would have seen Roxy. It was strange but Tess felt more comfortable with calling her sister Roxy than she did using the woman's birth name. It wasn't any different really than calling herself Susan. She hated the name and couldn't think for the life of her why their mother had made the choices she had. For a start both girls had the SS initial and there was nothing original about their names. Tess thought that maybe their mother had nothing original about herself. Her father on the other hand was a different matter and Tess had made the conscious decision, that if things worked out well with Roxy, then she would try and track him down next. Suddenly happy family images invaded her mind, images of the three of them enjoying a walk in the park, or a delicious Sunday lunch in some pub in the country. With difficulty she forced the images to go away. Tess wasn't stupid and she knew the odds of everything turning out rosy were very low indeed. The Middlesex hospital was established in 1745, although then it was very different from its eight storeys' of today. As Tess approached, the building seemed far more oppressive than it had earlier. She assumed it was just a case of nerves and inhaling deeply, climbed the front steps. After her initial emergency admission, Roxy had been sent to St Mary's ward on the second floor. Like the building, the ward was old and badly in need of refurbishment. It of course conformed to government guidelines but all the same Tess wouldn't have wanted to stay there herself.

Inquiring at the Sisters desk, she was taken by a nurse to a private side room that had been set aside for Roxy. She would later find out that it was Joe who had obtained the small place, in payment of a favour he'd done for the ward clerk. The man had been of dubious character and after his second pull for curb crawling, had been indebted to Joe for not being charged. The walls were plain magnolia but at least they were clean. The furnishings simple but somehow cosy, with the forget me knot detail. As Tess gingerly walked over to the bed, her heart was beating so fast she thought it was going to burst out of her chest. The member of staff who had shown her to this place resembled nurse Ratchet from one flew over the cuckoo's nest and Tess was glad that Roxy was still sedated. The ensuing conversation made Tess realise that nursing was no longer a vocation, though what exactly propelled people like this woman to follow up this career, she didn't quite know.

'Well here she is. I suppose you're one of them social workers, come to check her out. Her sort always has someone from the authorities following them about, though lord knows why. If she wants to end it all, who are we to stand in her way?'

Tess didn't have a clue what the woman was on about and her facial expression must have given her away.

'She's a self harmer, don't tell me you didn't know?'

With that the nurse pulled back the bedclothes and for the first time, Tess saw what Roxy's life was all about. Her arms from wrists to shoulders were covered in fine long scars. Even Tess's limited medical knowledge told her that many of the marks were years old.

218

'Why? Why has she done this to herself?'

'Self mutilation? who knows. Maybe even she couldn't give you a straight answer. All I know is that I'm sick of clearing up after them. Do you know that on average we deal with at least one case of this a day. As far as I'm concerned that's one case too many.'

The woman was shaking her head as she left the room. It wasn't a shake of pity but one of disgust and the action made Tess feel furious inside. Furious that someone could be so uncaring and furious, that her sister had to go through this without Tess knowing. After half an hour of sitting and stroking Roxy's hair, she started to come round from the sedation. Tess expected a mouthful of abuse but instead all she received was a weak smile. It was quite a while later that the two women spoke their first words but it was also a time Tess wouldn't have swapped for anything in the world. Roxy grabbed Tess's hand as she was again about to stroke Roxy's brow.

'Are you who I think you are?'

Tess nodded, her eyes filling with tears at the sound of her sisters voice.

'Carmel said you was a hard faced bitch but you don't look that way to me.'

Through her tears, Tess began to laugh and even though she must have been in great pain, Roxy grinned too.

'I know who did this to you Roxy and believe me when I say that I'll move heaven and earth to see he's brought to justice.'

That sentence brought the happy family reunion to an abrupt halt. The last thing on Roxy Baxter's mind was making Lenny pay. He was part of her and she loved him through and through. This woman, albeit her sister, didn't have a clue about what the two of them had been through together. She guessed Tess wouldn't understand

219

their relationship in a million years. Through gritted teeth Roxy began to talk, it was slow and it was painful but she had to say her piece.

'Don't even go there. I know you're my sister and I hope we can get to know each other but as far as Lenny's concerned, that's a part of my life that has nothing to do with you.'

Tess could again see the terrible marks that covered her sisters' arms.

'Maybe not but are you going to tell me that he didn't have anything to do with those.'

Roxy looked down and immediately tried to cover herself up. She was vulnerable and she didn't like it. Not even Carmel, had seen her undressed, at least not for several years and immediately she went on the defensive.

'I don't know why the pair of you are looking so fucking shocked, we all have vices and mine is to self harm.'

'Why in god's name? why do you do it to yourself?'

Roxy struggled to sit up in the bed. Her sides hurt terribly but for the first time she wanted to talk. Looking into the eyes of her twin, it was almost as if she was talking to herself. Not on a physical level, it was much deeper than that and something she couldn't explain.

'Why? You aint got a fucking clue what my life's like, so don't ask stupid questions. Look, sometimes I get scared, scared that this is all there is, then an unbelievable urge comes over me and I need to cut. I don't suppose you can understand that.'

Tess's eyes were brimming with tears but she had to carry on with the conversation.

'Of course I can. We all wonder from time to time, if this is all there is.'

Immediately Tess saw the angry girl from a few days ago, begin to emerge.

220

'Fuckin time to time! I wonder every minute of the bastard day but then our worlds are miles apart aren't they?'

Tess tried to embrace Roxy but she wasn't having any of it. She grabbed Tess's wrist when she tried to touch her face and held it in a vice like grip. Tess continued to talk, to try and sooth her sister but it wasn't easy.

'My poor poor baby. We've all travelled down roads to get where we are in life but yours has been hell and I'm so sorry for that.'

'What have you got to be sorry for?'

'That I wasn't here to stop all this happening to you.'

Tentatively Roxy swung her legs out of the bed and tried to stand up. The pain seared through her body, it was excruciating and all of her strength was immediately lost. Wearily she flopped back down onto the mattress again.

'You're not responsible for me or anything that happens to me, understand! It's not black and white you know. Shit happens and we just have to deal with it in the best way we can!'

Roxy emphasized the last part of her sentence and Tess understood what her sister was trying to tell her.

'I understand what you're saying Roxy but you must try to stop. I can't help you if you won't help yourself'

Whatever Tess said, seemed like a red rag to a bull and her last words were no exception.

'Help myself! How can I, when for the whole of my life, the world and his wife have been helping themselves to me, to my body, to every part of my being. You try living with that for a day and see how you fucking cope. I'm twenty eight years old but feel like fifty and I know I definitely aint going to see thirty.'

Tess's eyes were about to brim over with the tears, that she'd fought tooth and nail to hold inside.

221

'You're all mixed up and I know it's strange but you won't feel like this forever.'

Roxy began to laugh in a high pitched hysterical manner, every sound caused her pain like she'd never experienced before but she wasn't able to stop herself. The scene, was like something from a horror movie and just as Tess was about to call for help, the laughter subsided.

'This feeling isn't strange, it's normal, it's my life. Mine Tess and not yours, so don't fucking judge me alright!'

Suddenly the Tears that Tess had so desperately struggled to hold back flowed freely down her cheeks.

'I just want to try and make things better. Is that such a bad thing?'

Roxy looked deep into her sisters' face. She wanted to feel compassion, feel sorry that she was causing hurt but no matter how hard she tried, it wasn't forthcoming.

'Not if it had been twenty years ago but now, yes it is. Do you think that these scars can ever really heal, that I can ever feel normal again, the way you know as normal? Well, do you?'

The room was silent and for a few seconds the sisters stared into each other's eyes. Roxy was ready to fight but the answer to her question wasn't what she'd been expecting.

'I don't know Roxy but we have to try. It would be a crying shame if we didn't at least give it a go. People say that when you die, it's not the failures you regret but the things you never tried. God help me Roxy, I'm willing to try anything, whatever it takes, anything to break the vicious circle that you call a life.'

Now it was Roxy Baxter's turn and as her eyes began to brim with tears, Tess immediately hugged her. Roxy held on so tight that Tess didn't think she would ever let go and deep down she didn't care. This moment, this closeness, was something she'd dreamed of for weeks. The nurse, who had shown Tess to the room on her arrival, popped her head round the door. Seeing the two embrace, she made a loud tutting sound. Social workers were a disgrace as far as she was concerned. It was despicable having any kind of skin contact with a patient, especially a disgusting little whore like this one.

'If you'll excuse me I need to plump up the pillows.' Leading the nurse by her elbow, Tess physically pushed the woman from the room.

'Anything my sister needs, I will take care of. Oh and nurse, you should be a little more choosey about what you say to people regarding patients. You never know when someone might make an official complaint.'

The nurse scurried from the room and didn't bother to check on her patient until the next day. The last thing she needed was another black mark against her name.

'I don't think we'll be seeing anymore of nurse Ratchet tonight'

Roxy giggled.

'Why'd you call her that?'

'Haven't you ever seen the film, the one staring Jack Nicholson?'

Roxy shook her head.

'Lenny don't agree with wasting good money on the cinema or renting films and anyway it wouldn't be a lot of use as we don't have anything to play them on.'

Just the mention of the man's name made Tess's blood boil but with great restraint she held her anger inside.

'We'll that's just another thing I'm going to have to show you. Oh Roxy it's going to be great!'

Roxy smiled to herself. Yes it was, it was going to be so very great. Tess didn't go home that night; she slept beside her sister in a hospital issue armchair. It was a restless night for both the women but in the early hours, each would wake several times and in turn glance at their sister and smile. Finally they each had someone, someone who was theirs and wanted nothing more than to feel love from the other.

CHAPTER TWENTY THREE

The following morning, when she'd made sure that Roxy was comfortable and didn't need anything, Tess went home to change her clothes and freshen up. Agi Goldstein was clearing away the breakfast things when Tess walked through the front door. She could see the young woman was tired through lack of sleep and she could also see that something terrible was troubling her house guest. The past had taught her that it was best not to interfere, the time for talking and listening, was when Tess wanted to willingly unburden herself and not before. From the look on the young woman's face, Agi didn't think that time was too far away. She called out as Tess hung up her coat.

'Nice cup of rosy?'

'That would be wonderful please Agi. I just need to get changed before I go back to work but I'll be down in five minutes.'

Agi placed the kettle onto the stove and busied herself with the dishes until Tess walked into the kitchen.

'Sit down sweets, it's all ready.'

The older woman studied Tess's face. She noticed, lines that were not there before, now seemed to have magically appeared under her eyes in just a couple of weeks. It wasn't a pleasant sight and she sighed, making Tess look up from her drink.

'That was a big sigh Agi, is anything wrong?'

'Not with me Dearie but I bet I can't say the same for you. Now I'm not one to pry as you well know but if you ever need a friendly ear, then you know where I am.'

'I do Agi and thanks but it's just not the right time at the moment.'

Agi Goldstein grinned, revealing both rows of her ageing yellow teeth.

'Enough said, now don't let me make you late for work dear.'

Tess looked up at the large station style wall clock and seeing that she'd already been away from Roxy for over an hour and a half, stood up from the table.

'I don't know what time or even if I'll be back tonight. Is that alright?'

'It's your life Tess, just you take care!'

Tess didn't reply but gave a thin weak smile and nodded as she went into the hall. Leaving the house, Tess looked up and down the Street and couldn't face the long walk ahead of her. She was tired, desperate to get back to Roxy and another fifteen minutes was just too long to wait. Making her way onto the Charing Cross road, she was able to successfully hail a taxi in a matter of seconds. In the back of the cab, Tess phoned Joe on her mobile. It seemed like an age before her call was transferred but finally he spoke.

'Hi there! How's she doing?'

'Not so bad boss. Actually I'm on my way over to the hospital as we speak. It's the reason I'm calling to be honest. I don't think I can make it in today, if that's alright?'

Tess was being polite, nothing more. If she'd been told to get into work and fast, then she would have just hung up.

'I didn't expect you to come in for a second. Take the day off, take as long as you need. I'll clear it for you to have as much time off as you want.'

'Thanks Sir.'

'No need for that.'

Tess flipped the phone shut and sat back in her seat for

the rest of the journey. The hospital didn't look any more appealing in the fresh morning light and after paying her fare, Tess slowly climbed the steps. Entering the ward she was immediately spotted by the infamous nurse Ratchet, who hurried off in the opposite direction. The last person Tess had imagined she'd see as she walked into the side room was Carmel Jones. She thought that the woman would have had enough sense to make herself scarce, at least if she knew Tess was coming. The one thing Tess hadn't banked on was the depth of feeling that the old brass had for Roxy and after a terrible night's sleep, Carmel had decided that come hell or high water she was going to be there for her friend. Sitting on the opposite side of the bed, Tess took hold of her sisters' hand. Roxy looked at her friend then back to her sister. It was so painful for her to talk but that didn't stop Roxy Baxter from trying.

'In this room, I have the two people who care most about me in the whole wide world and I'm so happy.'

Carmel couldn't resist a cheap shot aimed at Lenny Layton and never being one to mince her words spoke out.

'Oh so you don't think that bastard cares about you then. Well thank fuck for that, it's about bleeding time you came to your senses.'

Roxy shot Carmel a piercing glare.

'If looks could fucking kill Rox, I'd be dead on the bleeding floor right now.'

Carmel didn't add anymore, she knew that talking about Lenny in front of the copper was a daft thing to do and she wished she'd kept her big gob shut.

'I can't wait to get out of here. The three of us have a lot of work to do but I think getting to know each other might be good for all of us. She squeezed the two

227

women on their hands and they both smiled at her. Several minutes later and Carmel Jones announced that she had to be on her way.

'A girl has to earn a living and there are men out there fucking dying for it.'

Roxy burst out laughing but Tess didn't find the comment the least bit amusing. Not wanting to miss her chance, she offered to walk Carmel to the main door. As soon as the two were away from the side ward and out of Roxy's earshot, Tess grabbed Carmel's arm roughly.

'I thought I told you to stay away!'

'You can fucking tell whoever you like, tell the fucking queen for all I care. I aint never taken orders from no one and I aint about to fucking start now.'

Tess turned to walk away but for selfish reasons she thought again. Looking directly into the face of Carmel Jones, she tried to put on her best smile and hoped that it was convincing.

'Look Carmel, I know we didn't get off to a very good start but at the end of the day. Well, we both have only Roxy's best interests at heart, don't we? I'm not saying we'll ever be the best of friends but we need to make the effort if only for her sake, so what do you think?'

Carmel let the words absorb in her head before she answered. This woman was good, very good but she wasn't a push over herself. Deciding to go along with the copper, at least until she knew the score, she nodded her head.

'That's good, now here's my mobile number in case you need me.'

Carmel took the small printed card and placed it swiftly inside her handbag.

'I suppose we need to work out who is visiting and when.

228

Have they said how long she'll be in this place?'
'Probably a couple of weeks.'
'Right. You let me know what shifts you want me to do
and I'll be here but obviously nights are a bit difficult.'
This time Tess did laugh and she continued to do so as
Carmel, in her canary yellow four inch high stilettos,
click clacked her way outside.
Back with Roxy, Tess broached the subject of where she
would go after her release from hospital. Tess tried to be
diplomatic, even suggesting they get somewhere together
but Roxy was having none of it.
'Tess I have a perfectly good place already. I don't know
if Lenny will come back, I suppose that's down to him.
Don't look so disappointed, I know you're only trying to
do what you think is best for me but living together
wouldn't work, well not yet anyway. We need to take
things slow, get to know each other bit by bit.'
Deep down Tess knew that what her sister was saying
was right but she hated the thought of her going back to
that hovel. With her own eyes she'd seen the state of the
place and it wasn't fit for a dog to live in.
'You're right and I'm sorry for being pushy. You can at
least give me permission to hold onto the key and clean
up a bit for you.'
Tess saw panic begin to spread across Roxy's face and
she wondered what she was going to find in the place that
her sister called home.
'You don't need to do that, I.'
'Don't argue Roxy. Before they let you out of here, they
need to know you have somewhere warm and safe to go
to. Don't worry about the mess; remember it's nothing I
haven't seen before.'
Reluctantly Roxy agreed. When the ambulance had left
yesterday, Tess had locked the door so she still had her

sisters' keys. Pulling them from her coat, she tossed them in the air before catching them again.

'I'd best get started then.'

She leant over and placed a kiss on Roxy's forehead.

'You rest and I'll be back tonight. I think Carmel's visiting again this afternoon and I'm sure you'll have things to talk about that you wouldn't want me to hear.' She winked at Roxy in a knowing way as she walked to the door. With her one good eye, Roxy tried to return the gesture but she couldn't manage it. She liked Tess and was glad they had finally met; somehow the future didn't seem so bleak now. Comforted by the thought, she snuggled down in the warm clean bed and drifted off to sleep.

Nervously Tess let herself into the Berners Mews flat. After calling out loudly, she was so relieved when there was no reply. Lenny Layton would have been insane to return here and she chastised herself for even thinking he would. Placing her carrier bags onto the kitchen table, she surveyed the room with disgust. The sink was filled to capacity with dirty pots, pans and plates. Over brimming ashtrays sat comfortably on the drainer, table and window sill. After removing bleach and cleaning cloths, Tess set to work bringing the flat some way towards looking respectable. Three hours later and every surface throughout the entire place shone. After hunting high and low, she wasn't able to find a vacuum cleaner and had knocked on the flat next door. Roxy had told her about Smiley Cosgrave and how she was a good sort if you needed anything. After what seemed like an age the door finally opened and Tess was shocked to see the woman's permanent grin. Roxy hadn't mentioned anything about a scar and Tess wondered if that had been done on purpose, or if it was just a case of she had known the woman for so long that she didn't notice it anymore. Explaining who she was and what she was doing, Tess was surprised when Smiley reached into her hall cupboard and brought out a vintage Hoover.

'Keep it as long as you need girl. I aint too fucking fond of housework myself so I don't suppose I'll miss it. How's Rox doing?'

'Fine, she's going to be just fine.'

'I'm glad. Aint seen hide or hair of that cunt Layton, perhaps he's slung his hook for good. Let's, fucking hope so anyway. I always had a soft spot for old Rox, though what the hell she ever saw in a tosser like him I don't know.'

Tess smiled and made a hasty retreat back into Roxy's flat. The last thing she wanted was to get friendly with an aging hooker who resembled the joker. By early evening, the sheets had been changed and the whole place smelled of sweet lavender air freshener. Taking a carton of milk from her bag, Tess put the kettle onto the cooker. Sitting down at the small table she drifted off in thought about all that had happened. When the sound of a key in the lock brought her hurtling back to reality, she stood up sharply. Lenny Layton had been sleeping rough for the last couple of days and all he wanted was to crash out on his bed. As he passed the kitchen, he spied Tess out of the corner of his eye.

'What the fuck are you doing here?'

'I could ask the same of you Layton, or then again I could call for back up and take you in!'

Lenny took a step towards Tess but she stood her ground and didn't move.

'Don't even think about it. Joe Reynolds will come down on you like a ton of bricks, if you so much a lay a finger on me.'

231

Lenny completely ignored what Tess had just said but all the same, he didn't advance any further.

'On what fucking charge!'

'The charge of beating an innocent girl into a pulp, or are you going to tell me that had nothing to do with you?' Lenny snorted with laughter and with that sound; Tess could feel her anger begin to build up inside.

'Innocent girl! There's nothing fucking innocent about Roxy. She'd sell her fucking arse to the highest bidder and enjoy it, would Roxy. I don't know what she's been telling you but this is my gaff.'

'Is that so! Do you remember what Joe Reynolds had in his pocket the last time we met?' That little packet can materialise at any time and after all, when Roxy gets out of hospital, she'll need this place far more than you will.' Lenny couldn't believe what he was hearing but he also knew he had Hobson's choice and it really stuck in his claw.

'You're one prize bitch!'

'That may be the case but I care more about that girl than you ever could. Tell me one thing before you leave. Do you feel anything for what you've done to her, any remorse at all?'

'Not one fucking iota, why should I? Life's a bitch and then it's over, get used to it.'

With that he turned and walked out of the flat. Tess lifted up her hands and could see that she was trembling. She carried on making the tea, in the hope that a hot drink would calm her nerves. It didn't.

Back at the hospital, Roxy was in fits of giggles at the stories Carmel was reciting. She strutted around the room as she spoke and Roxy found the sight hilarious.

'Carm you're a fucking tonic and no mistake.'

Suddenly Carmel Jones became serious.

'What you going to do when you get out of here Rox?'
'What you mean?'
Carmel walked over to the window and Roxy recognised the signs of nervousness.
'Are you going to carry on being on the game or what?'
'I haven't given it much thought. Just imagined I'd take each day as it comes, you know me Carm, ever the optimist!'
'That aint no good Rox! Fuck me girl, you have a chance to sort yourself out, take it!'
Roxy hated confrontation and here was her best mate doing just that to her.
'Aint I been through enough Carm? I've got Tess now and she's going to take good care of me, aint that enough?'
Suddenly Carmel Jones walked over to where Roxy lay and taking the girls face in her hands, she wore the look of someone serious in her intensions. It was a look that Roxy hadn't seen before and it unnerved her.
'I've lived this life for a thousand years and it's never going to fucking change. You've got a chance, a chance I never had and you're being blasé about it.'
'Blasé?'
'Don't be fucking funny Rox, you know what I mean.'
'Look Carm, its early days yet. 'Course I'd like to play happy families but we both know the chances of that happening are thin. Tess is lovely and I'd like to think she was in my life to stay.'
'I feel a but coming on?'
''Course there's a but there always is. I'm a fucking brass my twins a copper and the two definitely don't mix so I aint building my hopes up.'
'Don't you want to change?'
Roxy was tired and she didn't feel like talking anymore,

233

trouble was she knew Carmel wouldn't leave until she'd had her say.

'If I change, then I won't be me. Trouble is Carm, I don't know who me is anymore.'

Carmel Jones looked hard into Roxy's face, it was a serious look. Carmel was more serious than Roxy could ever have imagined.

'Then by god girl you have to find out. You've got an opportunity here, an opportunity most brasses would give their eye teeth for. For fuck's sake don't throw it away, because I tell you, you'll never get another one like it. You either have to fight for what you want or end up like me!'

Carmel spoke in a cold hard tone and Roxy knew the woman meant every word. She also knew she had some big decisions to make, decisions that would change her life forever. Trouble was she didn't think she was ready, didn't think she ever would be.

'I'm scared Carm!'

'I know you are babe but you just have to be strong and make the right choices. Remember, every action has a reaction.'

'What do you mean?'

'Whatever you decide, wont only affect you. It will affect Tess, me and anyone else who's in your life. Listen to me! a proper fucking Margery Proops. What I mean is, deep down, do what you want. Fuck everyone else, if you want to change then you will. If you don't, then that's how it's meant to be but don't look a gift horse in the mouth. Now that's enough of the heavy stuff I need to be out there knocking them dead. A girls got to do what a girls got to do and all that. Tess should be here soon, so you think long and hard about what I've just said, do you hear?'

'I hear you Carm and thanks!'

'No thanks needed, just make sure you make the right decision.'

'I will.'

With that Carmel left the room and Roxy fell asleep listening to the click clack of the woman walking down the corridor. Out in the cool evening air, Carmel decided to take the long route via Berners Mews. She didn't know if Tess had left yet but decided to call in and see on the off chance. The knock at the door made Tess jump out of her skin. The tea she'd made earlier sat stone cold and untouched. Slowly walking towards the front door, she asked who was there before opening up.

'It's me you daft mare, who the fuck do you think it is?'

When Tess at last opened the door, Carmel could see that she was badly shaken.

'Lenny came round while I was cleaning up.'

'He didn't hurt you did he?'

'Of course not, I'm a policewoman remember.'

Carmel shook her head and laughed.

'That don't mean diddly squat to the likes of him. To Lenny you're a woman and women are there to be pushed around. I'd say you got off lightly. Cuppa?'

Tess nodded and sat back down at the table.

'Lenny Layton's had Roxy flogging her arse every single night of the week since before I met her.'

'That's what I find so hard to understand Carmel. Why on earth, did she leave the safety of the Parsons, for a life like this?'

'You're having a laugh aint you. Robert Parsons was a kiddie fiddler. Oh, he hid it well beneath his religious ranting but he had his hand down Roxy's knickers within a week of her being placed there.'

'What about her foster mother?'

'Mavis? I suppose in a way she was kind to Rox but like a lot of them, she turned a blind eye. It was easier than confronting her bully of a husband and after all Roxy wasn't her child.'

Tess wanted to be physically sick. She'd thought the prostitution was bad enough but this! All she could think about was getting back to the hospital.

'Carmel I've got to go, I need to be with Roxy.'

''Course you do but a word of warning! Don't mention any of this to her, she won't thank you. Me neither come to that. By the way Tess, you've done a blinding job of this place.'

Tess didn't reply and picking up her coat and bag, stood waiting for Carmel to stand up. When no response was forth coming, she coughed loudly.

'Oh sorry, I was real comfy there for a minute. This place is a lot nicer than mine now, don't suppose you hire out your services?'

'Not a chance!'

The two women walked out of the flat together and Tess double checked that the door and windows were locked.

'Take care of yourself Carmel.'.

'All I ever do, it'd take a lot for any bastard to get one over on old Carmel Jones'.

Tess stood and watched for a few seconds as Carmel headed in the direction of Oxford Street. If anyone had told her just a few weeks ago that this was how things were going to turn out, she'd have laughed hysterically. Now here she was, having just said goodnight to a prostitute and finding that she was really warming towards the woman. Laughing to herself, she began to walk up the road towards the Middlesex hospital and her sister.

236

CHAPTER TWENTY FOUR

Tess never did reveal to Roxy that she knew about the abuse. It was something that was better left unsaid but Roxy wasn't stupid and she knew that an old gas bag like Carmel wouldn't keep her trap shut. Still she reasoned, they'd got their whole lives to find out each other's secrets. It was now almost two weeks since her hospitalisation and Roxy Baxter had healed well. Her injuries would not under normal circumstances, have required spending so long in hospital. Given the nature of her work and her history of self harm, the doctor had kept her in for an extended period, just to be on the safe side. The rest had done Roxy the power of good but now she was keen to be on the move. When the doctor told her she could go home, her bag was packed in seconds. Tess was due to visit at two that Monday afternoon but she'd hardly got through the door and Roxy was by her side, bag in hand.

'I can go Tess! I can finally go.'

Tess Davey was glad that her sister had been given a clean bill of health but she was worried about her going back to that flat. True she'd scrubbed it from top to bottom and it was a thousand times better than it had been but it still wasn't anything to write home about.

'Best be on our way then!'

Picking up the bag, Tess walked out of the room and along the corridor. Roxy followed but her pace was slow, she hadn't realised just how weak she was. Glad that she was going home by cab, Roxy sat back and stared hard out of the window. When they reached Berners mews and Tess opened the front door, Roxy couldn't believe the transformation of the place. Gone was the sour smell that had invaded her nostrils whenever she'd come in. In its place was a sweet spring aroma, which came via the numerous air fresheners Tess had installed. The nets were now a brilliant white, instead of the grimy grey that had infiltrated the material over the years. Walking into the kitchen, Roxy began to cry when she saw the vase of fresh flowers on the table.

'Oh Tess! Thank you so much. It's like a palace; I never dreamed it could look so good.'

'Well make sure you keep it that way, you won't have a servant from now on you know.'

Tess put the kettle on, while Roxy went into the bedroom to put her clothes away. Again the room smelled so good and her sister had even brought a new duvet cover and pillowcases. She didn't know what she'd done to deserve this but Roxy Baxter said a silent thank you all the same. Undressing she stood in front of the repaired mirror and studied her body. Running her hand down her left arm, she could feel all the lumps and bumps under her skin, from the scars that had been left as a permanent reminder. Suddenly she felt nothing but disgust at the sight before her. With the tea made, Tess started to get concerned and headed down the hall to the bedroom. Outside the door she could hear her sister whispering to herself. 'I need to be optimistic, I have to be. This life can't last forever, feeling shit can't last forever can it?'

Tess wanted to push the door open and comfort Roxy but she knew she couldn't. If her sister was ever going to break the cycle, then she had to do it herself.

When Tess was back in the kitchen she called out to Roxy that the tea was ready.

'Ok! won't be a minute.'

A loud rap on the front door distracted Tess from what she hoped wasn't happening. It was Carmel, as large as life and carrying a big bag of doughnuts.

'I phoned the Middlesex and they said she'd been discharged.'

'She's in the bedroom Carmel but I'm sure she's not right. Maybe they should have kept her in a few more days.'

'Don't be daft, they had to let her home sometime.'

'Home? you can't call this hovel a home!'

Carmel grabbed Tess's shoulders with both hands and turned her, so that she was staring directly into Carmel's eyes.

'Listen! This is the only home Roxy has ever known so don't disrespect it Ok?'

'Ok, ok! calm down.'

'I am calm but if she hears you talking like that, well it's as if you're ashamed of her.'

Tess walked into the kitchen and took another mug from the dilapidated wall unit.

'I could never be ashamed of her Carmel, no matter what she did.'

When Roxy appeared she was wearing the new dressing gown that Tess had brought for her. She took a seat at the table opposite Tess, Carmel stood with her back to the sink unit. She studied her friend and saw the small trickle of blood that was slowly making its way down Roxy's hand.

'What have you been doing in there girl?'

Immediately Roxy was on the defensive. She knew she had been rumbled but no one was going to make her admit it.

'Nothing!'

Tess hadn't seen what Carmel had and couldn't make out what was going on.

'What's the matter Carmel?'

239

'Look at her hand; she's been fucking cutting herself again.'

Tess grabbed her sisters' wrist and felt the warm sticky liquid on her fingertips.

'Oh Roxy! why?'

Roxy Baxter began to cry.

'I'm sorry, I didn't mean to. I was getting undressed and saw myself in the mirror. Suddenly I had the urge and there was nothing I could do. Sometimes the need to cut is so strong and I have to act on it. If I don't I feel as though I'm going to fucking explode.'

Tess didn't speak for a few minutes, she was deep in thought.

'It's not when something bad happens because today's been a good day. Is it when you see yourself?'

Roxy nodded her head as tears streamed down her beautiful face. Without a word, Tess stood up. Gently pushing Carmel out of the way, she opened up the cupboard under the sink and removed the heaviest pan she could find. She disappeared from the room and Carmel and Roxy stared at each other. When they heard the sound of breaking glass, they both ran out into the hall to see Tess coming out of the bedroom carrying the remnants of what was Roxy's mirror.

'What have you done?'

'If you only cut when you see an image of yourself, then we'll have to make sure that you can't see yourself wont we? There's no mirrors left in this place, I've even removed the small one in your make up bag.'

Carmel looked up towards the ceiling and shook her head.

'Jesus, Mary and Joseph, I don't know which one of you two is fucking madder.'

Three women, the most unlikely trio you could ever come

across, began to laugh until the flat had hysterical giggles bouncing off every wall.

Tess stayed at the flat that night and the next but over the following couple of days; she started to spend less and less time with Roxy. It wasn't something she wanted but she would have to return to work soon. If Roxy got used to being on her own again, it would be easier for her to handle, when Tess could only pop in for a short visit each day. By Friday, Tess had contacted Joe and told him she'd return to Agar Street on Monday. He was glad that he'd get to see her before he finished work; with only two weeks left he'd begun to think that wouldn't be the case. After her phone call to the station, Tess made her way round to Berners mews. Roxy was still in bed and Tess let herself in with the key her sister had given her. She made tea and warmed up the croissants that she'd picked up in the small bakery at the end of Manette Street. Ten minutes later and Roxy emerged from her bedroom. The smell of food warming had made her hungry and taking a seat at the table she filled up on several of the French delicacies. When not a crumb remained, Tess took her through to the small living room Leading Roxy by the hand she sat her down on the sofa.

'I have to go back to my job next week, so I won't be around as much.'

She could see the panic register on her sisters' face and she would have given anything to have been able to take it away.

'So this is, where it all ends then?'

'Of course not! We've got each other, this is only the beginning.'

'So if you see me on the Street turning a trick that would be alright?'

'No! it would not, Roxy why do you say these things.

241

Do you try to hurt me on purpose?'

Now it was Roxy's turn to be the comforter.

'I'm not trying to hurt you but it's a hard fact of life that we all have to make a living. The only way I know how, is on me back with me legs wide open.'

Roxy saw Tess cringe at her choice of words but nothing she had said was a lie.

'Roxy I earn enough for both of us, at least until you get sorted out with something else.'

'What if I don't? what if I don't want to. Maybe I like what I do, you've never even asked me that question. I get so pissed off with people judging me.'

'Now that's not fair Roxy! Not once have I judged you, not once. But now we're on the subject, do you like what you do?'

'Couldn't care less either way.'

'You must do!'

'Why?'

'Well, I don't know, self respect I suppose.'

'Tess I lost all self respect when I chose this as a career. Everyone gets fucked in this life by someone, the only difference is that I get paid for it.'

Tess rubbed her forehead with the palm of her hand. She'd realised in a small space of time, that her sister could be hard work at times.

'Look let's make a deal. I'll support you for two months while you look for work. If after that time you haven't found anything, then it's up to you what you do, deal?'

Roxy thought for all of three seconds.

'Deal.'

'Good, now how about I treat us both to dinner on Sunday night?'

'Where?'

'Anywhere you want it's your choice. You just book it

242

and I'll sort out a cab, you can tell me what time when I pop in tomorrow.'

Tess kissed Roxy lightly on the cheek before she left. 'By the way, there's a surprise for you in the kitchen.' Before Roxy had chance to say anything more, the front door slammed and Tess was gone. Curiosity got the better of Roxy straight away and she couldn't contain herself any longer. The black carrier bag looked expensive and when she peered inside, Roxy let out a squeal like that of a young child. She pulled out a soft pink dress that would have taken her a week's worth of punters to pay for. Tess had remembered to get something with long sleeves and that fact in itself made Roxy feel like crying. She held the dress up to her body but she couldn't see what she looked like, not since her sister had taken it upon herself to remove all the mirrors. For once she didn't need to look, Roxy could see it was beautiful and she held out one sleeve and danced around the room as if holding a partner.

By seven o'clock on Sunday night she was ready and waiting and when the cab finally pulled up, Roxy smoothed down her dress and made her way outside. Tess smiled when she saw her. Even if Roxy was still wearing her trademark platform boots, she looked absolutely stunning. The cab drivers eyes were out on stalks. Tess felt so proud that at last someone was admiring her sister for her beauty and not for what she would let them do to her.

'Where to Miss?'

'Old Compton Street please.'

Inwardly Tess groaned. She couldn't understand why Roxy would want to be in her old hunting ground but she didn't voice her opinion. The cab stopped dead outside the Three Greyhounds pub which was situated on the

243

corner of Greek Street and Moor Street. Tess paid the fair and the two stepped out into the warm summer air.

'Are we going for a drink?'

'Of course not Tess but it's such a nice night and I look so fucking gorgeous, that I thought it'd be nice to walk for a while.'

Tess giggled.

'Don't hide your light under a bush little sister, I mean there's no point in being shy about your appearance.'

Roxy gave Tess a funny look but when she realised that her sister was taking the micky out of her, she laughed.

'Why'd you call me little sister?'

'Because I'm the oldest by six minutes, so you have to look up to me and do as I say!'

'No fucking chance!'

The two women laughed as they strolled along arm in arm. Neither noticed Lenny Layton in the shop doorway on the other side of the road. He'd been on his way to the Kings Head when he'd heard Roxy's voice. Not wanting to be seen, Lenny had quickly ducked into a door way and watched the pair as they passed by. Roxy looked good in her new clothes and that fact alone made him sneer. She was going to pay for all the aggro she'd caused him and he was looking forward to making the first instalment. Slowly he followed behind them. The Street was beginning to fill up, so it wasn't too difficult avoiding being seen. The two women strolled through China town and Tess was mesmerized at the sights and sounds. Crimson Peking ducks hung in the windows of many of the restaurants. The sweet oriental smells, pungent and sometimes overpowering, had her taste buds drooling. There were crowds of all denominations mingling together, as the sound of woks sizzled from back doors. The foreign languages and laughter couldn't be deciphered but told anyone who cared to listen, that the people inside were happy. It was a warm summer evening, the type we all dream of and by the time the two sisters came back onto Greek Street, Tess was drunk with happiness. A group of about a dozen men were drinking wine and socializing outside the Admiral Duncan pub as Roxy and Tess passed by. Tess bit down on her lip when she noticed one of the men had his arm around the other. When the man squeezed his partner's bottom, she burst out laughing and Roxy had to grab her arm and move her on swiftly.

'Whatever's the matter with you, you can't go around staring at people like that. This is Soho and anything goes.'

'I'm sorry, it's just that I'm not used to seeing men being over familiar with each other.'

'Fucking over familiar! God Sis you don't half talk funny sometimes.'

They continued on their way until they reached Brewer Street. When Roxy stopped outside Aldo Zilli's fish restaurant, she felt like royalty.

'Here we are then!'

Tess knew this was going to cost an arm and a leg but she wouldn't burst her sisters' bubble for anything.

'So you fancy being a little high class tonight do you?'

Suddenly Roxy became serious and her brow furrowed as she struggled with what she was about to say.

'Every time I walked down this Street I would see people going inside. Not common people like me but people with real class.'

She smoothed down her dress and straightened her back, making herself appear taller and more elegant.

'They used to look at me funny from the windows, suppose they could tell I was a brass. One night one of

245

them waiters smiled at me, not a punter smile but a friendly one and I promised myself that someday I'd be a customer here. Well I'm here and tonight I can say hand on heart, I aint no brass.'

Tess tenderly touched the side of Roxy's face.

'You can that darling, now let us two sophisticated ladies go eat.'

Lenny's blood boiled when he saw them enter the posh eatery but he didn't leave. Instead he found a bar opposite, whose front window looked directly into the restaurant. The view was slightly restricted but he could still make out Roxy in her new pink dress. He didn't care if he had to wait all night for them to come out, as far as he was concerned it would be worth it.

CHAPTER TWENTY FIVE

Three hours later and with Tess's purse at least a hundred and fifty pounds lighter; the two sisters emerged from Aldo Zilli's restaurant. Roxy had been given a single rose by one of the waiters and as she stepped out onto the Street, opened her arms out wide and twirled around in a circle.

'Are you drunk Roxy Baxter?'

'Never in a million fucking years! I'm just soooooo happy. I've had a brilliant night Tess, thank you so much.'

'This is just the beginning darling, we have the rest of our lives to enjoy meals and spend time together. Shall we get a cab?'

'Let's walk Tess; it's such a nice night.'

'Ok but when we get to mine, you're getting a taxi.'

'Tess I've walked the Streets of Soho a million times. Now if you were on your own, that would be a time to worry. Roxy can take care of herself, besides I'm on first names with most of the druggies and muggers, so I'll be as safe as houses.'

'Roxy!'

'What?'

'Never mind, come on let's get going before the pubs empty for the night.'

The two walked back up Old Compton Street completely unaware, that Lenny Layton was following closely behind. At Manette Street Tess kissed her sister good night and stood for a while watching, as Roxy carried on towards Soho square. Tess was far from happy with the situation but knew Roxy was stubborn and if she wanted to do something, then come hell or high water that was exactly what she would do. Deciding that first thing in the morning she would telephone, just for her own peace of mind. Scanning the Street, something that was now second nature because of her training, she saw nothing out of the ordinary. Tired but happy, Tess Davey placed her key into the lock and went inside. Lenny had kept a comfortable hundred yards distance. When the women had stopped to say goodnight, he'd hid beside a parked car. Willing Tess to go down Manette, he knew he couldn't continue following until she had. When he finally caught sight of Roxy again, she had reached Oxford Street and was about to cross over. Lenny wasn't planning on revealing himself in such a busy area and was happy to keep up his surveillance for a while longer. Finally when Roxy was in sight of her flat, she stopped to search for her house keys. The road wasn't that well lit and she fished several times inside her bag before she found them.

'There you areeeeeee!'

Clasping the keys in her fist she took a step forward but was instantly stopped. With his right hand, Lenny had grabbed the back of Roxy's new dress. His left hand clamped hard over her mouth to drown out any protests and as he lifted Roxy off of her feet, she felt the dress begin to tear and she didn't know how but one of her platform boots left her foot. Lenny didn't walk her, with all his might he hauled Roxy along the pavement. Her instep and toes scraped along the tarmac surface and she could feel the skin begin to quickly rub off. All the time Roxy knew who her assailant was, even though Lenny hadn't uttered a single word. At the door, he briefly let go of her dress to snatch the keys from her hand. Once open, he slammed her hard in the back and she fell forwards onto the hall floor. While all this was going on and Roxy knew the worst was yet to come, all she could think about was Tess. Life was so cruel; they'd only just found one another and now it was all about to be snatched away, before they'd had time to get to know each other. Of all the things in her sad life she'd been through and there were so many, this thought alone was the worse. Rage began to build up and she tried to stand on her one good foot but Lenny was too quick for her. Forming his hand into a fist, he back handed her across the cheek and she again fell to the ground. Looking down she saw the beautiful dress that Tess had brought, was now in shreds. Miraculously she'd still managed to hold onto the rose and unclenching her hand, Roxy saw that it was in a worse state than she was. The petals were all but gone and the once beautiful bloom, hung down in a sad submission that it was about to die. A missed thorn, dug deep into her palm and when she saw the tiny droplets of blood that had begun to swim with the sweat that was forming, she felt doomed. Lifting her head, she looked up at Lenny as tears trickled down her cheeks.

'I have a chance, for once in my miserable life I have a chance. Please let me take it, let me find out what real life is like.'

'Never! you wouldn't last five minutes without me and you fucking know it!'.

'That's where you're wrong Lenny. For years I thought it was that way but now I have my sister and she loves me.'

He took a step closer to her and Roxy cowered.

'Fucking sister! she's a copper and when you're back on the game she'll bang you up faster than the speed of fucking light.'

'You're wrong Lenny and I aint going back on the Street. Tess is going to take care of me and one day we're going to get a place together.'

Her whining was starting to annoy him now and he decided that the time for talking was over. Now it was time for Roxy Baxter to pay her long overdue debt.

Tess had gone straight to bed; she was so worn out but at the same time deliriously happy. Agi and Geoffrey were already tucked up and she crept upstairs like a teenager who was late home from a date. The moon shone through a chink in her curtains and Tess watched as the illumination made patterns on her bedroom wall. She recounted every moment of the night, never wanting to forget her first special time with her twin. Things had turned out better than she could ever have imagined and she couldn't wait to tell Joe all about it tomorrow. She'd been thinking about returning to Spalding but only if Roxy would go with her, though she knew that was a long way off at the moment. Taking things a day at a time was best for now but she still couldn't help dreaming. Before she knew it, Tess Davey was in a wonderful deep sleep. There was nothing bad, no nightmares and no monsters, yet she woke up an hour later in a cold sweat and couldn't work out why. Wrapping her arms tightly around her body, Tess shivered as if someone had just walked over her grave. Roxy was still huddled in the hall in a foetal position, not daring to move. Lenny had disappeared into the kitchen but she didn't try and make her escape. When he returned carrying a selection of knives, Roxy realized that this was very different from before. Before it had been just the odd beating but even then, Lenny had sometimes gone so far over the mark, it had taken her weeks to recover. This time Roxy Baxter didn't know if she would escape with her life. Grabbing hold of her hair, Lenny pulled her round so that she was lying on her back. He climbed on top of her and used the force from his knees to pin her arms and back to the floor. Roxy stared into his eyes and seeing his pupils were dilated, knew he was high on something. When Lenny was high anything could happen and he would have no recollection of his actions in the morning. The realization of this did nothing but fuel Roxy's fear, that here in this cold dank hallway, she was probably going to die. Lenny placed the knives in a neat row on the floor beside him. Slowly and methodically he selected a small vegetable knife. He was holding Roxy still by nipping her cheeks together with one hand and she could see from the corner of her eye why he'd taken so long in the kitchen. Each knife had been sharpened with the old stone that he kept in the cutlery drawer. The blades looked rough and she knew that whatever was going to happen, would hurt more than she could imagine. As the knife came towards her face, Roxy's eyes opened wide. She tried to struggle but he held her in a vice like grip. Slowly he drew the blade down her left cheek from just below the eye and finished in a crescent on her chin. The flesh parted easily and Roxy screamed out like a wild animal. Smiley Cosgrave was at home next door and heard the commotion from where she sat in her arm chair. She liked Roxy Baxter but history and her own permanent smile, had taught her long ago not to get involved. Reaching for the remote she turned the volume up on the television, until the sound of Clint Eastwood's voice coming from the movie that was showing, was all that could be heard. Roxy's cheek lay open like a piece of raw meat but the pain was disappearing quickly. When Lenny slit her right nostril, blood spurted all over him and only caused his rage to heighten.

'You bitch! Now look what you've done. Don't need

me? Who the fucks going to give you a second glance now?'

With every ounce of strength she possessed, Roxy fought for her life and managed to break one arm free. With nails like talons, she drew her hand as hard as she could down the side of Lenny Layton's face. The lines began to fill up with blood and she knew she'd marked him good and proper. Stunned that she'd dared to try and fight back, he spat in her face and again back handed her, slamming her head sideways. Picking up a larger knife, he began to cut away at the front of her dress to reveal her breasts. In a frenzy he sliced at each one in turn and even his grip on Roxy's mouth couldn't hush her screams. Lenny was enjoying inflicting pain, he'd never realized before that he had a taste for it. Maybe this was his vocation and he thought that perhaps he'd try his hand working for one of the big boys. Finally when Roxy passed out, he became bored. Standing up he surveyed his handy work and was pleased with what he saw. Roxy resembled a carcass that he'd often seen in the back of a butchers van down the market. For a few seconds Lenny stood in a trance but when he saw her leg twitch, realized he had to finish what he'd started. Lenny didn't know if she was dead or alive. Maybe it was just a last nervous spasm but he couldn't take the chance and bending down, plunged the knife into her side. Turning round he walked out of the door, oblivious to the fact that he was covered in blood. He'd killed her and to anyone else, it was just another brass being topped by a punter. At least fifty percent of attacks on prostitutes go unreported but he knew that as she was dead this would be different. Lenny rationalized, they wouldn't delve too deeply even if her sister was a plod. He decided it would be best to lay low for a few days. An old mate over in Marylebone owed him a favour and as it was a night for repayments, Lenny thought he might as well call in one more. Yes, Lenny Layton would take a little holiday and come back all shocked and acting the victim, when he learnt of his woman's demise.

Smiley Cosgrave peered from behind her sitting room curtain and saw Lenny leave the flat. She was desperate not to get involved but Roxy's screams had been so bad, that she knew to do nothing, would be a disgrace and more than she could live with. Sheepishly she made her way outside and pushed open the front door. The sight that confronted her was nothing less than a blood bath and she had to clamp a hand over her mouth to hold in the vomit. Pacing up and down she tried to think of what to do next, when suddenly an image of Carmel popped into her thoughts. The two went back years and Smiley knew how close the woman was to Roxy. With no land line and a fear of mobiles, Smiley had no alternative but to walk over to Old Compton Street. It was now very late and Soho was winding down. Smiley didn't dare go through the square; it was too dangerous at this hour. Instead she ran all the way down Dean and at the end looked left and right, desperately trying to remember exactly where Carmel's flat was. Lady luck must have been shining on all of them that night because suddenly she heard Carmel's shrill laughter coming from further up the Street. Running, Smiley Cosgrave was just in time to see Carmel bidding farewell to her last client of the night. About to close the door, Carmel saw the funny looking little woman standing on the pavement.

'Smiley! how the fuck are you? I've had a right good touch tonight. That prick couldn't get it up so I got fifty for a chat, mind it's about time I had some fucking luck I.....'

Carmel was stopped mid sentence when she saw the expression on Smiley's face.

'What's up! oh fuck me don't say its Rox? I couldn't take it if it was her.'

Smiley nodded, tears streaming down her face. Carmel grabbed her warm coat from the downstairs cupboard and slammed the door.

'Best we get over there and see what the damage is then!'

'Carm I think she's dead.'

Carmel Jones stopped abruptly and grabbed Smiley by her coat lapels.

'Don't fucking say that, just don't say it alright!'

Again Smiley nodded, though this time it was more out of fear for herself, than for concern regarding what had happened to Roxy Baxter. Due to the late hour, there were no cabs on the street and the two women had to run back to Berners Mews. Carmel was soon ahead by a good hundred yards due to Smiley now being exhausted. By the time she entered the flat huffing and puffing, Carmel was on the floor sobbing over Roxy's battered body. Smiley made her way into Roxy's sitting room and nervously picked up the woman's mobile. She knew how to use it but was frightened to death of them, since she'd seen the documentary on radiation and brain tumours'. One look back into the hallway and seeing the heartbreaking sight before her, she switched it on. About to dial the boys in blue, she was stopped by the sound of Carmel shrieking.

'She's alive, Oh fucking hell she's still alive. Smiley call an ambulance. Oh my poor poor baby who did this to you?'.

For a second Roxy opened her eyes and Carmel saw her mouth the word "Lenny" and then she slipped back into unconsciousness.

'I fucking knew it! That bastard, that cruel fucking bastard!'

It was another twenty minutes before the ambulance arrived and Carmel cradled the poor beaten girl in her arms, all the time Smiley Cosgrave looked on but never said a word. While the paramedics were doing all they could for her friend, Carmel was about to phone Tess, when she thought better of it. She decided to wait until they were at the hospital and she knew what was happening and could relay actual facts. The last thing she wanted was to build up Tess's hopes, only to have Roxy go and die on them. Carmel Jones had never been religious in any way shape or form but in the early hours of Monday morning, she prayed as if her very life depended on it.

CHAPTER TWENTY SIX

At the same hospital where only a few days earlier Roxy had been discharged, Carmel was ushered into a waiting room set aside for families. Smiley Cosgrave hadn't joined her, she'd figured that she'd done her duty for one day and had declined the paramedic's offer of a lift to the A & E. Carmel paced the floor as she chain smoked. The nurses had told her time and time again that it wasn't allowed in the building. Finally they had decided to turn a blind eye, when she had fixed the last one to reprimand her with a steely glare. Ladies of the night or at least that was the term the charge nurse had used, were not to be challenged, due to their volatile temperament. Carmel was used to being treated as a second class citizen but these people looked on her as if she were from another planet. Under normal circumstances she would have given them a mouthful but this wasn't normal circumstances. Roxy Baxter was just a few feet away fighting for her life and that was the only thing Carmel could focus on. By six thirty that morning, Carmel had managed to fall asleep only to be woken an hour later by a grim faced surgeon.

'Miss?'

Carmel shot up from the row of chairs she'd made into a makeshift bed and rubbed hard at her eyes with the backs of her hands.

'Jones, Carmel Jones. I'm the closest thing Roxy has to family. How is she?'

Carmel hated not mentioning Tess but she knew that if she did, the doctor would refuse to speak to her.

'Miss Jones your friend is gravely ill. The knife entered at a very unusual angle. It narrowly missed her Iliac artery but did cut into the large intestine. As for nerve damage, there may have been some to the Sacral but as yet we don't know. I'm afraid it's just a case of having to wait and see.'

His word went straight over Carmel's head, what did she know about arteries and intestines.

'Listen fucking smart Alec, just tell me how she is. Is she going to fucking die or what?'

Even at this early hour and after a mammoth round of surgery, her outspoken tone brought a smile to the surgeons face.

'Your friend is very lucky to be alive, very lucky indeed. Apart from her injuries, she's lost a considerable amount of blood and is very weak. The next few hours are crucial but I must warn you that even if she survives, we can't tell what the long term damage will be.'

Carmel nodded, at last she could now understand what was being said to her.

'Don't you worry about that. Roxy Baxter's a fighter and if any fucker can get through this, she can!'

Glancing at her watch she saw that it was almost eight am. Tess would be up now but at the same time Carmel didn't want to leave, for fear that Roxy may take a turn for the worse.

'Can I see her?'

'It wouldn't be wise and in any case she's so heavily sedated that she wouldn't know you were here. Take some time out and come back in a few hours, maybe then we'll have some news.'

Carmel didn't argue, she was dog tired and her brain felt like jelly, so doing as the doctor now advised, she hailed a cab and made her way home. The need for forty winks, a wash and a change of clothes was desperate and she decided that after that she would go and see Tess.

257

They could then go down to the hospital together and show a united front.

Tess Davey had been up with the larks. She was looking forward to seeing Joe and even Agi's banquet of a breakfast wasn't putting her off. By eight thirty she was on her way to work and after last night, she had a spring in her step. The sun was shining and if the heavens had opened or it was blowing a force ten gale, it wouldn't have mattered. Tess Davey had everything in the world she wanted and nothing could dampen her feelings of happiness. It was business as usual at Agar Street nick. Tommy Radcliff was on desk duty and his grin brightened up the room when he saw her enter.

'Tess! good to see you girl.'

'Thanks Tommy, is he in?'

'Here before I was love, don't seem to be able to keep away from the place these days. Lord knows what he'll do when he has all that time on his hands.'

Tess laughed but didn't reply. Instead she ran up the stairs in her eagerness to see her boss. Walking into the office, she wasn't surprised to see that nothing had changed. Joe was asleep surrounded by papers and the place was a mess. She made her way over to the small unit that housed the tea things and proceeded to make them both a drink. Tess had a lot to tell and it was always best done over a cuppa. Quietly she filled the kettle and removed the cups from the cupboard. So intent on not waking him, she nearly jumped out of her skin when he spoke.

'Nice to see you as well D.C. Davey!'

'Sorry Sir, I thought you were asleep.'

'You know what thought did? Now how's that sister of yours?'

The following hour was spent going over everything that

258

had happened since Roxy's hospitalisation. Tess hardly stopped for breath but Joe Reynolds could see that she was enjoying every moment. When she finally relayed the events of the previous evening, he could see that there was a remarkable change in his new prodigy. Where before she'd been quiet and reserved, now she had a new lease of life and it pleased him to see her so happy.

'I'm glad everything's turned out well Tess, I can leave the force on a happy note. What are you going to do now?'

'I don't know Sir; take one day at a time I suppose. One thing I do know is that I can't wait for tomorrow and the day after that. Something I never thought I'd hear myself say.'

While Tess was revealing all and feeling euphoric at what the future could possibly hold, Carmel walked over to Manette Street. Knocking on Agi Goldstein's front door, she could see that Tess didn't rough it like her and Rox. Agi came to the door laughing as she did so, that laughter instantly disappeared when she set eyes on Carmel Jones. Agi had been on the game years earlier and it had been long enough for her to recognise a brass when she saw one. Today she was a respected member of the community but until Mr Seaman had come on the scene, Agi was as loud and up front as the woman standing before her. It wasn't something she liked to be reminded of and her thoughts were relayed in the tone of her voice.

'Yes!'

'Sorry to bother you love but I'm looking for Tess, Tess Davey do you know her?'

'I'm well aware of who Tess is but what she's doing associating with the likes of you, I don't know.'

Carmel took a lot in her life but with what had happened in the last few hours, Agi's words were like a red rag to a

259

bull.

'Now you just hold on a bleeding minute Mrs. I'm looking for Tess pure and simple, I aint disrespected you and I expect the same in return. Now do you know where she fucking is or not?'

Suddenly Agi felt ashamed and it showed.

'I'm sorry, please accept my apology. Tess has already left for work but if you'd like to leave a message, I'll make sure she gets it.'.

Carmel was sarcastic in her reply. She'd just about had enough and this old hag of a woman and she was starting to get right up Carmel's nose.

'Thanks but I'd rather deliver it in person, at least I'll know that she'll get it.'

Without giving Agi a chance to reply, Carmel walked off in the direction of Charing Cross road. When Tess had given her card to Carmel, it had contained the Agar Street nick address and hailing a cab she told the driver where to go. He smirked and couldn't resist having a pop at his fare.

'I know the likes of you are down the nick more often than not but I didn't think I'd see the day when a brass would ask to be taken to one.'

Carmel didn't know if she'd woken up on another planet but something was wrong. Every conversation she seemed to have today turned nasty towards her, well she wasn't having it.

'Do you want this fucking job or what? because if you don't there's plenty out there who do!'

'Alright love, keep your knickers on.'

Sensitive to his comment, Carmel turned in a second and flew down the man's throat.

'Don't take the piss.'

'Calm down, I was only trying to have a laugh, no

offence meant.'

The cabbie was a typical 'Sheenie' and if his hands hadn't have been on the wheel Carmel knew he would have been rubbing them together as he spoke in that whiny voice. She hated the Yid's more than any others. They always wanted something for nothing and tried to haggle on the price of a shag even if your rates were rock bottom.

'Just drive will you, I aint in the fucking mood for small talk.'

The driver did as he was asked and ten minutes later the black cab pulled up outside Agar Street station. When Carmel entered the reception, she knew she was in for a tough time when told that Tess and Joe had left a few minutes earlier. The desk sergeant had looked down his nose at her and he wasn't too pleased when she said she'd wait. Tommy Radcliff couldn't stand the Toms. The cells were full of them most nights and the mess they left was unbelievable. He tried hard to discourage Carmel from staying but nothing he said made a blind bit of difference. In the end he gave up trying and pretended that she wasn't even there. The station clock showed midday as Tess and Joe Reynolds entered the reception area and as soon as Carmel saw them, she stood up and rushed over. Just as they were about to disappear behind the security door she called out.

'Oh Tess love, I've been waiting here ages, I tried your mobile but it was switched off.'

'Carmel! Sorry about that it's playing up; I couldn't get through to Roxy this morning.'

The mention of her sisters' name brought a feeling of foreboding over Tess and she grabbed hold of Carmel's shoulders.

'What's happened?'

'He's done it again, only this time it's much fucking

261

worse. Tess I don't know if our girl is going to pull through this time.'

Joe had stood by and listened to all that Carmel Jones had to say. When she'd finished, he walked over to the main doors and held them open.

'Come on you two, let's get down there then.'

Back at the hospital, Roxy had been moved to the intensive care unit. She was starting to come round from the aesthetic and the doctor was waiting to have a word with her next of kin. As the unlikely trio entered the unit, they were met by Doctor Rahj Zeta.

'Miss Jones I've been waiting to.'

Tess cut the man off in mid sentence.

'I'm Tess Davey, Roxy's sister, how is she?'

'As I said to your friend earlier, we won't know the extent of the damage for several hours if not days. She's begun to regain consciousness and her vital signs are good. I'm afraid that's as much as we dare hope for at the moment.'

'Can I see her?'

'For a few minutes but she may not be aware that you are even here.'

'That doesn't matter; I just need to see her.'

Doctor Zeta beckoned to a small ward containing five or six beds. Carmel began to follow but was stopped when she felt Joe's hand on her arm.

'Let her have a few minutes Carm.'

Carmel Jones nodded her head and took a seat on the row of chairs that had been provided for grieving relatives. Tess walked up to the bed and let out a gasp when she saw the state of Roxy's face.

'Don't be alarmed Miss Davey, the surgeon did an excellent job with the stitches. Of course there will be scaring but at the minute our main priority is keeping her alive.'

262

Tess had to take a second to comprehend what the man was saying.

'Do you mean she really might not live? I thought Carmel was over dramatising like she does with everything else.'

'It's very early days. We've done all we can, now it's down to how much fight your sister has.'

Tess stroked Roxy's hair and smiled.

'All her life my sister has had to fight harder than you could ever imagine. If her survival is down to her will to live, then she'll be fine, believe me she'll be fine.'

Gently Tess kissed Roxy before leaving the room.

Outside Carmel and Joe waited apprehensively. When Tess emerged, they simultaneously stepped forward.

'How is she?'

'She's holding her own, for the moment at least.'

The sentence was directed at both but Tess's next was for Carmel alone.

'Are you sure about who did this.'

'According to Smiley, she heard the screaming then watched him leave the flat.'

'And would she be a willing to make a statement?'

Carmel lets out a huge exhale of breath and puffed out her cheeks as she did so.

'It don't make much difference. Tess you know Roxy wont press charges and if you go ahead anyway, then she'd just say it wasn't Lenny. You're flogging a dead horse love believe me.'

'Joe I need some air, come with me.'

Carmel watched as they walked away, she knew when she wasn't wanted and anyway she needed to see Roxy.

Outside in the cool afternoon air, Tess sobbed like never before. She cried for Roxy, for all that could have been and she cried with pure rage at what that low life was being allowed to get away with. Joe Reynolds didn't comfort her or offer any words of wisdom. Instead he let her get it out of her system, before he spoke.

'So, what now?'

Tess wiped her nose on the cuff of her coat before looking up into his face.

'What now?'

'As I see it you have two choices. You either wait until Layton finishes off the job or you put a stop to it once and for all.'

'You heard Carmel, Roxy would never press charges.'

'I'm not talking about charges and prison here Tess. I'm talking about removing the problem for good, either that or the next funeral you'll be going to will be your sisters.'

Tess tried to take in what was being said to her but every word of it went against the grain. The only trouble was she knew that he was right. She struggled to justify to herself the option he was suggesting. It was something she'd been against, had fought against for the whole of her life. Now when faced with a black or white situation, she had to make a very big decision. Wait for some evil bastard to take away her flesh and blood and as far as she knew the only living relative she had, or get in there first and eradicate the problem.

'Ok what do you suggest?'

'You don't need to know that but I do have one question for you and the outcome will depend totally on your answer. How far are you prepared to go?'

Tess ran through the various scenarios in her head. She thought of the injustice, being caught and what that would entail but finally she thought of Roxy. The mental image she had of her sister, lying helpless in that hospital bed with her beautiful face scared forever was enough to make up her mind.

'Whatever it takes!'

'Are you really sure?'

Tess didn't speak but moved her head up and down in acknowledgment.

'That's all I wanted to know. I will deal with this Tess I promise but for now let's get back inside and see if there's any news'.

As they walked along Tess's appeared to be slumped over and Joe could see that she'd well and truly had the stuffing knocked out of her. With his arm around her shoulders he tenderly squeezed her and when she looked into his face, he gave her a knowing wink.

CHAPTER TWENTY SEVEN

Tess and Carmel spent the rest of that day and the
ensuing night at Roxy's bedside. It was a futile exercise,
Roxy Baxter was so heavily sedated that she wouldn't
have know if the sky had come crashing down on her. At
six am the next morning they were woken by the senior
intensive care nurse, who advised them both to go home
and get some rest.

'You'll gain nothing by staying here. Experience has
shown us, that the families of patients, who stay around
when their relative is unconscious, are generally fit for
nothing when the patient finally comes round.'

Tess could see the nurses' logic but she wanted to be
there if Roxy woke up.

'I couldn't bare it if she came to and we weren't here
nurse.'

The nurse smiled and it was a true caring smile. She'd
been on the Intensive unit for over ten years but she still
became personally involved with each and every patient
in her care. It was something she'd been advised not to
do but all the same, something she couldn't stop, no
matter how hard she tried.

'Miss Davey, I promise as soon as your sister shows
signs of waking, you will be the first person I will call. I
have your home, work and mobile numbers, not to
mention those of Miss Jones.'

Carmel preened at being called Miss. She liked this
nurse and could tell by her manner that she was a caring
sort. They were rare attributes in today's society,
especially when it came to dealing with Brass's. This
nurse wasn't bothered what you were or what you did for
a living, the only thing she did bother about was her care

for Roxy. In Carmel's estimation that was all that mattered.

'Tess I think the lady's right, we won't do right by Rox if we're knackered when she opens up her mince pies. Let's go home and come back later, what you say?' Tess stood up and wearily pulled on her coat. Picking up her bag, she smoothed down Roxy's hair and tenderly kissed her beside the dressing that covered her poor scared face. The two shared a taxi home and after dropping Tess at Manette Street, Carmel proceeded home to Old Compton. Entering her flat was like waking up from a long sleep. The stagnant smell of sex hit her from all sides and she slumped down on the dirty sofa and cried. For Carmel Jones life was one long ride of sex, drink and having a good time. Over the years she'd made friends and some of them were good friends. The trouble was, no one had touched her as much as Roxy Baxter. In the cold light of day, sitting in this rancid place she had no option but to call home, she didn't know how she would manage if the girl wasn't here anymore. Carmel now realised just how low her life had sunk and the only sweet thing in it, was her lovely Rox. If her girl didn't survive this latest episode then Carmel didn't think she could go on in life. Joe Reynolds had called in sick. He had one week left on the force and had hoped it would be a quiet one. That had all changed last night and he knew that he was going to help out Tess Davey, if it was the last thing he did. Since the day he'd first joined the force, justice was the only thing that had mattered. Naively Joe had thought he could change the world, somehow make it a better place but that ideal had disappeared within a few months of leaving rookie school. The world was a bad place, full of bad people who never seemed to get their

267

comeuppance. Sometimes you had to take matters into your own hands and regardless of what all the lecturers and physiologists told you, sometimes the end did justify the means.

Joe Reynolds took no pleasure whatsoever in what he was about to do but after he weighed up all the alternatives, knew there was no other way. Heading west on the Marylebone road, Joe's destination was only a few miles away but with traffic as it was in the smoke, his short journey would take nearly an hour. The delay gave him time to think, time to at least try and understand why he was about to do what he was. All the bad things from the last few years flashed before his eyes and ended with the image of Tracey Woods. Suddenly it all became clear, oh he liked Tess, knew she was a good girl but it went deeper than that, much deeper. Joe realised that he didn't want anyone to be scared like he'd been and if he could make a difference, then he would. He couldn't do anything about Tracey Woods but he could stop another human being suffering as he had and if a small amount of self healing came into the equation, then so what. Accepting that it could have been anyone and he would have done the same, he was glad it had turned out to be for someone as nice as Tess. The twin towers of Wormwood Scrubs were smaller and less foreboding than they appeared on the television. If it hadn't of been for the prison, then the street was like any other in the smoke but it didn't make Joe feel any happier about the visit. Parking in the visitor's car park, he lit up a cigarette and again went over everything in his mind. There would be no going back from what he was about to do. Tracey Woods once more came into his thoughts and the fear that one man, could instil on another scared him. Joe didn't want anyone else to live as he had and after

268

nipping out his cigarette and locking the car door, proceeded towards the reception building. It didn't matter that he was in the police force; he had to take his turn in the strict regime that was required at visiting time. A small makeshift hut that housed a canteen had been set aside for visitors and resembled something the local scout group would use. The canteen was full of brasses and wives, all too scarred not to visit. Women with snotty nosed kids, who knew this was all the future they had to look forward to. Prostitutes aware that if they didn't do their duty and visit every two weeks, would have no future at all, at least not once their pimps were free. When called, Joe made his way over to the inner compound. The visiting process was something he had become used to over the years when he came to interview prisoners. That said he still got a shiver down his spine when he walked through the gate. Today was heightened by the fact that he knew a man's life hung in the balance. Stanley Pritchard had been on the police force for over thirty years and Joe had known him for the last two. Joining up at the age of twenty, he'd done more than the obligatory twenty years and after retiring was now seeing his timeout as a prison warden. As soon as he set eyes on Joe, it was like old times and he was quick to latch onto this particular visitor.

'Hi there mate, how you doing?'

Joe was at least grateful for a familiar face, although it was something he would later come to regret.

'Hello Stan!' nice to see you mate. I didn't know you was doing this for a living, thought you'd gone to live in the country?'

'I wish Joe, no I'm destined to take care of the criminal fraternity for the rest of my days, or at least that's what the missus says at any rate. What brings you to this neck

269

of the woods?'

'Need to interview a suspect Stan, though I aint looking forward to it I can tell you. His names Maxi Trueman, ring any bells?'

'Does it? Starting to become a main man on the wing already the black bastard.'

Joe didn't like Stags manner. Maxi was supposed to be in the man's care but his attitude didn't seem very caring as far as he could see. Trying to lighten the mood, Joe changed the subject.

'Anyway what made you choose this for a living?'

All at once Stanley Pritchard became serious.

'It's not a vocation anymore; it's just a fucking job. Do you know Joe that every day it's like we're under fucking siege? Staff shortages mate, I tell you it's just a matter of time.'

'What do you mean?'

'Before this whole place, no I take that back, before the whole system fucking blows. They're all fucking paranoid, not the staff, I mean the inmates. They're a fucking danger to themselves and us. It's all prisoner on fucking prisoner violence but then again what do I care. I mean at least I go home to the missus every night. Mind you I'd probably be better off here, know what I mean?'

The men talked as they walked through the wings to a small room which was set aside within the heart of the prison. Joe was grateful at least, that he didn't have to sit in the muggy overcrowded visiting room with all the others. Official business called for special privileges and as far as anyone knew, this visit was strictly on an official basis. All the while they walked; Stanley Pritchard opened and closed doors with the enormous set of keys that were chained to his waist.

'They deal between wings you know. I tell you they're

270

onto a fucking good thing and it's all because of staff shortages. There aint nothing,' we can do about it. We're hanging on by our fucking finger nails here Joe! I mean would you fucking work here? The bastards have mobile phones to carry out business, can you believe that. I tell you these bastards have it better than we do.'

'Why do you stick it Stan, I mean it can't be for the money.'

'It's in my blood Joe. I was having a conversation with Eric from C wing in the mess just the other night. He asked me the same question and the only explanation I could come up with was 'it's in my blood'. Fucking hooch is another big problem you know. It's all a fucking nightmare here mate, sorry to go on but sometimes it gets to you, know what I mean?'

Joe wasn't given time to reply and he could instantly see that this man, this exemplary officer, had become as institutionalised as the men he was now guarding.

'Well! I suppose it keeps them quiet and at least it makes it easier on us.'

Joe had forgotten where the conversation was at and just nodded in agreement to anything the man said.

'It's all about us I suppose, they use us, and we use them.'

Joe Reynolds was having difficulty in believing what he was hearing. An ex member of the force and he'd become bigoted and racist in his views. The sad thing was, Stanley Pritchard didn't even realise it. It only confirmed to Joe, that he'd made the right decision regarding his resignation.

'I thought the inspectorate advised treating the inmates with respect?'

'Fuck that for a laugh mate! It's each for his own in this place.'

Stanley continued to run on and on for the entire time it took for Joe to reach his interviewee.

'The bastards who commit suicide are the worst. At least you're man aint a worry on that score. Most of the cunts that do it, don't give a fuck about anyone and then guess what, it's us who get the blame. Pity their mothers didn't drown them at birth if you ask me.'

Joe wanted to say that he hadn't asked but decided against voicing his opinion.

'Anyway, as far as I'm concerned, if these cunts want to hang themselves, let them go ahead. Are you going to the bridge on Saturday?'

Joe couldn't believe what he was hearing. Stan was talking about someone killing themselves, like you'd talk about the weather or the football. He could now see that the problem was systematic and it only refuelled his belief in what he was about to do. If the prison service acted like this, then what chance did justice have. The interview room was tiny but at least it was clean. Maxi Trueman had already been seated at the table when Joe Reynolds entered the room.

The two men, stared at each other for several seconds before either spoke and it was Joe who broke the silence first.

'So how are they treating you Maxi?'

Maxi Truman's response was to say nothing but he gave Joe a look of contempt that spoke volumes.

'I know you must think it fucking strange that I've turned up like this but I felt you had a right to know who grassed you'.

Joe's words were like music to Maxi's ears. In the days that he'd been incarcerated, he'd had only one thing on his mind, to find out who was responsible for sending him to this hell hole. Maxi wasn't stupid, he knew that he

272

was in for a long stretch. That stretch would be a little easier to handle if he was happy in the knowledge that whoever did this, wouldn't ever get the chance to do it again. Sitting back in his chair and with his hands clasping the back of his head, Maxi tried not to appear overly interested. He knew how to play the game and it was obvious this filth wanted something in return.

'Why'd you think I should care? Not as if I'm going to see the light of day for a few years now is it?'

For Maxi to show any interest at all, told Joe that he had the man hook line and sinker. With any luck, he'd be out of this shit hole of a place in the next few minutes.

'Maxi as far as I'm concerned you can rot in here with the rest of society's wanker's. I only have a few days left on the force and I thought I'd do you a good turn. 'Course if you aint bothered then that's fine, I might as well get out of here?'

'I didn't fucking say that copper.'

'Good! So let's carry on shall we? It's a fact that Lenny Layton is an even bigger scum bag than you. Now I wouldn't want any young rookie coming up behind me, having to deal with the likes of him. I've also become a firm believer that the law is an ass and this is my way of leaving the world in a bit better state.'

'What makes you think I'll do anything?'

Joe laughed smugly and stood up from his seat. Pushing the chair neatly under the table, he spoke as he turned towards the door.

'Because Maxi, your sorts always do. I don't know if it's a cultural thing or only that it just boils down to pride. Either way, I know your conscience wouldn't allow Lenny Layton to go unpunished.'

'Tell me copper, is this a personal thing?'

'Makes no difference if it is.'

273

Maxi scratched the back of his head and laughed at the same time.

'Maybe not to you but how do I know you don't just want a fucking free hit?'

'You don't Maxi but then why would I go to all this trouble. There's plenty out there who'd do the job and it would cost me far less aggro than having to come to this shit hole of a place.'

With that Joe walked out of the room and as quickly away from the prison as he could. He didn't bother saying goodbye to Stanley Pritchard. Joe didn't know if he'd have been able to look the man squarely in the eye for a start. Suddenly he felt dirty like soiled goods and he needed to get out in the fresh air. Driving back along the West way, Joe switched the radio to the classical channel and made himself as comfortable as possible. He was in no doubt that his mission had been successful, all he had to do now was to sit back and wait for the shit to hit the fan. Maxi Trueman didn't go back to his cell, he spent the next half hour out in the recreation area, mulling over what Joe had told him. Something didn't quite add up but he couldn't put his finger on it. At the same time, he couldn't let the information go and he definitely couldn't let Lenny get away with grassing. He'd never liked the slimy little grease ball and if it turned out he was just someone Joe Reynolds wanted rid of, then it wouldn't do Maxi's Street cred any harm either. Removing a phone card from his back pocket, Maxi Trueman dialled the number. The call was connected but no one spoke on the other end, it was Maxi who did all the talking.

'It's me, I need a favour.'

CHAPTER TWENTY EIGHT

Tess was on tender hooks the whole time she was at her digs. Carmel was due to collect her by cab in a couple of hours that was unless they received a call from the hospital any earlier. Agi had run her a bath and made a plate of sandwiches but other than that she had said nothing. As far as Agi was concerned, it was blatant that Tess was involved in something that was causing her a great deal of pain. She'd taken an instant dislike to the woman who'd come round looking for her lodger the other day but hadn't dare broach the subject with Tess either. As much as she liked Tess Agi hoped and prayed that whatever she was involved in it wasn't something that was going to bring trouble to Agi Goldstein's door. Thirty minutes before Carmel Jones was due to arrive; Tess Davey's mobile sprang into life. With her heart in her mouth, she answered the call.

'Hello?'

'Hi Tess! It's nurse Crawford from the Intensive care unit. Don't panic it's nothing to be worried about, quite the opposite in fact. I'm just ringing to tell you that your sister has woken and is asking for you.'

Tess didn't reply and snapping the phone shut, ran out of the house and up to Charing Cross road, where she hailed a taxi. Carmel was just about to close her flat door when the phone began to ring. For a second she dithered as to whether to answer but after deciding that it could be important, went back inside. Tess was phoning from inside the cab and her signal wasn't great. For a minute Carmel thought she had a pervert on the line but then she at last recognised Tess's voice.

'Carm it's me! The hospital's just called to say Roxy's

woke up. I'm on my way round now, sorry I couldn't wait but I have to get there and like yesterday!'

'Of course you do! Give her a kiss from me and tell her I'll be over as soon as I can.'

Tess hung up again and sat back in her seat for the remainder of the journey. Carmel reasoned that she might as well walk over to the Middlesex. It was a nice day and besides those two needed a little time on their own. Added to the fact that a cab fare saved, was a good few vodkas later on, she was happy to walk.

Lenny Layton had made his way to Marylebone after the attack but the old mate who owed him a favour, wasn't so keen to see him. Lenny had to almost force his way inside the small bedsit that his pal Jimmy Barnet, now shared with his overweight Peroxide blonde girlfriend. Lenny's personal hygiene was nothing to write home about at the best of times but even his nose was offended at the rancid stink omitting itself from inside. Jimmy's bird was called Geraldine and he was totally bowled over with her, though Lenny couldn't for the life of him see why. Her fat belly and legs were so gross; they filled the armchair that she sat in. Her white hair was greasy and lank and she had an unwashed smell about her, which made Lenny feel physically sick.

'So long time no see Len, what can I do you for?'

'I need a place to crash for a few days Jimmy and I figured that as you owe me, you were a safe bet.'

Jimmy walked behind the armchair and stood resting his hands on Geraldine's shoulders. She nestled her plump cheek against his fingers in an affectionate gesture and Lenny rolled his eyes upwards at the disgusting sight.

'I'd love to help you out Len but now that my Duchess has moved in, well you can see their aint a lot of room.'

Lenny Layton curled his lip into a snarl and stepped a

pace forward. Like greased lightning big Geraldine was up and out of the chair, ready to fight to the death to protect her man. Lenny wasn't afraid of any woman but he wasn't about to pick a fight with one the size of Everest.

'Jimmy you're a fucking cunt.'

Geraldine moved forward and Lenny retreated towards the door.

'Just don't come running my way, when you're in trouble again. I hope that ugly fat bitch suffocates you the next time you're on the fucking job.'

Quickly and before any repercussions, Lenny ran out of the flat. He slept rough that night and cursed Roxy to hell and back, for every minute of it. The following morning he sat in a small café, being eyed suspiciously buy its owners. His clothes were dishevelled and his normally combed back greasy hair, hung down limply into his eyes. Running over all of his options, he realised they were limited. In fact options wasn't really the right turn of phrase, Lenny didn't have any. He had no one to turn to and he couldn't go back to the flat for fear of the police. Instead he made his way to Soho Square in the hope of scoring a freebie from Denzel Howard. He was down to a twenty and didn't want to waste it on heroin, not if he could help it. Denzel was nowhere to be seen and after hanging around for a few minutes, Lenny walked towards the squares main gates. He was due to collect his prescription for methadone and although he usually sold it on in favour of the real thing, if it was all that was on offer, then it would have to do. The chemist was situated on Wardour Street and Lenny was well known. He'd been a regular since the last time he was released from a stretch at her majesties. Lionel Gates was a small man in stature but well respected in the

277

community, if only by the majority of drug addicts that resided there. Inheriting the business, he had trained and qualified as a pharmacist but had little interest in the world of pharmaceuticals. The shop was busy and when Lionel saw Lenny approach the counter, muttered under his breath 'Not today'. Lenny always created a scene. He always refused to drink his measured dose on the premises and Lionel handed over the small bottle, rather than have confrontation in front of a packed shop. Outside Lenny caressed the bottle as he placed it inside his jacket. He could have taken the liquid inside but he knew of something, that when added to the methadone, would blow his mind. The only side effect was a massive headache afterwards but he reasoned it was well worth it for such a high. Heading back to the square, he stopped at the first wino he came to. Seeing that the old boy was downing Meth's, he swiftly moved on. It wasn't long before Lenny found what he was looking for. Jock Mackenzie nestled in the porch of Soho Squares central structure. Years earlier the quaint building had housed the green keeper's tools but today was locked and empty. Jock was a well known local figure and liked by most. Having come down from Glasgow in the seventies in search of work, he'd soon slipped into old habits and spent his days smashed out of his skull on whatever he could lay his hands on, alcohol wise. Lenny knew Jock by a nod of the head basis only but even that didn't stop him being unkind to the old man. Spying the four pack of special brew that Jock had recently acquired, he went in all guns blazing. Stooping down, he snatched up the pack and wrenched one of the cans from its ring binder. When Jock stood up swaying and began to voice his anger in a more than colourful manner, Lenny kicked the man squarely in the groin. Jock fell onto the floor and

groaned out in pain. Clutching his manhood as if it was about to be stolen and rolling about, he screamed and cursed at his attacker. Throwing down the remaining pack of beers and rendering them useless to the man for at least a couple of hours, Lenny went on his way. Jock continued to scream out obscenities but a scene like this was an everyday occurrence in Soho and no one took any notice. A small alleyway just off Sutton Row was the perfect place to get out of your brains and Lenny had used it on more than one occasion. Resting his back against the door of one of the now defunct offices, he sat down and poured his methadone into the can that he'd just stolen. The buzz took a little longer than his usual fix but within fifteen minutes, Lenny Layton had nothing on his mind but pure intoxicating bliss. He was oblivious to the stale urine that was now penetrating his trousers from the hard concrete. Several pools of vomit from last night's drug users, flanked him on either side and when his hand fell loosely down and landed in a regurgitated curry, he didn't pull away. Lenny was so out of it, that the disgusting smell from the disturbed pile made no connection with his nostrils. Drayton Livingston had as usual, been holding court in the back room of his coffee house. When the phone rang he picked up the receiver but as was Drayton's way, he didn't speak. When he heard Maxi's voice on the other end he smiled. The two went back a long way and it was good to know that his friend was well. He listened intently to what he was being told and apart from a 'No worry's!' comment at the end of this one way conversation, nothing else was said. Beckoning to Donny Fletcher, one of the many young men that filled the place these days, the two walked outside and got into Drayton's black Discovery.
Donny Fletcher felt he was king of the walk after the

main man had told him to drive. With a gold cross bigger than most churches housed hanging from his neck and sparkling over the top bling on each finger Donny thought to himself that he had at last made it. Drayton on the other hand couldn't give two hoots about the stupid little idiot sitting beside him. It was easier to look for Layton when he didn't have to drive and Donny had been the first face to come into view. The boy hero worshiped Drayton to such a degree, that it didn't hurt to build up his loyalty. He reasoned that at least this way if it came to the crunch, Donny would defend him to the hilt, stupid little fool that he was. After driving around Soho for over an hour, Drayton realised it was like looking for a needle in a haystack. Maxi had given him an address but that had proved a dead end. About to give up for the night, he spotted Denzel Howard exiting the square. Opening his window Drayton called out. Denzel Howard was more frightened of this man, than he was of Maxi Trueman and that was saying something. He glanced from left to right but Denzel knew there really wasn't anywhere to hide. The likes of Livingston didn't give up and in the end would hunt you down like a wild animal, no matter how long it took. Hoping that whatever he'd done wasn't too bad, the small time dealer made his way over to the four by four.

'Hello Mr Livingston, don't normally see you in this neck of the woods?'

Drayton was tired and in no mood for niceties, he didn't bother being friendly to Denzel and came straight to the point.

'Am in a reaal bad mood mang. Ting is a need ta fand a mang call Lenny Layton, would ya be able ta help ol Drayton owt?'

Denzel was no grass but he wasn't a fool either. If this

280

nutcase even caught the first whiff of a lie, then he'd be a dead man walking. Deciding that in this instance, honesty was the best policy, he revealed all he knew. 'I saw him disappear down Sutton Row about an hour ago. A lot of them use the place because it's quiet but whether he's still there? Who knows!'

Drayton didn't bother to say thanks and Donny sped off seconds later, leaving a scared but relieved Denzel shaking in his boots. Lenny was beginning to come round from his stupor. Smacking old Jock had been well worth it and he just needed somewhere to crash for the night and he'd be sorted. Staggering to his feet, Lenny began to wobble along the alleyway towards the top end of Sutton Row. He was now aware that his hand felt sticky and wiped it haphazardly on his trouser leg. This time the rancid smell infiltrated his every sense and he began to gag. Bent over double, Lenny retched hard but it was a dry retch and nothing came up. Glancing up and trying hard to focus at the same time, Lenny could make out a hazy figure coming down the alley.

'Who's there?'

The figure didn't reply and Lenny placed his offending palm onto the wall to steady himself. Everything seemed blurred and in slow motion as he desperately tried to gain coordination and focus. Seconds later his full vision had returned and he recognised the man as Drayton Livingston. He was also aware, that this man never went out of his way or manor come to that, for anything trivial. Lenny gritted his teeth; if he was lucky then he'd survive this with only a bad beating. If not, well he didn't even want to think about that. Drayton Livingston was a tall thick set man and even though Lenny wasn't exactly small, this man appeared to tower over him. Lenny waited for the standard lecture before receiving his punishment, but none came. About to speak, he was instantly silenced when Drayton pulled out a light weight steel baseball bat that he had hidden behind his back. With the speed and power of such a large man, crazed with desire to inflict pain on his unsuspecting victim, the first blow made contact. It came at a cutting angle across Lenny's face and instantly the cheek and skin split wide open. The cracking sound of bone could be heard by both and it was a sound Drayton took enjoyment from. A shower of blood shot out and only stopped when it made contact with the nearby wall. Lenny screamed out just as any victim would.

'Please! Please don't hurt me. Please don't hurt me anymore!'

That initial blow had sunk Lenny to his knees and his face was already bludgeoned beyond recognition. The second came from the opposite direction and this time he fell flat to the ground. Lenny realised this was serious when the usual body blows to the arms and legs were ignored. Drayton was aiming for the head only and Lenny wondered just how much he would be able to take. The third and fourth strikes came via a downward action and Lenny screamed out as his nose and mouth vertically split wide open. Drayton laughed out loud at the sight. His victim resembled something from a freak show and the way his mouth now hung, made him look like he had four lips.

'Na ma talking to da filth fa you ma mang!'

Drayton Livingston could feel the first stirrings of an erection and it was a feeling he liked. Violence always had that effect on him and the more vicious the attack, the better the orgasm. This one was going to be good, he could tell. Drayton loomed over Lenny Layton, who was still trying to protect his head with his arms. Even Lenny realised his actions were futile, he wasn't going to get out of this one alive and he just might as well get it over with. Placing his arms by his side, ready to take his execution, he stared up defiantly into Drayton Livingston's face. The next blow was the last Lenny felt but not the last to be administered, by any way shape or form. Drayton continued his assault until the walls and floor were sprayed with brains and bone. Finally when he realised that all life had left Lenny's body and he had reached his own sexual peak, he removed a razor sharp flick knife from his inside coat pocket. Holding Lenny's mouth open, Drayton sliced quickly across and pulled out the man's tongue. It was a practice Drayton enjoyed, was well known for in fact and he kept a supply of plastic bags in his breast coat pocket, for whenever this situation arose. Placing the now silent tongue inside the bag, Drayton returned the small plastic container and knife into his coat. Just for good luck, he tapped his top pocket flap twice and strode off back to the discovery. Donny Fletchers eyes were as wide as saucers when he saw Drayton approach. His new found boss was covered from head to foot in blood and other sticky substances that had come from somewhere, Donny couldn't begin to imagine. Silently he waited for Drayton to replace the bat inside the boot and get into the vehicle. Knowing better than to ask questions, Donny drove cautiously back to Camberwell and the coffee shop. Drayton didn't enter into conversation with his driver but he wore a weird grin on his face that only he could reveal the reason for. He was due a visit to Maxi in the next few days and he had a little gift for his friend, which was sure to bring a smile.

CHAPTER TWENTY NINE

At around five pm that night, Joe Reynolds received the call he'd been waiting for. It had been a day of doing nothing. He couldn't eat, couldn't sleep, in fact he couldn't do anything and all because he was starting to feel guilty. True Lenny Layton was a leech, clinging to life on the back of modern society. This leech needed to be burned and Joe tried to reason that being no use to man or beast, he'd done the right thing. Trouble was his conscience was also asking, what gave him the right to play god? Joe Reynolds was starting to doubt his actions, something he hadn't done before and it was a feeling he didn't like. When the phone burst into life, he was sitting on the sofa in darkness. The curtains were closed, even though it wasn't yet nightfall and the shrill ring made him jump out of his skin.

'Yeah?'

'Joe! It's Annette. There's been a brutal murder on our patch.'

'Annie I phoned in sick'.

'I know you did and I wouldn't have bothered you, except the deceased prints have come up as those of Lenny Layton. The system shows that you brought him in within the last couple of weeks. Joe you know the protocol!'

'Give me an hour and I'll be at the nick, Ok?'

'See you then.'

Joe wasn't exactly in a state of panic but he knew things could be tricky if he didn't play his cards right.

Showering, he dressed quickly and within thirty minutes he'd arrived at Agar Street police station.

Annette Windsor stood looking out of her first floor

window. She knew there was more to this and she paced up and down waiting for Joe to come in and explain things. As usual, Tommy Radcliff was on desk duty but his normal jolly greeting wasn't there. The place was abuzz with officers; all called in from time owed or holidays, which didn't make for good spirits. A policeman's private time was his own and they really didn't appreciate it being interrupted, for anything! Nodding to Tommy but offering no words of a greeting, Joe made his way upstairs. He'd begun to perspire and before entering his boss's office, removed a handkerchief and wiped his brow. As was the norm for Joe, he didn't knock and walked straight in. Annette Windsor was glued to the spot in front of the window. She had her back to him and didn't attempt to turn around when he entered.

'I hope you haven't got any involvement in this Joe?'

'Involvement, why would I have?'

'You pulled him in and don't try to tell me it wasn't anything to do with Tess, because I know damn well it was.'

Walking over to where she stood, Joe desperately tried to embrace her but Annette shrugged off his advances.

'I wasn't about to say anything of the sort. Yes, I do admit that we hauled him in for a few questions but that was all. Why all the fuss anyway, Layton was the scum of the earth and not worth worrying over.'

His last sentence was the one that tipped her over the edge. Annette Windsor spun round in a flash and her words came out with more spite and venom than he'd ever seen before.

'Not worth fucking worrying over! The poor bastard had his brains splattered half way down an alley off Sutton Row. Not to mention the fact that whoever did this, cut

285

out his tongue as a trophy. You have the gall to stand there and tell me he wasn't worth worrying about. I'll tell you one thing Joe! come the day that I stop worrying, then you might as well put a bullet in my brain.'

Joe turned and walked back across the room, with his back to her, she wasn't able to see his expression. He was trying to buy time but was fast running out of explanations.

'Annie you don't think I could be involved in this, well do you?'

She didn't answer and he knew that he was in deep shit. There was no proof, at least he hoped there wasn't and he only thanked god that his last few days on the force were nearing to a close.

'Where's Tess Davey?'

'At the hospital with her sister I suppose, why?'

'Because, I want to speak to her. I'll give you one hour to get her back here, after that a squad car will call round to the hospital. For your sake and mine Joe, don't let me down.'

Without another word, Joe Reynolds was out of his boss's office and driving towards the Middlesex hospital in record time.

Roxy Baxter's face was a picture when she saw her sister enter the intensive care unit. Roxy had more tubes coming out of her than a science lab but still she managed a smile. Tess ran over to the bed wanting to hug her sister so badly but not knowing where was safe to touch and where wasn't.

'Oh Roxy! Whatever am I going to do with you?'

'Hu ma.'

'What? What do you want?'

'Hu ma.'

'Oh hug me! Sorry darling I couldn't make out what you

286

were trying to say.'

After just a few words, Roxy was exhausted and Tess too afraid to embrace her. Sitting down gently on the side of the bed she held her sisters hand. Minutes later and the door to the unit swung open and bashed heavily against the wall. Carmel never did make a quiet entrance and today was no exception. She wore a smile that stretched from ear to ear and Tess couldn't stop herself from giggling at her first line of greeting.

'My fucking feet are killing me. I didn't realise what a bastard of a walk it was, anyway babe how are you doing?'

Roxy formed her thumb and index finger into the ok sign but didn't attempt any conversation. Right now she was just glad to be alive and be in the company of two wonderful women. As Carmel tottered towards the bed, Tess glanced down at her shoes and saw that she was sporting four and half inch high stilettos.

'Whatever are you wearing those for? No wonder your feet hurt, surely you possess a pair of flatties?'

Flopping down on the bottom of the bed, Carmel looked almost as needy as Roxy Baxter.

'My dear Tess, those words are blasphemous to a working girl. No respectable brass would be seen dead without her makeup and heels. No pain no gain or so the saying goes, though what made me think I had a fucking chance of pulling on me way over here, god only knows.'

Tess burst out laughing but was instantly stopped when she saw Joe Reynolds standing at the door.

'D.C. Davey I need a word.'

Walking over to the door she stopped and waited for whatever it was he had to say.

'Not here, outside.'

Turning back so that she could see Roxy and Carmel, she

287

mouthed the words 'back in five minutes', then left the room. Roxy and Carmel stared at each other and Carmel shrugged her shoulders as if to say 'wonder what's going on there then?' Outside on the main steps, Joe took out a cigarette. As he lit it, Tess could see that his hands were shaking.

'What's wrong?'

Tess expected Joe to maybe beat around the bush a little as bosses tend to do but instead his next sentence shook her to the core.

'Layton's dead and the Chief somehow thinks I may be involved.'

'You're not are you?'

Joe shot her a piercing glance and she knew the answer to her question. About to question him further, Tess was flabbergasted at what he said next.

'It's what you wanted isn't it?'

'I can't believe you've just said that. Of course I wanted him stopped from hurting Roxy again, but dead, I never asked for that Joe.'

With smoke coming out of his nostrils, Joe now stood directly in front of her.

'And how do you think that was going to be accomplished? A slap on the wrists from us maybe?'

'There's no need to be like that. I asked for your help but this, well it's just plain crazy. Whatever did you do?'

'Firstly you said "whatever it takes" and it took this, or are you too naive to see that?'

Tess began to tremble. She was caught up in something that she didn't want and didn't know how to get out of.

'And to answer your next question, no I didn't kill him.'

'So why does the chief think you're involved?'

'It's laughable really. She knows we brought him in and that it was something to do with you, I didn't deny that.

Said we just asked him about your sister but didn't get anywhere. Anyway she wants to speak to you straight away and I mean like now!'

'Ok! I'll come but you didn't answer me when I asked you what you'd done.'

Joe walked in the direction of his car and Tess ran along beside, desperate to hear what he was going to say and hoping all the while that he wouldn't.

'I went and paid a visit to Maxi in the Scrubs. Told him Lenny had grassed him up and the rest is history.'

'So you didn't actually do it yourself?'

Her words cut Joe like a knife and turning to face her, she could see the pain in his eyes.

'Fuck me Tess! What do you take me for? I'm a copper first and foremost. Alright, some of the things I do are border line sometimes, but murder! People like Maxi Trueman educate themselves and think they're a cut above the rest. Trouble is you can't polish a turd and their street cred will always be the most important thing to them. If they have even an inkling that they've been grassed, well you know the outcome.'

They drove back to the station in silence and Joe only spoke again when they pulled up in the car park. Unclipping his seat belt, he turned to look at her.

'Say what you want up there but just remember one thing. Lenny Layton would never have stopped, his sort never do. I made a decision and it was the right one. If I hadn't of done what I did, then it would have ended up with your sister lying in the morgue instead of him. Now go and see Windsor and let's get this mess sorted out once and for all.'

Tess walked across the car park, her thoughts darting in every direction. She knew what Joe had said was right but still it was wrong, all wrong. Silently she entered the

289

building and was able to slip up to the first floor without being noticed. Tentatively she knocked on the door and waited for a response.

'Come!'

Chief Windsor sat behind her desk with a pair of designer spectacles perched on the end of her nose. She didn't look up as Tess took a seat in the strategically placed chair.

'So D.C. Davey, what a mess we have here! Now what do you know about it and I want your words and not those of Joe Reynolds.

Tess took offence at the woman's choice of phrase and it was reflected in her tone, which didn't go unnoticed.

'I can assure you Ma'am that if I thought Joe had anything to do with this in any way shape or form, I would bring him in myself. As you are aware, we did haul Lenny Layton in and asked him a few questions. He didn't know anything and if he did, then he wasn't saying. I'm sorry to disappoint you but that was the end of it. Layton was a small time drug dealer and there's the rub, you know the saying "live by the sword, die by the sword" and I guess that's what ultimately happened.'

Annette Windsor studied the young detective as she would a piece of evidence. When there was nothing forthcoming, she continued.

'It all seems too suspicious to me, to neat and tidy somehow.'

'It may well appear that way but sometimes it's just how things are. Sometimes there isn't anything sinister, nothing untoward, it's just what happens. Now if there isn't anything else Ma'am, my sister is very ill and I need to get back to her.'

"Yes I heard about the attack Davey and I hope she makes a full recovery."

Annette Windsor again studied the young woman's face. The girl was either a very good liar or she believed every word she'd just said. Either way Annette wasn't happy but there was very little she could do about it.

'Ok Tess you can go. I'm glad D.C.I Reynolds will be leaving us soon as he's a bad influence and you are a promising young officer with your whole career ahead of you.'

'Thank you Ma'am.'

Tess walked over to the door and even got as far as turning the handle, when something stopped her. Glancing over her shoulder, she spoke to her superior, who was again studying paperwork.

'You're wrong about Joe Ma'am! He's one of the finest officers I have ever worked with and put in a tight spot, there wouldn't be anyone else I'd want by my side.'

Tess didn't wait for a reply and when Annette Windsor looked up to make a comment, the room was empty. Back out in the corridor Tess took in a deep lungful of air as she steadied herself against the wall. Lying had never been something she'd agreed with or had ever been particularly good at but this time she thought that she'd pulled it off. Back in the car park Joe Reynolds had been smoking himself stupid waiting for her to return. When Tess opened the door so soon after getting out, he breathed a sigh of relief.

'Good god Joe! it's like Chernobyl in here.'

He ignored her comments. Desperate for information, his eyes were wide and animal like.

'So?'

'She swallowed it hook line and sinker, even if she didn't want to. Now can we get back to the hospital?'

Joe didn't reply but the car was in gear and driving away before Tess had her seat belt on. Ten minutes later they pulled up outside the Middlesex hospital. Tess got out but didn't thank her boss for all the trouble he'd gone to. The only thing on her mind was Roxy and anything or anyone else, could go to hell as far as she was concerned.

CHAPTER THIRTY

As Tess walked back into the Middlesex and made her
way along the corridor to the intensive care ward, her
face was still flushed. Her adopted mother had always
drummed into her that a liar could be spotted a mile off
and that thought now hung heavy on her mind. Before
she had chance to press on the electronic entry button, the
nice nurse from earlier that day, emerged from inside.
'Oh hello Miss Davey. Your sisters been moved.'
Tess started to panic and her eyes instantly had a terrified
look about them.
'It's OK! calm down Miss Davey, Roxy's fine. In fact
she's doing so well, that they decided to move her to a
side room just over an hour ago. If you continue down
this corridor it's the third door on the left.'
Tess was speechless and squeezed the nurses' arm in a
gesture of thanks. Following the nurses directions, she
soon found Roxy's room, though successfully seeking it
out had been more from the amount of noise being
emitted, than from being shown the way. Carmel was in
a fit of giggles and Roxy was trying desperately to join in
with her. Every time she laughed, the stitches in her face
pulled tight and she winced in pain. Carmel Jones was so
funny and she didn't even realise it. It wasn't something
she practiced, being comical came naturally to her, even
when she was trying to be serious.
'What's going on here then? You two can be heard from
all the way down the hall!'
Roxy pointed towards Carmel but had to place a hand
across her mouth in a desperate attempt to stop laughing.
'I was just telling Rox here about the stroke of good luck
I've just had. A nice little touch really and it brought in

fifty quid. I went to get myself a cuppa from the vending machine and some old boy who was visiting asked if I was doing business. Well Rox was snoring her head off so I thought why not!'

Tess gasped out loud and this only made Roxy want to laugh even more.

'Carmel! Oh please tell me you didn't.'

'Too fucking right I did. Found a quiet store room and hey presto fifty smackers in my hand. The old bastard must have been eighty if he was a day, so it was over in a matter of seconds. Means I don't need to go out on the trot tonight and god bless the old cunt, that's what I say. Anyways, where have you been, or is old Joe a bit more than a work colleague?'

Tess could feel her face begin to colour up again and it was something Carmel took as a blush. She couldn't have been further from the truth but for the moment Tess thought it best to let the women surmise what they wanted. Anything was better than having to tell the truth.

'There! I fucking knew it Rox. While I've been out there earning, your sister here's been giving it away for fucking free, daft cow.'

Again Roxy had to place a hand across her mouth as tears of laughter streamed down her cheeks. Tess didn't see the funny side but had to bite her tongue for her sisters' sake. She hated it when Carmel Jones talked dirty but it was something she was going to have to get used to. It was obvious to any onlookers that Roxy loved the older woman like a mother and that the two came as a package, or not at all.

'I had to go back to the station to deal with an important matter if you must know. Sometimes Carmel you can have such a filthy mind.'

'Not just sometimes, hey Rox?'

Roxy once again bit down on her bottom lip but instantly cried out in pain.

'Now look what you've done Carmel, honestly!'

Tess was about to chastise the woman, when they were interrupted by a nurse popping her head round the door.

'Sorry to be a kill joy but our patient needs her rest and judging by the amount of laughter that's been coming from this room, she's had quite enough excitement for one day.'

Carmel looked shame faced and stared down at the bed clothes as she spoke.

'Sorry sister.'

'I'm only a nurse and thank god I am. If Sister Lomax had heard you lot, you'd have been out of here with a flea in your ear.'

With that the nurse disappeared and Tess gave Carmel a look that told her it was best if they got on their way. Kissing Roxy good night, the two women began their walk home together. Strolling along Berners Mews and passing Roxy's flat, neither woman said a word. Carmel had been waiting for Tess to speak, even if it was something sarcastic, at least it would have been conversation. When none was forthcoming she studied the young woman's face.

'What's wrong?'

'Nothing!!!'

'Don't try and pull the wool over my eyes love. Your reply was just a bit too fucking sharp for someone who's got nothing troubling them.'

Tess didn't know what to say, she knew she'd been rumbled and wondered how best to back track her way out of it. Deciding to tell a half truth she unburdened herself as much as she dare.

'Layton's dead.'

295

If Tess was expecting a barrage of questions, then she was about to be disappointed. Carmel continued to walk along in silence and a few minutes later when Tess could stand it no more, she challenged the woman.

'Well?'

'Well what?'

'Don't you want to know what happened?'

'Not really interested. He was a cunt through and through and probably got exactly what he deserved. The only thing worrying me is how our girl's going to take it.'

'Roxy will be fine. I suppose Layton was paid back in a way, for what he did to her and at least he won't get the chance to hurt her again.'

Carmel Jones shook her head and Tess caught the gesture out of the corner of her eye.

'What?'

'Tess you aint got a clue about Roxy Baxter. I've known her longer than most and sometimes I feel as if I don't know her at all.'

'Maybe you don't but I feel I do. Don't forget we're twins Carmel and we have a bond that can't be broken.'

'I wouldn't be so sure about that Tess. Lenny and Roxy had an unusual relationship, one I could never fathom out, I can tell you.'

They continued to walk until suddenly Carmel stopped dead in her tracks. Turning to Tess she took both of the woman's hands in hers.

'Promise me one thing Tess!'

'I have to know what it is first.'

'Don't tell Roxy about all this until she's well. Mark my words this is a disaster waiting to happen and if you tell her now it's going to fucking set her back big time.'

'If you think it's for the best then of course I won't tell her. To be honest, it's something I was dreading

296

anyway.'

Carmel dropped Tess's hands and as they fell to her sides, the women continued on their way.

'You aint off the hook sweetheart! She has to know, just not yet that's all. The only thing you've done is bought yourself some time.'

Three weeks after that fateful day, Roxy Baxter had improved enormously. She was now able to sit up in bed and was eagerly looking to the future. Joe Reynolds had left the force and Tess had even managed to attend his leaving party, although their relationship was now strained. Entering the ward, Tess was met by one of the doctors who'd been treating Roxy.

'Miss Davey!, how nice to see you. I have some good news regarding your sister. She has made such a remarkable recovery that we are considering discharging her tomorrow.'

Tess grabbed the doctors' hand and shook it until he thought it would fall off.

'Thank you! Thank you so much doctor, does she know?'

'No not yet. I thought it would be nice if the news came from you.'

Tess's smile lit up the foyer and she almost ran to Roxy's room. Roxy Baxter lay on her stomach flipping through one of the many magazines that Tess or Carmel had brought in over the last few days.

'Hi darling! you'll never guess what I've just been told.'

Roxy stared at her sister but didn't inquire any further.

'The doctor said you can go home tomorrow, isn't that fantastic?'

Roxy shrugged her shoulders as if the words she'd just heard were no big deal.

'Oh come on Rox, aren't you excited?'

297

'What's to be excited about? I mean at least here I'm safe and warm and not earning a living out on the Street.' Tess sat down on the edge of the bed and gently took Roxy's chin between her thumb and index fingers. Slowly she tilted her sisters' head upwards until their eyes met.

'I told you before; you'll never have to earn a living that way again.'

'Don't hold your breath Sis because it's in me and I aint never going to change. I'd be kidding myself to believe any different. It was in our mother and it's in me.'

Tess's jaw dropped open so far and so quickly, that Roxy thought it would hit the floor.

'Oh don't look so shocked, are you honestly telling me you didn't know that she was a brass, just like me?'

'No! No I didn't.'

'Well you learn something new every day, or so they say.'

'Why are you being so hard all of a sudden? Anyway Roxy I don't want to talk about this now, there are more important things to discuss.'

'Like what?'

Tess stopped holding her sisters face and placed her hand by her side.

'You said you were safe here and that was something I've been waiting to talk to you about. Carmel said it was best left until you were well but now as we've had such good news, it seems as good a time as any.'

Roxy could tell by Tess's tone that she was nervous and she was more than a little interested, in what her sister had to say.

'Come on then, don't keep me in suspense!'

Tess swallowed hard and after taking in a large mouthful of air, told Roxy what to one twin was brilliant news but

298

to the other, would be totally devastating.

'Lenny's dead Roxy and he will never be able to hurt you again.'

If Tess had been expecting a happy reaction, she didn't get it. Roxy shrank back against the metal headboard, trying to gain as much distance as she could from her sister. Her eyes filled with pools of tears and from nowhere came a howling sound, like that made by a wounded animal. Tess stood up and tried to get close to Roxy but the girl pulled away, as if Tess was infected with a deadly disease. The wailing was so loud and heart rendering that two nurses quickly ran into the room. Tess waved them away with her hand.

'It's fine, she'll be fine honestly! I've just had to break some bad news that's all.'

The nurses reluctantly left the room and Tess turned back to where Roxy sat huddled.

'Come on sweetheart, it's not so bad. He was never any good for you, look at what he did. I'd say Layton got what he deserved.'

Instantly Roxy Baxter turned from a grieving young woman into something from a horror movie. Curling back her lips, she snarled her words to such a degree that Tess stood back from the bed.

'What the fuck would you know about what he deserved?'

'I know what he did to you and no one should be allowed to get away with that. The only way he would ever stop, is when he's six feet under.'

'You stupid stupid bitch! What the fuck have you done! Oh god, oh god in heaven help me please!!!!!!'

The wailing began all over again and Tess could do nothing but stand and stare. Slowly it began to subside and Tess thought Roxy was beginning to adjust to the

299

news, though why she was so upset, Tess couldn't understand. Wiping her nose on the cuff of her pyjamas, Roxy sniffed in deeply.

'So what part in all of this did you play?'

'I don't know what you mean.'

'Fuck off Tess, 'course you do! You mean to tell me that I'm put in here and suddenly Lenny's dead and it's all down to coincidence.'

'Well I wouldn't say that but believe me Roxy, I was only trying to help. I couldn't bear what he'd done to you and I was scared he would do it again. Only next time maybe you wouldn't survive.'

'Soooo! what did you do and you'd better tell me the truth Tess.'

Roxy Baxter almost shouted her last words and Tess was frightened that someone outside would hear.

'Calm down and I'll tell you.'

'I am fucking calm!'

Tess leant over the bed, her face so close to Roxy's that the woman could feel Tess's breath against her cheek.

'No you're not. Now listen and promise that you won't over react.'

Roxy nodded and swallowed hard. She was dreading what she was about to hear but she knew she would never rest until she'd heard the truth first hand.

'Someone had a word in Maxi Truman's ear and the rest was taken out of my hands. You above all else should know what these people are capable of. I suppose if Trueman thought he'd been grassed up, well then he would want his revenge.'

Roxy wrapped her arms tightly across her chest and began to rock back and forth.

'Oh Lenny my poor poor Lenny what have they done to you.'

Tess put her hand out and tried to touch Roxy's shoulder but it was instantly slapped away.

'Roxy you'll get over this and in time meet someone knew. Lenny was a bad apple and you're better off without him.'

Roxy started to sob again and Tess thought her heart would break at the sight.

'You don't know what you've done, oh dear god in heaven, you don't know what you've done!'

'Yes I do and I'm not sorry in the least. The world is a better place and you will have a better life, without that scum bag in it.'

Roxy jumped from the bed and dived on Tess. Kicking and punching until she was exhausted and all the time Tess offered no defence. Finally when Roxy could hit out no more, she flopped back down onto the bed.

'I loved him more than anyone in the world and deep down I know Lenny loved me. You come along and within a few weeks you've taken him away from me. What gives you the right Tess, tell me that, what gives you the fucking right?'

'I have the right because I'm your sister Roxy; it's as simple as that.'

'And what about Lenny's rights?'

'Lenny? what are you talking about?. Why would Lenny Layton have any rights?'

Roxy stared hard into her sisters eyes for several seconds before she answered. When she spoke again her words came out like poison.

'Because Tess, he was our father! Our fucking flesh and blood, that's why.'

It was again Tess Davey's turn to swallow hard for the second time, as she tried to hold onto the bile that was building up in her throat. Glancing at the door she saw

301

Carmel propped up against the frame and that sight alone made her feel totally alone.

'I don't get this, I don't get it at all! Lenny Layton was your partner, your pimp. For god's sake you were having sex with him and now you tell me he was our father!'

Roxy shrugged her shoulders and her face was hard but also expressionless as she spoke.

'When you live all your life without love and finally it comes along, well you grab it with both hands, no matter what form it comes in. Don't stand there looking so high and fucking mighty Tess, you've never been lonely have you? You've always had your job and your dad. You haven't got a clue what it was like, so don't stand there and look down on me. Lenny loved me like no one ever has or will again.'

Tess didn't know how to answer, so turned her attention to Carmel.

'Did you know about this?'

'I had an inkling but I never asked outright.'

'An inkling! And you didn't think to say anything!'

'How could I. Roxy would never have forgiven me, and you, well honestly Tess how would you have reacted?'

Tess didn't know how to answer the question and she stared down at the floor and away from Carmel's gaze. The room was silent except for Roxy's continuous sobs and Carmel walked over to the bed. Unlike the distance between the two sisters, Roxy would allow her friend to comfort her and again Tess felt alienated.

'So what now?'

Roxy pushed Carmel away.

'I want you to go and never fucking come back, because I swear Tess, if I ever clap eyes on you again, I'll fucking kill you.'

Silently Tess stepped from the room. Out in the corridor

and with her shoulders slumped; she began to walk towards the exit but was stopped by Carmel's voice. Clacking along the linoleum, the older woman soon caught up with her. Instantly noticing the tears in Tess's eyes, Carmel's heart went out to her.

'I'm so sorry things have turned out this way babe, it's bad news all round.'

'Oh Carmel! It's like I want to wake up from a bad dream, only I can't because I'm already awake.'

'I know darling but there's nothing you can do about it.' Tess gently shook her head and tears began to flow thick and fast down her cheeks.

'No Carmel you don't know but promise you'll take care of her? I couldn't bare it if she had no one watching out for her.'

'You don't even have to ask, I love that girl as if she were me own. I'll try and talk to her when she's calmed down a bit. Tess just for the record, I for one think you did the right thing.'

'Do you Carmel, I'm not so sure.'

'Well you're certainly not to blame in all of this. The only one who is, is dead and gone and good fucking riddance if you ask me. I could never say that to our girl but I know if he hadn't of snuffed it then Roxy would soon be dead.'

'Maybe Carmel but the only thing I want is Roxy's forgiveness and I know deep down, that's something she will never be able to give.'

With that Tess Davey walked out of the Middlesex hospital and Roxy Baxter's life.

THE END

303

EPILOGUE

SIX MONTHS LATER

Tess had gone back to her old position in Spalding but it wasn't the same. Her interest was little above zero and it was becoming a problem with her fellow officers. She'd been called into Chief Inspector Shepherd's office on no less than three occasions and she wasn't once able to justify her lack of efficiency. Nothing had changed, the work was still the same but she just didn't have any enthusiasm. Sophie Milligan had tried and tried to get her old friend back on track but all her efforts had fallen on deaf ears. Tess felt totally and utterly lost and wasn't interested in anything, least of all work. Visiting her dad's grave had brought little comfort. When Margaret Davey had turned up unexpectedly, it had been the straw that broke the camels back as far as Tess was concerned. She couldn't bring herself to call the woman mum and the two had all but had a stand up row in the cemetery. Tess really didn't want to be in Spalding or anywhere else come to that, the only trouble was she had nowhere else to go. Nowhere except to her old boss and just lately that idea was becoming more and more appealing. Thinking back to London and her last few days in the place that had caused her so much heartache, Tess grinned when an image of Agi Goldstein entered her head. The old woman had always been so kind and in the end, Tess had felt it her duty to come clean about who she was and what she was doing there. To begin with Agi had acted shocked but that had only lasted a few seconds. When she'd finally revealed her own past, the two women had laughed until their sides ached. With her cases finally packed, Agi had seen Tess to her taxi and gently kissed her cheek.

'You take care Tess Davey. It's been a pleasure knowing you.'

'Same here Agi and give my love to Mr Seaman.'

'I will! As a matter of fact I give him love most nights.'

'Oh Agi you are incorrigible! I'm really going to miss you.'

'Likewise sweetie, likewise.'

Tess felt as though she was leaving part of herself behind and for once she wasn't thinking of Roxy. In the short time that she'd been in London it had become her home and now that she had left she didn't feel that she belonged anywhere. Waving as the cab pulled away, she had known that her life was never going to be the same again.

Joe Reynolds had retired from the force a couple of weeks before Tess returned to Spalding. Within a month he'd sold up and had moved to a small villa in the Valencia region of Spain. He hadn't regretted the move for a minute, although he often thought of Annette and what might have been. Leisurely days were spent at the beach and when he'd heard that Tracy Woods had received a sentence of twenty-five years, it had brought about an inner peace that he never thought he'd feel again. Recently Tess Davey had begun to enter his mind more and more often and he wondered how she was doing. It had been an instant admiration and he couldn't for the life of him understand why. Maybe it was his fatherly instinct but maybe he had just seen a thoroughly nice human being. In Joe Reynolds estimation that was a rarity nowadays. As soon as he was settled, Joe sent her his address but as yet hadn't received a reply. He hoped everything was well and that maybe she would visit. So much had happened in both their lives and it was time to put a few ghosts to rest. Sitting outside a small bar that he'd come to favour at lunch times, his mobile began to vibrate. Glancing at the screen he smiled when he saw who was calling.

'Hi there girlie! How's things'?'

'To tell you the truth, not that well boss. I was wondering if you were up for a visitor?'

Joe's face beamed. The locals were friendly enough but it could never make up for seeing one of your own.

'Are you joking? When are you coming girl?'

'Tomorrow if that's all right?'

'Fine by me sweetheart. Ring me when you land and if you don't mind me saying, you sound as if you could do with a little holiday.'

'See you tomorrow boss.'

Joe Reynolds was immediately concerned. There was no way Tess Davey would have ended a call so abruptly, not unless she was in some kind of trouble. It would take a fortnight for Joe Reynolds to find out what that trouble was, a whole fortnight before he would realise that this visit was more than a holiday. Tess Davey had handed in her notice and had no intention of returning to the place where she'd grown up. The police force held nothing for her now and the only chance she had was to move on or at least that's what she told herself. Tess was lonely, lonelier than she could ever have thought possible and suddenly she began to understand what Roxy had meant.

On leaving hospital, Roxy Baxter had returned to Carmel's flat. Within a couple of weeks, things on the financial front were once again tight. Before leaving London, Tess had left a cheque with Carmel. It was a small inheritance she'd received from her dad and she had wanted Roxy to have it. Up until now there was no way on earth that Roxy would accept, that was until there was no bread or milk left in the flat. Carmel Jones soon came up with yet another of her hair brained schemes but this time she was sure her friend would go for it. After many rows and much cajoling, finally Roxy had relented and had allowed a deposit to be placed on a small two-bedroom apartment in Kensington. The area was smart, upmarket and a good place to run a business from. Carmel had wanted them to move in but Roxy was adamant that it was to be a place of work and nothing more. After furnishings and decorating, there was still enough left over in the kitty for Carmel's place to be spruced up. For the first time in their entire lives, the unlikely pair had somewhere decent to live. After a local raid, Roxy had befriended two eastern European girls that had been left high and dry by a pimp. They had agreed to work for Roxy at the new address and at long last Carmel would be able to retire. Roxy soon got into the swing of being a madam come maid and putting everything aside, didn't hanker for her old line of work. Her scars had healed to such a degree, that with clever concealer they were nothing more than faint lines. Carmel had smoothly moved into the world of being a kept woman. She baked and cooked, albeit limited and having a family even if it was only Roxy was something she'd always dreamed of. Business boomed and the duos clientele were rich and sometimes even famous. The amount of money coming in was far more than Roxy had ever earned before. It was so good, that she and Carmel even managed a couple of weeks away on the Costa's. Neither could have imagined that they would have ended up in Spain at the same time as Tess Davey. It was destiny that had brought the two sisters together and destiny that would stop their paths ever crossing again. For separate reasons, both wished that things could have been different but nothing would stop them thinking of the other every day for the rest of their lives.

12004073R00175

Printed in Great Britain
by Amazon.co.uk, Ltd.,
Marston Gate.